W9-CIR-774

Twisted
Pieces

Also by Lew Stonehouse

Twisted Intentions
Twisted Pieces

Twisted Pieces

By

Lew Stonehouse

HOLLISTON, MASSACHUSETTS

TWISTED PIECES
Copyright © 2016 by Lew Stonehouse

This book is a work of fiction. Names, characters, places and incidents are products of the author's imagination or are used fictitiously. Any resemblance to actual events, locations or persons, living or deceased, is entirely coincidental.

Printed and bound in the United States. All rights reserved. No part of this book may be reproduced or transmitted in any form or by any means, electronic or mechanical, including photocopying, recording, or by an information storage and retrieval system—except by a reviewer who may quote brief passages in a review to be printed in a magazine, newspaper, or on the Web—without the express written consent of Silver Leaf Books, LLC.

The Silver Leaf Books logo is a registered trademarks of Silver Leaf Books, LLC.

All Silver Leaf Books characters, character names, and the distinctive likeness thereof are trademarks of Silver Leaf Books, LLC.

Cover Art by Sam Ezzo.

First printing February 2016
10 9 8 7 6 5 4 3 2 1

ISBN # 1-60975-098-5
ISBN-13 # 978-1-60975-098-5
LCCN # 2015942589

Silver Leaf Books, LLC
P.O. Box 6460
Holliston, MA 01746
+1-888-823-6450

Visit our web site at www.SilverLeafBooks.com

Acknowledgements / Dedication

As we move forward in the John Harvard series, I am compelled to dedicate this book to my father, Jack Carlisle Stonehouse. Always an avid reader, he devoured my books and read the raw manuscripts many times over. Even so, he was never lacking in criticism I might add, but with an eye toward making what he felt was a good book even better. So here's to you Dad and I'll try to send more your way.

Jack Carlisle Stonehouse
November 6, 1926-March 2, 2015

Twisted
Pieces

CHAPTER

1

The power from the massive 766 cubic inch engine reverberated throughout the cabin. The operator of the colossal machine, that weighed in right around 32,000 pounds, sat in a comfortable chair, surrounded by a bank of video and computer monitors. Rows of gauges reflected information gathered from a variety of sensors, measuring such things as speed, ground clearance, flow rate, and every other bit of data the operator would need to perform his task. He didn't even have to steer if he didn't want to. A cutting edge GPS, or Global Positioning System, could do that with far greater accuracy than a mere mortal. With the mundane tasks being handled by circuit boards and sensors, the operator could concentrate on more important matters such as which song he should play next through his equally powerful and sophisticated sound system.

Danny Forrester was ensconced in the climate controlled, glass encased control center of his combine tractor, snapping up rows of corn faster than a contestant at the local hot dog eating contest that was held each year at the county fair. He sat, listening to music and enjoying the scenery, while the machine worked its way tirelessly through the unending rows. Danny was a farmer, as was his Daddy, as was his Daddy before that, as was his Daddy before that, and so forth.

The Forrester's had been farming this land since Thomas Forrester had received a land grant for his service with the Continental Army in the Revolutionary War. Danny's son, Todd, would almost certainly do the same. Danny was young, only twenty-three, but his father had died of a heart attack last year and he inherited the ancestral land much earlier than he normally would have. Fortunately, the Forrester's were very successful in their business and they had little problem dealing with the exorbitant estate taxes that caused many farmers to lose the land that had been in their families for generations.

He liked the work. It was peaceful, rewarding, and he dearly loved the land. He could not dream of doing anything else and took all of the hard work and the pitfalls of the job in stride. The only thing that really bothered him was the wanton destruction of his crops, and he was seeing signs of that right now. Off in the distance, but getting closer with each pass, was an obvious path through the corn to the approximate center of this particular field. Obviously, someone had driven a car from the road right through Danny Forrester's corn field and into the middle. There was a large blank space in the corn at the end of the path as well.

Danny had seen it before, too many times for his liking. A group of kids looking for someplace to party, safe from the prying eyes of cops and other adults. Or perhaps some lovers who also wanted to be safe from the searching eyes of cops, other adults, and in some cases, spouses. Whatever the reason, the results were the same.

As the combine got nearer on every successive pass, he looked closer at the damaged area. The downed corn had been young when the destruction occurred, so whatever had happened here had happened some time ago, obviously months earlier. Danny had gotten his crops planted early this year, dangerously early, and a cold spell nearly ruined his efforts. This vandalism had to have been done shortly after planting. One area in the center of the field looked particularly barren. That was strange. He wondered what had been done there to cause that. Bonfire perhaps? One more pass and he would be over it. He looked straight down from his lofty perch on the last roll by and noticed something that glinted in the sunlight, a sudden, bright flash, then it was gone. '*Probably a beer can,*' he thought. Still, there was something about the way the sun reflected off the object that didn't set right with him. The flash appeared too tiny, too bright to be cast from something as coarse as aluminum.

The big machine turned around at the end of the field and started chomping its way back, heading directly for the barren patch. Just before it got there, Danny stopped the machine and clambered down the ladder to the ground. He walked over to the area in question and stood, looking around for the object that had caught his eye. He didn't see anything, so he ventured further in. The ground was crusty from a massive amount of rain a few days back and it crunched as he walked.

There! Something caught his eye again. He walked closer to it. It looked like a wedding ring, a huge one at that, attached to a stick. He bent closer and picked it up.

Like most farmers, Danny was a hunter. He had hunted for as long as he could remember, as long as he could walk, he supposed. He'd seen lots of bones, old and new, in the woods and the fields that surrounded his home. As soon as he picked up the ring and the "stick," he quickly saw it was not what he had at first thought. It was the bone from a human finger.

In shock and disgust, he half dropped and half threw them away as if they were red hot. Eyes wide and heart pounding, he looked down and saw what appeared to be the top of a human skull protruding slightly from the ground.

Danny Forrester didn't see anything else. He was too busy running back to his combine with all the speed he could muster. He went up the ladder with a bound that would have made any Olympic broad jumper proud. He tore open the cabin door, reached for his cell phone, and dialed 911. He guessed that his corn was about to get more messed up than ever.

John Livingston Harvard was sweating profusely. He was on his fourth lap around the small body of water upon which his house sat. There weren't many homes on the lake, which meant that the majority of his run was on rough, natural terrain. He was forty-five years in age, but with a body of a thirty year old, just over six feet tall and built like a running back. Big, but full of speed and muscle. His hair was dark and full, in a Reaganesque fashion. He'd been athletic all his life, with the usual bouts of laziness that caused his stomach to expand into the typical middle age pouch.

Every couple of years or so, he'd get sick of looking at himself in the mirror and start a workout regime to make himself respectable again. Only this time, it was for a different reason. He'd had a little "*run in*" this last spring that had required him to defend himself, as well as some other folks. Though he'd put up a respectable showing, he'd promised himself that he would get back into shape as soon as that little episode was finished.

Of course, he'd run into a bit of a snag on that. That *snag* being that he'd been shot and cut with a knife to the point that he had been in a coma for several days. He couldn't decide which had been worse, the bullet wounds to his head, arms, and legs, his broken ribs, the knife slice to his calf, or all the laying around he had done while he was recuperating.

So now he was running... running... running, punctuated by *kata's,* martial art movements designed to build and maintain speed, flexibility, strength, and timing. He'd done a *lot* of them, as well. Next time he wanted to be ready, though in reality, he thought the odds of that happening were slim to none.

What John Harvard refused to admit to himself was that he was getting in shape not so much to be ready for the next time, but because he felt guilty that he hadn't been able to save *Her*. She kept coming back to him in his dreams. What compounded the problem was the fact that when she came to him in his dreams, she didn't blame him for not saving her. On the contrary, *that* may have been easier to deal with. Instead, she apologized! "*I'm sorry*," was all she would say before she would fade away into dreamland once again. *That* only made things worse. Had she betrayed him? Yes. But there had been special circumstances and in the end, she had given her life to save his. She didn't deserve to die. So, he was running *away* from the memory of *Her,* and run, he did.

That said, it wasn't the whole story. There had been the man who had killed *Her*. A cold blooded killer, an ex-special forces soldier who had accused John of being no different than himself. The only difference being, the assassin had said, was that John had chosen one side of the thin blue line that marked the good guys, while he, Gregory Harris, had chosen the other side. Killing, Harris informed him with a sadistic smile, was just as pleasurable to John as it was to him.

In the end, John had, in fact, killed Harris, violently, viciously, and not with a remote, dispassionate bullet, using instead a knife. Up close and personal and true to Harris' insights, he took great pleasure in doing it, because Harris had killed *Her*. He had been extremely angry at Harris. He *wanted* to kill him. But he hadn't made some wild, vengeful attack. No, he had turned that anger into speed and ruthless efficiency. John consoled himself with the knowledge that he had killed to save himself and others. Hadn't he? It was only the adrenaline rush of combat that had made it seem so pleasurable. Wasn't it? He took a life merely to prevent the death of others so the pleasure he had felt in seeing Harris die didn't really count. Did it?

As Harris lay in the ever widening pool of his life's blood, he looked up at John, mustered his remaining strength, smiled, and croaked feebly, "*I told you.*" He died then, still smiling, content with the knowledge that he had left John with a moral conundrum. Had Harris been right? Was there actually no real difference between men who killed for their own purposes and the men who in turn killed them? Both killed. And in the end, at least in this instance, both had taken great pleasure in their victory.

John knew it was an age old philosophical question. One that he had thought he had come to terms with a long time ago as a rookie cop. But that was before *Her*, before Harris. Now it went beyond theoretical discussions amongst priests and scholars. Now, it was personal.

So he ran. So he worked out to the point of exhaustion so that he could, at least temporarily, sleep and flee his demons.

Susan Browning was watching John from the deck of his home. She was a slender woman, with long brown wavy hair, and green eyes. She had never been married and even though she had just turned forty, neither of those facts bothered her in the least. Nor should they have. Susan was one of those women whose looks seemed to get better with age, like a fine wine, as the man who she was currently watching would have said. As far as marriage was concerned, she hadn't minded being single, but John Livingston Harvard was changing that notion.

John's daughter, Mary Kate, was sleeping uncharacteristically late and Susan was taking advantage of that circumstance by drinking her coffee on the deck and watching him as he glided over the wooded terrain. His movements were quick, natural, and he reminded her of a deer moving gracefully through its unrefined environment. She had seen firsthand how well he blended into a wooded setting such as the one in which he now ran. And quite unlike a deer, how deadly.

He was a driven man, but a tormented one. She'd heard his restless, muted, cries in the dark. She had stood at his bedroom door in the middle of the night and watched as he tossed and turned and valiantly fought the fiends that had besieged him since that day at the cabin. She wanted to help him but knew that in reality, there was little she could do.

She could only be there for him if he wanted to talk about it, which he rarely did. At times, she wanted to crawl into bed with him. To hold him. To comfort him. However, she also knew that would not work right now. They didn't have that kind of relationship... yet. For now, she was merely a guest at his home. She hoped that would change one day, one day soon.

Susan was a programmer and she had developed the ultimate hacking program. She hadn't done it for personal gain.

There was a word for what she had become, '*Hacktivist.*' The word is a combination of two well known words. "Hacker," which everyone knows is a computer geek that breaks into computers. And "Activist," which everyone knows is someone who is trying to bring about a political or social change. Hacktivist is a new word in the English dictionary. Oxford has one of the most blunt and to the point definitions, "A person who uses computer crimes to further social or political ends."

She had committed no real crime and the only social change that Susan had attempted to bring about was an end to hacking. It enraged her to think of how a few bad people had hijacked something as awe inspiring as a computer and the internet and had turned them into a source of fear and mistrust. She decided to do something about it.

With that goal in mind, she had created the ultimate hacking program. She had done this with the logic that if she could fashion the absolute best, most devious program ever devised, then create a program that could defeat it, she would give it away and screw all the hackers. Unfortunately, it hadn't worked out quite the way she had planned.

In her obsession with the technical aspects, she hadn't stopped to think just how dangerous the hacking part of her program could be in the wrong hands. As is the normal way with the world, the "wrong hands," had indeed discovered her program and had kidnapped her in order to force her to give it to them. Unbeknownst to her, her estranged father had discovered the plot and had hired John Harvard to get her back.

Actually, there had been a lot more to it than that but suffice it to say, John succeeded in finding her and her captors in a remote northern cabin. There had been gunplay and a terrible fight in which all of her captors had been killed.

He had survived that initial onslaught, only to be viciously cut down by the Deputy Chief of his old police department, who it turned out, had actually worked for her captors as well. Only the fortuitous intervention by Nick Giovanni, one of John's police pals, had saved his life.

The other casualty that day had been Emily Stone, a gifted programmer in her own right. She had worked for Peter, Susan's father, and had been supposedly helping John find Susan. What John didn't know was that Emily had actually been working for the kidnappers, albeit at that point, not willingly. In the end, she had given her own life in a successful attempt to prevent Gregory Harris from shooting John.

What brought him to his present, demon filled condition, was that he and Emily had, in the short time they had known one another, become lovers in the truest sense of the word. John had talked about it enough for Susan to know that Emily had come to him, still came to him, in his dreams, to tell him she was sorry for her betrayal. And *that*, somehow, made it even worse for him.

After being flown out of the woods that day by a medical helicopter, John had spent days in the hospital in a coma. No one, not even the doctors, would venture a guess as to his survival. During those times, Susan sat by his side day and night. At first, she felt beholden to him for having saved her. Then she started to recall the look of regret he had given her when it had appeared that he had failed in his mission to rescue her. He had been ordered to his knees at gun point by Harris and as he dropped down in compliance, he looked up at her, their eyes met. She didn't see fear in them. She saw compassion for her and regret that he'd been unable to save her. In the twinkling of an eye, she knew that this was a worthy, strong, dependable man and she had to try and help him.

During the dreadful time when they didn't know when, or if, he would come out of his coma, she had listened as his friends came to his room and laughed as they talked about him and his exploits. She started to learn just what a special man he really was. Mary Kate, his daughter, loved him unconditionally, and to Susan, that in itself said something about him. By the time John had awakened from his deep sleep, she was starting to have some definite feelings for him that had nothing to do with his role as rescuer.

She had come home with him from the hospital to help while he recuperated, mostly out of a feeling that she owed him something. He had saved her life, almost at the expense of his own. However, that didn't explain it all. She had never known a man like John Harvard. He was strong, always wanting to help others, and he expected nothing in return. His quiet, assured demeanor reminded her of some character out of a John Wayne movie.

She had felt a powerful animal magnetism toward him almost the instant they'd met. Of course she realized, her feelings might have had something to do with the fact that

John had just shot dead two of her captors and had been in the process of calmly planning their next move to facilitate her escape. Shortly after, he had been captured by Harris. When her eyes had locked with his during that brief moment while he was on his knees, his capable aura had descended upon her and quelled the panic that she had been vainly attempting to fight off up to that point. She had made up her mind right then and there that she would save John Harvard or die trying. Though he didn't know it, he then had the assistance of two very capable women who would try to save him that day. A wistful smile came across her face. Between her, Emily, and John himself, Gregory Harris never had a chance. Special Forces training be damned!

After she had moved in to help while John recuperated, she began to know him in ways that two people can't learn unless they are living together. She watched as he interacted with his daughter and others in is life. All of this did nothing but deepen her respect and her feelings for him. Now, she was ready to love him. But she needed some sign that he was willing to accept that love. He didn't need her help anymore and she dreaded the day when he would ask her to leave. He never did and though she had come close to bringing up the subject, she always backed down at the last moment for fear of what he would say.

She didn't want to breach the wall that John had built around himself. She wanted him to take it down of his own accord and intuitively, she also knew that would take time. Time for his feelings for Emily and his guilt over having failed to save her to fade. Time for him to come to terms with the moral dilemma that Harris had burdened him with. Just... Time.

Harold and Jenny Watson were both a spry seventy-one years old. They lived in town, had all their lives in fact. They had known each other since grade school and had been high school sweethearts. He had gone to the local junior college and had become a heating and air conditioning specialist. He built a small company of eight employees, which was successful and provided a generous income for the Watson family. It was now run by one of their three sons. Their one daughter worked there as a secretary.

Jenny had been a school teacher, a profession that she had temporarily given up to raise their family, but as soon as they were old enough, she returned to her beloved occupation. Now, both were in a thoroughly enjoyable retirement. They were as much in love now as they were the day they had gotten married.

Harold and Jenny had a not so secret passion: mushrooms! During the mushroom season, they were rarely at home. They could be found combing the woods for their little prizes. Dark areas with undisturbed, rotted logs, were the best and they would walk for hours in their quest, which explained their excellent health.

Be that as it may, their family insisted that they carry a cell phone with them on their daily treks, in case one of them should fall and sprain an ankle, so their family said.

But all knew the real reason. They were prime age for a heart attack. Therefore, they carried it, but never used it, and everyone knew not to call unless it was a dire emergency. That emergency had never come because everyone also knew that calling could bring the possible onset of one of Harold's infamous tirades, which were rare but nonetheless loud and quite prolonged. So, they were left to themselves, together and happy as they enjoyed the peacefulness of the woods.

On this particular day, they were intent on working their way around a large raspberry patch, attempting to get to a group of rotted logs they had spotted at the bottom of a ravine. Jenny announced that when they got there, she wanted to stop and have lunch. Harold was feeling a bit hungry, so he agreed. When they arrived, he removed his pack and Jenny began to go through it, spreading out a blanket for them to sit on, removing their meal and placing napkins at each place setting. Just because they were in the woods didn't mean they had to eat like cave people, she would say. Harold decided to take a quick look at the logs as Jenny went on with her preparations, which included a cup of red wine for each. He was looking forward to that.

He moved over to the logs and immediately spotted a group of beautiful mushrooms, just asking to be collected. It was going to be worth the strenuous work it took to get here. He was just turning away when he spotted something colorful a few logs away. Blue. What on earth is that strange hue of blue in the woods? Nothing! That's what. Nothing natural anyway.

He decided to move closer and see what it was. They were pretty far away from where the average person would normally hike, too far for the usual trash they sometimes encountered on their travels. As he got closer, he could see that the blue object was really the arm of a shirt. 'That's odd.' he thought.

Closer still, and he could make out that it wasn't just a sleeve, but an *entire* shirt. After climbing over a particularly large log, he was able to look down at the shirt.

Meanwhile, Jenny had completed her task and was a little irked when she saw Harold working his way over the logs, still going away from her. "Harold," she yelled, "It's time to eat some lunch. I thought you said you were hungry!"

Harold didn't answer her. Instead, he stood looking down at the ground. *'How could he not hear me?'* she wondered. "Harold! Are you going to answer me? Come on over here so we can eat. We'll get the mushrooms later."

Harold still didn't answer, but he did turn and look at her. His face was pale and he didn't look good at all.

Jenny shot to her feet. "Sweetheart! Are you alright?" *'My God,'* she thought, *'Is he having a heart attack?'* She began to move toward him.

He held up his hand. "Stay there!" he commanded. "Call the police. Call them now, Jenny."

She was confused. "Why? What's wrong?"

She stared in shock and disbelief at his answer. "There's someone here, Jen. It's a body. A dead body."

CHAPTER
2

Susan Browning was once again sitting on the deck of John Harvard's home as he ran his laps around the lake. Only this time, she was reading the paper while she sipped her coffee. The mornings were getting cooler and the hot coffee felt good as she felt it working its way through her torso.

They had found another body, not far from here. That was two in the last week. Both had been dead a while, most likely sometime last spring. The paper also said that one was a man and the other a woman. They were found miles apart and other than that, the police knew nothing. They had identified neither body and they didn't know if they were related killings. There was no mention of a cause of death.

The papers were all concerned about whether or not they had a serial killer on the loose. The police representative said it was far too early to be jumping to that conclusion, which, Susan thought, was probably quite correct. John had shown her a new perspective in the past few months which brought with it a thorough distrust of the news media.

John had related story after story of incidents he had seen

and heard through the media that had involved him directly. Many times, he wondered if they were reporting on the same event that he'd been at. It hadn't seemed like it.

Before she met him, she had pretty much taken everything that came from the news at face value. Why would they lie? She learned from John that usually it wasn't so much a case of outright lying as it was a case of slanting the facts to sell more papers. In this case, what was more interesting and would therefore sell more papers? Two dead bodies located miles apart with no connection, or a serial killer on the loose, possibly getting ready to kill again? The answer was obvious.

She was just putting down the paper when the doorbell rang. '*Who on earth would be here at this hour of the morning?*' she thought. She hoped the sound wouldn't wake up Mary Kate.

She walked to the front and looked out a window. A familiar form, carrying a brief case, smiled and waved at her. She smiled back and went to open the door. Nick Giovanni walked in and gave her a big hug. "How are you doing, Sue?" he asked.

She hugged back. "I'm fine. What's happening over by your way? You involved with those bodies they found?"

The smile faded from his face. "Well, sort of. That's kind of why I'm here. I need to talk to John."

Susan's smile also drifted away at this news. Nick Giovanni was John's ex-partner at the police department. They had remained fast friends even though John hadn't worked there in years. It was Nick who had called in the state

S.W.A.T. team last spring and saved John from an untimely end. When Deputy Chief Ramsey had been shot by a police sniper while trying to kill a then helpless John, the whole ugly mess of Ramsey's involvement had come to light. The chief was asked to step down because of the political backlash and Captain Giovanni had been fingered to replace him. He was now known to most people as "Chief Giovanni," but to John and Susan, he was just "Nick." To Mary Kate, he was "Uncle Nick."

She stepped away and said, "He's out running right now. He should be done soon. Let's go out on the deck and wait. Would you like some coffee?"

"Please." he replied as he walked through the house and onto the deck. Susan joined him a moment later and handed him his cup. They stood by the railing and he soon spotted his friend through the trees, watching him as he ran.

"How's he doing?" he asked somberly, without taking his eyes off John.

"Better, I think. He's starting to lighten up a little, starting to laugh, and more importantly, starting to talk. But he spends little time just enjoying himself. If he's not helping me around the house or paying attention to Mary Kate, he's out running or doing kung fu stuff or whatever it is."

"Or he's down at the shooting range," finished Nick. He turned and looked at her. "I talked to the range master the other day. Other than the fact that John is one of the best combat shots he's ever seen, he's a little worried about his targeting."

"Targeting?" she asked with a quizzical look.

"Yeah. As you probably know, the targets we use are in a human form. You're suppose to shoot at the largest part of the body, that being the easiest to hit. All of our training dictates that is where you shoot, it's drilled into us from the beginning. It's for public relations reasons as well, a shot to the torso isn't necessarily fatal, thus we're not intentionally trying to kill anyone, just disable them."

"That's all very well and good, but you're not making this any clearer Nick. I feel a 'but' coming on."

Nick sighed and turned back to look at John, who was still running. "There is. The *But...*" he paused. "John isn't shooting at the torso. He's shooting at the head." He looked back at Sue. "And he rarely misses anymore."

"Oh," she said weakly and sat down in the nearest chair.

"On a cheerier note," Nick continued, attempting to lighten the mood, "what's going on with you two?"

Her slight smile indicated a partial success. "Nothing really. There have been a few times recently where I thought he was going to kiss me. But always, he changes his mind at the last minute. It's almost like someone physically grabs him and says, 'What are you doing?' I think there is something there, but he just won't let it come out."

A look of compassion crossed Nick's face. "Don't let it get you down, Sue. He needs you and I know him well enough to know he cares about you a whole lot more than he's letting on. I've given the matter some thought and I've come to the conclusion that it probably isn't just Emily that is preventing him from showing it."

She looked at him with eyebrows furrowed, again confused.

"I think he's afraid of something happening to you. He's doesn't want to be responsible and he doesn't want to get emotionally hurt himself. He wants to be completely ready next time, no excuses." He turned back toward where he had last seen John. His eyes scanned the area, but failed to find him. He turned back to Sue again.

"Unfortunately," he said with a rueful smile, "I think that time is now."

Susan's eyes flew wide open, "Oh no Nick, you can't. He's not ready."

"I'm sorry Sue. I agree with you, but something's come up and I think John is in a unique position to help on this one. He moved over to her and sat down. "I... the department, needs his help."

"Help with what?" came John's voice from behind him.

Nick bolted to his feet and spun around. "Jesus Christ! What the hell are you doing? You scared the shit out of me."

John laughed. A big, hearty laugh that Nick hadn't heard in a long time and one that Sue had never heard. It was a good laugh that lifted the spirits of everyone involved, including John. '*Yes,*' John thought to himself, '*that did feel good.*' He said to Nick, "I haven't seen you look like that since the time you jumped the balcony three stories up, looking for that fugitive and found him lying on the sofa jacking off."

John looked at Sue and saw her smiling, but obviously wondering what on earth he was talking about. He explained. "Nick and I were looking for a fugitive out of Miami. Miami P.D. had called us and said that they had information that he was hiding out at an old girl friend's apartment here in the city and they gave us the address. We looked for this asshole for about a month, couldn't find hide nor hair of him. Then one night, we saw the girlfriend go out and shortly after that, a TV came on in the apartment.

"First we tried calling the apartment and no one picked up. We knew the guy was pretty skittish so we didn't try knocking. We were standing in the hall trying to decide what to do when the owner of the adjoining apartment came home. Nick identified himself and asked to use his balcony. The guy was confused but gave us permission.

"So we went out onto the balcony and Nick, three stories up mind you, jumped to the girlfriend's balcony so he could look in the window. All of a sudden, he gets that look you just saw and says to me, 'He's in there.'

"'How do you know?' I asked. 'Trust me.' Nick says, 'He's in there. Go around to the front door.'"

John continued, "So I went around to the front, knocked and identified myself as a police officer. All of a sudden I heard a terrible screaming. I bashed in the front door and ran into the apartment, gun drawn, ready for a shootout. I find the fugitive rolling around on the floor screaming his head off in obvious pain. Nick is standing just inside the balcony door laughing his ass off."

Nick spoke up. "This guy was lying on the sofa, eyes closed, wanking his weenie. When John knocked on the front door, the guy opened his eyes and saw me, three stories up, standing on the balcony. In a state of complete shock, he quickly put his pecker away and zipped up his pants in a flash. Problem was, his pecker wasn't completely put away and he zipped right on over it."

The two of them were laughing so hard at this point that Sue couldn't help but start laughing herself. "What's so funny?" They all turned and saw Mary Kate standing in the doorway.

Through his laughter, John replied, "Aw Angel, I'm sorry we woke you up."

She walked over to him and he picked her up. "You didn't really wake me up," she said. "I woke up a little while ago and I was just playing in my room. Daddy, you were laughing real hard, what was so funny?"

Now it was Susan's turn to pump the laughter up a notch. "Go ahead John, tell her what was so funny." and with that, Nick's laughter went to a higher level as well.

"This ought to be good," Nick grunted between laughs.

"Well, sweetheart," John said with as straight a face as he could muster, "we were just talking about a guy who fell down, that's all."

"What's so funny about that," she asked.

Nick and Susan looked on in amusement as he said, "It was just the way he fell down. He was hurt and he was rolling all over the floor like one of your rubber toys. It's just funny when an adult does that. Have you ever seen an adult do that?"

She was smiling herself now. "No, I haven't. That would be funny, Daddy."

Nick started clapping. "Nice recovery there buddy," he exclaimed as he and Sue started laughing all over again.

Smiling, John turned to look at Nick, "You want some breakfast?"

Nick looked at Sue for her unspoken approval. She nodded. He looked back at John, "Sure, if you promise to stop telling bad stories about me."

"What bad stories, Daddy."

"Oh no," said Sue. "Here we go again. You guys excuse me while I start breakfast." She got up and moved into the kitchen.

"It's the same story, Angel." John said to Mary Kate.

Mary Kate got down and started to play on the deck. Nick and John talked about what was going on in the department. Who was dating who. Who had gotten into what trouble. Who got caught cheating. Who *didn't* get caught cheating. Most people don't realize that cops are as big a bunch of gossipers as anyone else and in a lot of cases, bigger. They're all in to drama and intrigue. John couldn't believe it the first time he went into roll call and heard a bunch of big, burly cops talking about the latest happenings on the noon hour soaps! Cops watching the soaps? Seemed like an oxymoron, but it was true.

Sue came in with breakfast a little while later and they all had a very pleasant time. She was seeing yet another side of John that had not been revealed in her presence before. She had heard others talk of his sense of humor and she had in fact seen glimpses of it. But nothing like the easy going, relaxed man that sat before her now. She wished Nick wasn't going to ruin it.

When they were finished eating, everyone chipped in to help with the dishes. After the last crumb had been wiped from the table, Sue turned to Mary Kate, "Why don't we go for a ride in the paddle boat?" She got an eager reply and off they went.

When they were gone, John looked at Nick. The laughter was gone now and in a serious tone he said, "Alright, first, you come over here early in the morning when you should be at work. Then I overhear you saying you need my help. Last, but certainly not least, Sue rushes Mary Kate off to the paddle boat, leaving us alone. What's up? I have a feeling it's not good."

Nick sat back, crossed his arms and slowly, loudly, let out a long sigh. "It's not. Buddy, I feel bad bringing you into this. But I've got a really bad feeling about some things. I think its trouble with a capital 'T,' and I think you should be involved for more reasons than one. First of all, I want to know... do you think you're ready? Say the word and I'll figure out another way."

"I'm ready Nick. It must be important or you wouldn't be asking," he replied grimly. "Get on with it."

"Okay. You hear about the two bodies that were found this week?"

"I heard of one, some woman in a cornfield. Didn't hear about the other. What's the woman got to do with you? That's county territory, or is she from the city?"

"Well," Nick returned, "she was from the city. So is her husband."

John's eyebrows arched. "Do I know him?"

Nick nodded, "Judge Walton."

Now John's eyes opened wide in amazement. "You're shitting me! I heard she took off with another man. She was cute as a button as I recall and what, twenty-five years younger than him? Now she turns up dead? Not good for da' Judge, I'd say."

"Yeah, well... it's not quite that simple." Nick replied. "Normally, this would be a pretty much open and shut case. But you know the dangers of having blinders on in an investigation."

John looked like he'd been shot with an arrow. He looked out at the lake as he replied in a mournful tone. "You know that I know the dangers of that."

"Right, so there's no need to go there. Sorry I brought it up, buddy." Both men remembered an incident, so long ago, but not so long ago. It had stressed both of them and had caused John to voluntarily resign front he department. The most important thing for an investigator to keep in mind, was to keep an open mind. Don't suppose anything. Don't leap to conclusions. Just follow the facts to wherever it is they lead you, regardless of where you *think* they should lead you.

"Don't worry about it," he told Nick as he turned his gaze back to his old partner. "At this point, that's the least of my worries. So you were saying?"

"Okay, here's the fly in the ointment. She was naked when what was left of her was found last week. Her cloths and her shoes were underneath her. Everything was going along nicely until one of the evidence techs found a piece of paper in the toe of one of her shoes."

"And?"

"And it had a phone number on it. It was the number to Ramsey's personal cell phone."

John's jaw dropped. "You... are... kidding... me!" Nick shook his head. Ramsey! Was the man ever going to be out of his life? Ramsey had been the department's deputy chief. Well known within the department as a tainted cop, it had been learned after his death that he had been working for the folks who had kidnapped Sue. He had been the one who had bushwhacked John, putting a bullet into his head, side, arm, and leg. He had stood over John's prone body and was about to finish him off when a sniper from the state S.W.A.T. team blew his head off. For as long as he lived, he would never forget the sight of the deputy chief's head suddenly exploding into a bloody, mangled mess. Now it appeared that perhaps Ramsey may have finished off someone else before attempting to cancel John's ticket.

"Which kind of brings us to the second body," rejoined Nick. The second body was a male and he was found in some woods a few miles from the woman. What connects the two is the fact that they were both killed the same way, a single shot to the back of the head. Both by a .38 caliber weapon. A bullet was recovered from the guy. It was too deformed for an individual match, but class characteristics indicate that it could have come from a Smith and Wesson, stainless steel model 640."

John looked out at the lake. He could see Mary Kate and

Susan merrily maneuvering the paddle boat about around the dock. They looked like they were having fun.

A model 640 was a five shot, .38 caliber, snub nosed revolver. The gun was also what is known as, "hammerless," meaning that there was no hammer protruding from the rear of the gun. It was specifically designed that way so that the wearer of the gun would not have their cloths torn up from the friction of the protruding hammer constantly rubbing on the fabric. John himself had many suit coats that had torn inner linings from the hammer of his guns. Some guys went so far as to have a piece of leather sewn into the lining of their coat to combat the problem.

But what stuck in his mind right now, was a "flashbulb" moment. He could see, as though it were yesterday, Ramsey pointing his gun down at John's head as he lay bleeding on the ground in front of the cabin last spring. Ramsey had said the words, "*Okay, good enough for me*," raised his gun and pointed it directly at John's head. He remembered looking directly at the weapon that was about to take his life. It was a Smith and Wesson, stainless steel model 640. Thing was, not too many guys carried them to begin with for most had traded them in for one of the more modern automatics, such as the Walther PPK that John himself preferred. He looked back at Nick.

"Shit," he said. "Not that it makes much difference at this point, but it sure would be nice to match that bullet to dick-wad's gun."

"Ahh, that's why I'm here John. It does kind of make a difference."

John's forehead creased in confusion. "Why?"

Nick shifted nervously in his chair. "When I replaced the Chief, after he was forced to step down because of the embarrassment of Ramsey's involvement in your little affair, there were some in the city council who didn't feel that I should have been given the post. After all, they knew nothing about me. More to the point, they knew nothing of my political leanings or what political aspirations I may have. They weren't sure if I was... '*controllable*.' They were miffed because the mayor, who was caught up in the moment, had just gone ahead and appointed me Chief without so much as discussing it with them.

"Sure, they could have raised objections and probably put enough pressure to bear that the Mayor would have to reconsider. But that was dangerous. After all, I was the 'hero,' for taking the initiative in calling out the state S.W.A.T. team. Even though the Chief tried to take the credit, everyone knew I was the one responsible.

"So now they're in a quandary. They can't just start bitching about me without risking a political backlash for coming down on the '*hero*.' They don't like leaving me in there because by now they know that I refuse to be anyone's lackey. Unfortunately for them, I've given them absolutely no reason to criticize me for the way I'm running the department."

"And now they think they may have one," finished John.

"That's right. I've already heard rumblings about a possible accomplice that Ramsey might have had. I've already fired two people who were tied in with Ramsey and criminal charges have been filed on one of them. There may, in fact, be more. There is an ongoing investigation into the matter, but they have turned up nothing new for several weeks. Now I'm stuck with a few potential problems.

"What if there *are* more, that I don't know about? What if one of the guys conducting the investigation is actually *one of them*? What if someone on the city council is tied up in all of this and actually *knows* there are more? The Coeptus Guild would be more than happy to sacrifice one of them for the sake of getting me out of there. They lost Ramsey, a *Deputy* Chief. What if they could replace him with an honest to god *Chief*? The only way open to them right now would be to show that I've done something to warrant being removed, something like maybe the murder of a judge's wife or at the very least, proof that I haven't done enough to uncover the crooked cops at the department."

John rubbed his face, deep in thought. The Coeptus Guild was the group of people responsible for kidnapping Susan. They were a shadowy consortium of individuals who came by the rights of sale-able goods, hardware, software, or whatever else they wanted, by whatever means possible. Kidnapping Susan was how they tried to get her program. They had tried to buy it outright. When she refused they had kidnapped her. If she had then agreed, they would have released her, with threats of dire consequences if she told anyone. Of course they paid handsomely in addition, so having one of their victims go to the police wasn't likely. If Susan had continued to refuse outright... well, in all likelihood, she would not be out on the lake right now.

After the shootout at the cabin, the F.B.I. had gotten involved in trying to nail Coeptus Guild to the wall. However, the F.B.I. was notorious for not sharing information, so the actual status of their progress was still a mystery. But from what Nick had been able to tell, they weren't getting very far. Coeptus Guild was very good at the smoke and mirrors routine.

And now he could see Nick's problem all too clearly. Who could he trust to find out, quickly, who else may have been involved and prove the two bodies they recovered were the work of Ramsey, and Ramsey alone? And, if his thoughts on someone else in the city council being involved were correct, it was just a matter of time before they got their way. In this case, time was on the side of Coeptus Guild.

Nick sat as he watched John work this all out in his head. When it was obvious that he had, Nick asked, "You ready for this, or should I think of something else? If you're not, just say so buddy. Don't worry about me. I'll get it figured out."

John shook his head. "No way. Look, you put your ass on the line big time for me and we all know I wouldn't be around today if it weren't for you. I owe you, big time. Besides," John's eyes began to brighten noticeably, but his face took on a look that would freeze molten lava, his voice went down several octaves and became hard as nails, "I wouldn't mind a chance to take a chunk out of the Coeptus Guild. Wouldn't mind it at all." He smiled then, but there was nothing comforting or happy in that smile.

Nick was taken aback by the transformation. He'd known John for a very long time and they had been through a lot together. He had seen John in more tough situations than he could count, but he couldn't recall ever seeing a look like the one John now wore on his face. Nor had he ever heard his voice sound quite so brutal. In spite of his friendship with the man, he shuddered deep in his core and he wondered what kind of hell fire had just been spawned. He was suddenly very glad that John was on *his* side.

Nick shook himself out of his self induced trance and responded. "I can't pay you very much. I..."

"You don't have to pay me anything." John shot back. The look on his face did nothing to qualm Nick's fears about the monster that he had just released.

"Well... keep track of your time anyway. If this all turns out okay, I'll have the city pay for it. I'll justify it by telling them that I needed an independent investigator that I knew I could trust. Who better than the hero of the OK Corral."

John's face lightened slightly. "OK Corral?"

Nick laughed, part in humor but mostly in an attempt to lighten the mood. "Yeah. After the shootout at the cabin. The news media dubbed it the shootout at the OK Corral. The good guys versus the evil men in the black hats. The good guys won and there was a stack of bodies and a rescued heroine to prove it. Again, once it comes out that you're helping to find any more nasties that may be around, the council may not like it, but the public will eat it up. Their hands will be tied."

A sound alerted them both of the return of Susan and

Mary Kate. They looked up as the two came up onto the deck. Susan wore a look of concern. "Are you guys finished or should we entertain ourselves a little longer?"

"Daddy, we saw a *huge* bass," Mary Kate said with an equally huge smile.

The transformation in John was as sudden as it was dramatic. His entire demeanor changed in an instant as the terrible instrument of death vanished, replaced by that of a loving father overjoyed by the sudden appearance of his child. He held out his arms and Mary Kate promptly jumped into them. "Really?" he said. "Should we go get our poles and try to catch him?"

"Yeah, that would be cool."

"Okay. I just have to talk to Uncle Nick here a little longer. Then we can go."

"*Yes!*" Mary Kate exclaimed while merrily clapping her hands together. She jumped off his lap and ran over to Susan. "Sue, Daddy says we can go fishing. Will you come too?"

She laughed. "Yes, I know. I heard him and yes, I'll come too. Let's go into the garage and get the poles ready. Then we'll fix a snack to take with us." She looked at the men. "Let us know when you're ready. Nick, would you like to come too?"

"No," he chuckled. "I have to get to work, but maybe Janie and I will come over tonight." Janie was Nick's wife and was a bubbly, slightly portly Irish woman who loved to laugh almost as much as she liked her beer. She was a good match for Nick.

After the girls had left, John asked, "So what information can you give me?"

Nick lifted his brief case onto the table and opened it. He removed a file folder and handed it to John. "Here's what I have so far. I'll give you more as I get it, for as long as I continue to get it. Remember, this isn't our investigation and the information that I'm getting is only as a courtesy because of the fact they found Ramsey's phone number in the woman's shoe. My fear is that if the city council somehow manages to turn this into an investigation of me, even that information will dry up. I've got a pretty good relationship going with the lead investigator from the county right now. I told him that we're still looking into any ties to Ramsey that may be left at our department. He understands the need for secrecy. He seems like a pretty straight up guy who's doing his best to help me out. His ass is slightly out on the limb on this as well since he's really giving me more information than he should. Remember, everyone is pretty much taking a wait and see attitude on our whole department right now, though no one will say it to our face. John, we have to convince the world that we've rooted out all the bad apples and everyone that's left is one of the good guys. This is for the department as much as it is for me personally."

"To me, at this point, you and the department are one in the same, Nick." John said as he rummaged through the file, without looking up. Nick was relieved to see the harbinger of death had not returned. He looked like his normal self as he sat looking through the file. In fact, John looked more normal now than he had since his return from the hospital.

He wondered if maybe they hadn't been going about this all wrong. Instead of protecting John from any intrusions, maybe it would have been better if they'd thrown him into the mix and given him something to do other than brood about the recent past.

Nick closed his brief case and stood up. "I'd better get going." He smiled. "Who knows what evil brew the city council has been cooking up in my absence," he said, only half in jest.

John closed the file and stood up with him. They started walking to the front door and were met by Susan and Mary Kate. "Can I see your police car?" she asked Nick. She loved Nick's unmarked squad, with its hidden emergency lights and radios and all sorts of stuff to amaze a six year old.

"Sure." He turned to Nick and Sue. "See you guys later."

Sue gave him a quick peck on the cheek and watched him as he and Mary Kate walked to the car and got in. That would keep Mary Kate occupied for a few minutes. She turned to John. "Well? How'd it go?" She too saw a light-ness in John that hadn't been there before. She had nothing to compare it to, since she hadn't known him before the inci-dent at the cabin, but she could see a bounce that hadn't been there before. There was also something else, hidden just below the surface and she wasn't quite sure of what it was until he began to speak.

He related everything Nick had told her. It wasn't until he started talking about Ramsey and the Coeptus Guild that she began to see what Nick had seen. Though it wasn't nearly as pronounced as what had been displayed to Nick, it was enough to chill her to the bone. His self doubts appeared to have evaporated, replaced by a grim determination that, like Nick, made her glad that she wasn't the object of his obvious and deeply rooted wrath. It was a part of him that she had never seen before. Even when he killed those men at the cabin, it had been with ruthless efficiency and with no sign of obvious emotion.

The mention of the Coeptus Guild had made her heart skip, but not nearly as much as the look on his face. As always, she was going to be there for him and help him in any way she could. But, she was going to stand back and not get in his way. Because Susan Browning decided right then and there, it would not be a good idea for anyone to get in the way of John Livingston Harvard at this juncture. Not a good idea at all.

CHAPTER

3

Mary Kate had gone to school. Susan was doing Susan things on her computer and John was sitting in the sun room going through the files Nick had given him. The woman's name was Sally Jane Walton and she had been thirty seven years old at the time of her death. He looked at the pictures that Judge Walton had given to the city investigators at the time of her disappearance last spring. She was pretty, strawberry blonde hair, trim figure, and eyes that danced in merriment. But there was something else in those eyes that belied that initial assessment.

John was a big believer in eyes. The saying goes that the eyes were the gateway to the soul and he was a devout follower of that way of thinking. The mouth could lie. Given enough practice, the language of the body could be made to tell a convincing lie as well. But the eyes, that was a much more difficult thing to control. He'd met a few individuals that could master it, but just like those who could fool a polygraph at will, it was a rare occurrence indeed.

She had met the Judge at a social gathering in the city and it had been a whirlwind romance that ended up in marriage one year later. The Judge was a widower with two adult children from his prior union, neither of whom attended the wedding. Apparently, the children didn't approve. Was it strictly the age difference? Or was there something else?

John always thought of an investigation as a jig saw puzzle. An investigator started with clues that could be thought of as pieces of that puzzle. Some were big, obvious, important pieces. Others were smaller, less significant, but pieces all the same and therefore important to the finished picture. One never knew when one of those smaller pieces would fit with another small piece and suddenly, together, the little pieces formed a bigger part of the larger picture. Little things like grown children who didn't approve of a wedding may provide a valuable clue to Sally's death.

Of course, when analyzing those pieces, the investigator always had to keep in mind that some of them may be twisted from the influence of lies and deception. Or, they may be twisted due to erroneous information given by well intentioned witnesses. Eye witnesses often, unintentionally, gave a distorted version of events. To a lay person, a handgun may look huge as it is pointed at them and they will swear that it was a .44 magnum or bigger. Later it is found to be, in fact, a .22, a much smaller weapon. Or they may swear that a given person in a police lineup is the perpetrator, only to have that person cleared later in DNA comparison. So the reasons are many, but the fact remains that it is up to the investigator to straighten out those twisted pieces and add them to the puzzle in their true form.

He looked through the detectives' notes and didn't see any reference to the children other than the fact they had been interviewed and didn't have anything pertinent to say about her disappearance. John knew both of the main investigators on the case and he judged them to be competent enough. But they had been looking at the case as a probable runaway wife, not as a homicide. It was yet another instance of preconceived notions. An upstanding Judge said that his young wife had split with another man. What reason had there been to doubt him?

With any normal person, there would have been few reasons for it ever to have come to police attention. It was different for a Judge when his wife was suddenly not around. People notice. So there had been a cursory investigation and it was decided that yes, she had apparently gotten tired of the older man and went looking for younger pastures. Shit happens. Too bad for him.

John turned his attention to the crime scene photos. It was obviously a corn field and he could see a gigantic combine tractor rig sitting near the spot where the body had been found. It loomed over the area like some huge prehistoric monster. He took that to mean a farmer had found her while harvesting his corn. Not an uncommon occurrence. Cornfields provided a good, remote, dumping ground with easy access, though, looking at the pictures a little closer, this crime occurred before the corn had grown very much. Hmm, that was a little unusual. Possibly an indication of haste. A likely indication that someone had killed her without much forethought and wanted to dispose of the body as fast as possible.

That would be consistent with an act of passion and not a well thought out crime. However, if Ramsey did kill her, and John believed that he did, passion would not be a motive. Nick said she had no clothes on when she was found. John could see Ramsey raping her, but only for his own personal enjoyment as a prelude to killing her. But why? What would Ramsey have to do with the wife of a Judge?

Suddenly, the picture came into focus all too clearly. Click! A piece of the puzzle fell into place. Coeptus Guild! It was their typical MO, or modus operandi, the normal way they operated. Most people had two big, overwhelming weaknesses, sex and money. Coeptus Guild took full advantage of both. It was how they conned Emily into working for them and it was how they had gotten close to Susan just prior to kidnapping her. In both cases, they had used good looking men to seduce the women. They were not impatient people. They realized that though effective, this method took time. They were willing to wait. Now, John realized what the other thing was that he saw in Sally Walton's eyes... deceit.

The Judge had been conned, pure and simple. It didn't take a rocket scientist to figure out what they would want from a judge. The question was, how far had things progressed? Was there a particular case they were interested in or was he part of an overall contingency plan? Had they sprung the trap yet? Was he part of Coeptus Guild now? Or had he still been living in ignorant bliss, convinced he had found, then lost, true love when she disappeared? And what was she doing with Ramsey's phone number in her shoe? That indicated that she didn't know Ramsey, or at least his phone number. So what had happened that she suddenly had to call Ramsey and meet with him, then have him kill her? Finding the answer to that, would probably be a key piece of the puzzle.

He turned his attention back to the crime scene photos, studying each meticulously for any clues that had been overlooked. The bones were pretty clean, only a few mummified remnants of skin adhered to them here and there. Her shoes and clothes had been thrown into the makeshift grave first, then her. The grave itself wasn't very deep, which explained why the tremendous torrent of recent rain had uncovered it. It looked like animals had begun to scatter the bones before they had been discovered.

He turned to the preliminary autopsy report. Nothing much there, a Caucasian female between the ages of thirty to forty. Her approximate height around five feet, five inches. Damage to the head indicated that a bullet had entered the back of the skull and exited around the area of her left eye, damaging the eye socket slightly as it went through.

John sat back in his chair. '*Typical*,' he thought. He now knew of three people that Coeptus Guild had used to get close to their targets. They had killed two out of the three of them. Guess they weren't much for pensions. But somehow, he didn't think this was planned and he doubted Ramsey did this on his own initiative. Something must have occurred to make them take drastic action. What? An idea began to formulate in his brain.

He picked up the file on the man that had been discovered in the woods. Since they still didn't know who he was, he was listed as a "John Doe." The crime scene photos indicated that he was left in a heavily wooded area. Crime scene sketches showed he was several hundred feet away from the nearest path. It appeared that this was an even more hastily arranged grave site than the woman. He was barely in the ground, earth and leaves had been piled on top of him. As with the woman, the recent heavy rains had probably exposed him to the point that he was easily discovered. At least by someone who would be that far off the beaten path. Who had found him anyway? Who was wandering that far into the woods and for what reason?

John rifled through the file until he found the answer. Ah, now he understood. An older couple looking for mushrooms. As with the farmer, a fairly common occurrence. Mushrooms just happen to grow in just the right place to hide a body. Dark, damp, undisturbed, and far from prying eyes.

He looked at the preliminary autopsy report on this one. The man was a white male, between the ages of twenty five to thirty five. He was approximately six feet tall. Damage to his skull was consistent with a bullet fired into the back of his head. Burning and stippling on the skull indicated that it was a loose contact wound.

John sat up straight. A contact wound? He picked up his cell phone and called Nick. As it rang, he began to quickly look through Sally Walton's file. He was looking for a date. Nick answered on the third ring.

"Yeah."

"Nick, that you? That's a hell of a way to answer your phone."

"I'm not having the best of days, John. I'm feeling the hot breath of the wolves on my ankles. I gotta feeling they're getting close to biting."

"Well, we'll see what we can do about that. Do you know if they found any blood on Ramsey's gun?" Even though it had been obvious that Ramsey had shot John and then had been killed himself by the S.W.A.T. team, the gun should have been routinely processed by the crime lab to back up the officers testimony on the events.

"It was processed by the State crime lab, but I don't know what they found. It was pretty much an open and shut case. Why?"

"I just saw the preliminary autopsy report on the dead guy. He had a contact wound to his head. The gun may have blow back on it." 'Blow back' was made when a gun is placed directly on, or at least very close, to a victim when fired. Gases from the gun enter the body and the skin literally explodes from the trapped gases, sending particles of skin, blood, and sometimes bone backward onto the barrel of the gun.

"That," Nick responded, "would mean that if Ramsey was the one who killed him, he never cleaned his gun afterward? That would be pretty careless. It doesn't make sense."

John countered with the idea that had been coming together in his mind, "It would if he killed him the same day he came after me. You said he disappeared for several hours. What if he was getting some things done first? He probably thought he could clean his gun when everything was finished."

Nick didn't answer right away. John waited patiently for Nick to mull it over while he continued going through Sally's file. Finally, Nick said, "We're going to have to get DNA from the dead guy."

"It doesn't look like there's much left for DNA, but you can pull the teeth and get it from there, right?"

"Yes we can, or from the bones," replied Nick. "But I'm not going to do that unless there's something on Ramsey's weapon. We have a few problems here. First of all, we have to make sure there's enough on the gun for analysis. Second, it's been several months. Hopefully, the sample won't be degraded to the point where no usable DNA can be obtained. Lastly, the city council hammer is starting to come down. I don't know how much longer I'm going to have access to the information. "

"Well, see what you can do. If DNA can connect Ramsey's gun with your dead guy, we're more than halfway there. That would mean we have Ramsey's cell phone number with the dead woman and that Ramsey's gun was used to kill the guy in the field."

John found the date he was looking for. "Ah, Nick?"

"Yeah?"

"Nicholas my man. Guess what the date of disappearance for Sally Walton is?"

"I know it was around the time of your deal up north, but I don't know the exact date... don't tell me..."

"You guessed it!" John exclaimed. "It was the night before my shootout at the cabin."

"No shit! I guess with everything that was going on, no one ever put the two pieces together. Why should they? A judge's wife takes a powder and you have a shootout miles away. Now that you've connected the dots, it's obvious, but you're probably the first one to look at the two events together. I have to admit, it looks good. First, let me call the lab and check on the gun. I'll call you back."

This was exactly what happened on 9/11 when terrorists flew the planes into the World Trade towers and the Pentagon. The clues were out there. Different agencies looking at different things for different reasons. At the time, there was no one to look over all the events at the same time. If they had, they too would have connected the dots and the whole terrible incident could have been prevented.

"Good," said John. "I'll be waiting. I think I want to talk to the Judge's kids first. I'll let you know what they say. Bye." He hung up then and began looking up the phone numbers for the Walton children.

He found them and dialed the number for Debra, the Judge's daughter. It rang twice before being picked up. "Hello," a female voice answered.

"Hi," replied John. "Is this Debra?"

"Who is *this*?" she countered. She seemed cautious, but still polite. He supposed that having a judge as a father was bound to develop a sense of vigilance in a person.

"My name is John Harvard and I'm sorry to intrude on you right now, but I am a private investigator and I've been hired to look into the death of your step mother. I realize that you are probably still in mourning, but I'm calling to see if I could set up a time to meet with you for just a few minutes." He had intentionally included the "mourning" part, to see what kind of reaction he got from her. He wasn't disappointed.

"I read the papers, Mr. Harvard. I'd have to be living under a rock to not know who you are," she said lightly. Then her voice firmed up as she continued, "But you don't have to worry about intruding on my *mourning* time. I never liked my step... whatever she was, and I'm not the least bit upset about her passing. In fact, I'm quite happy that she's out of my father's life."

"Oh, I see." Her reaction was what he was hoping for. He could probably get some very straight answers out of this one. However, he still wanted to be present when he questioned her. He wanted to be able to "read" her as she answered his questions. He was pretty sure that she had nothing to do with the murder, but on the other hand, nothing was a certainty at this point, and until he talked to her, he wasn't willing to rule her out. "Well," he continued "when would a good time be?"

"Whatever is a good time for you. How does four o'clock this afternoon sound?"

John thought for a moment before answering. "Sure, that's fine. Where?"

"If you don't mind, would you like to meet me at my house?"

Normally, John would have preferred a more neutral

place. People felt more comfortable and in charge in their own house, making it easier for them to stick to a prefabricated story. Having the meeting away from there would put them a little more on edge and make it easier to "work" them during the interview. However, in this case, John really didn't think he would have to "work" Debra, so he consented. He confirmed her address and hung up.

Next, he dialed the number for David Walton, the Judge's son and the older of the two siblings. David answered on the first ring with an abrupt, "Hello!"

John immediately felt that this phone call may not go as easy as the last. He identified himself and asked David if he would meet with him for a few moments to discuss Sally Walton. His reply was terse, "No. I don't have anything to say to you, Mr. Harvard, and I certainly do not want to discuss my deceased step mother."

John's internal warning system went on full alert and he chose his next words carefully. "Look, Mr. Walton, I'm sorry if I caught you at a bad time. I realize that you just became aware of her untimely demise and I understand how you may want some space while you deal with it. I'm merely looking into what happened and I..."

"I don't need *space*, as you put it." David snapped back. "I could care less that she's dead and I could care less who killed her. The world is a better place with her not in it. You're not a policeman anymore, Harvard. I don't have to talk to you and I won't. I have better things to do than waste any more time discussing that tramp."

There was a click on the line and John realized that he

had been hung up on. Now *that* was an interesting development. He sat back in his chair and reviewed the entire conversation in his mind. Very interesting. Either the man was a complete asshole, or something was going on.

After further consideration, John decided that if the man wasn't an asshole, then either he was completely exasperated with the whole affair, or, he was hiding something. Maybe Ramsey didn't kill her. Or maybe Ramsey was somehow tied in with David Walton. Like, maybe he hired Ramsey to kill his stepmother? It certainly wouldn't be the first time a family member was responsible for having a stepmother or even a mother killed. John himself had handled several contract homicides involving family members.

If that was the case, why did he want her dead? Was David the only one of the Walton's involved? Or was the Judge himself in it up to his neck and David handled the details? That would make sense. The Judge looking for a contract killer would be a lot more likely to attract attention than if David did.

But if the death of Sally Walton was nothing more than an inner-family squabble, then what was Ramsey's phone number doing in her shoe? Why was she calling the man who would ultimately do her in?

And if David Walton was involved, was his sister Debra involved as well? He thought of his conversation with Debra. If she was, she was certainly better at playing the game than David was. Speaking of David, John assumed he was an educated man, so if he was hiding something, one would think that he would at least make a pretense of cooperating.

John shook his head. This case was definitely looking to be FUBAR, big time. FUBAR was an acronym for "Fucked Up Beyond All Recognition," and it certainly appeared that that particular shoe was going to fit this time. He was going to have to learn more about David Walton and he was going to have to revise his approach with Debra Walton.

John pulled his SUV into the driveway of Debra Walton's modest home on a quiet, tree lined cu-de-sac. Though the homes themselves were only slightly above average, John knew that the property values in this old neighborhood made the dwelling well above the price range of the average income. The house and the grounds were well maintained and it was obvious that someone spent a lot of time caring for them. Whether it was Debra or a service, he didn't know.

That question was answered a moment later when she came to the door. The main door was open and he could see through the screen door that she was a pretty brunette, wearing a gardening apron with the name "Debra" emblazoned in green across the chest. She began removing it as she approached. "I'm sorry Mr. Harvard. I was working in the garden and lost all sense of time. I just realized how late it was and hadn't been in the house for more than a minute when I heard your truck in the driveway."

"Please, call me John. I was just looking at your garden.

You've done a great job with it. I like those red flowers over by the tree. You've got a ton of bees and butterflies on them. What are they?" He knew what they were, but gardeners love to talk about their creations and he wanted her to relax and feel comfortable with him.

"First, let me return the favor by saying, please call me Deb, or Debra, whichever you prefer. As for the flowers, those are called Mars Midgets and they pretty much bloom all summer. You just have to keep snapping the heads off when the color from the flower is nearly gone. I love them. Are you into gardening too?"

He shook his head. "Not really. I just appreciate a nice layout when I see it. I think it adds a lot to a house."

"It sure does and I find it very relaxing as well as reward-ing. I thank you for the compliment. Now, let's go into the kitchen. Would you like something to drink?"

"No thanks. I don't want to intrude anymore than I have to. I just wanted to ask a few questions, then I'm out of your hair."

They walked into the kitchen and sat at a breakfast table near a large bay window. The backyard was small and en-closed in a dense hedge that provided a surprising amount of comfortable, intimate privacy. The size of the bay window was such that it almost felt like one were sitting outdoors.

"What did you want to ask me, John?" she said with a most pleasant smile. '*If this woman has anything to hide,*' he thought, '*She certainly is hiding it well.*' He looked at her eyes for signs of deception and the side of her neck for the telltale throb of a nervous individual. He could see nothing but a perfectly calm woman at peace with herself.

"Well, I just wanted to discuss your relationship with Sally Walton."

He noted that the corners of her eyes creased slightly upon hearing the question. Whatever her response, he could tell that he'd hit a nerve.

She didn't respond. Instead, she looked out the window at her beautiful backyard, as if she were looking there for answers, or maybe strength, or maybe both. He waited patiently.

Eventually, when she did respond, she continued to look out the window as she spoke. "Right after she disappeared, some detectives interviewed me about anything I might know about her disappearance. They wanted to know facts. I don't think that I knew anything that would have been helpful and they seemed to agree. You are the first one to ask me about my feelings and my relationship with her, or at least anything beyond the surface. I suspected that your purpose for coming here might be a little more in depth than those first interviews and I thought I was ready for it. I can see now, I was wrong."

She turned to look at him once again and it was obvious that she was a jumble of emotions. But he still could see no signs of deception. She continued, "My relationship with Sally was... flawed, to say the least. Sally seemed the perfect woman. Smart, beautiful, funny, and she made a good showing of being loving and caring. She always did and said the right things."

"But?" John pressed.

She returned her gaze to the backyard as she answered. "But, it just never felt right. At first, I thought that it was probably my own emotional problems dealing with her as a replacement for my mom."

She looked back at John as she continued. "Physically, she was very similar to my mother. A younger version of course, almost thirty years younger. But she made my father very happy, so I tried to deal with the situation as best I could. It forced me to do a lot of soul searching, and when I did, I began to realize that her as a replacement for my mother was not the problem." She momentarily stopped again and stood up, "I'm going to fix myself a cup of tea. Would you like one?"

"No thanks." he replied. He watched as she moved to a cupboard and removed a cup and a box of tea. Then he continued. "So what was the problem?"

She walked to the microwave and began preparing her tea as she answered. "It was nothing I could put my finger on really. That's what made me question my own self doubts for so long. It was little things, like bragging a little too much about the price of an expensive purchase they had made, or the cards and gifts she would get for birthdays and other various occasions. The cards and gifts always seemed... not quite right. Almost like she was doing it because she was expected to, not because she wanted to. There was no true feeling there and therefore her selections were always... off. To sum it all up, I guess you could say that I felt a calculated coldness in her that she kept clothed in her outward appearance of frivolity and caring." She started the microwave and turned to him while it ran. She smiled and grimaced all at the same time. "Am I making any sense?"

He smiled. "As unbelievable as it may sound, yes. You're making perfect sense. It's called intuition and it's how any good policeman or detective operate. I understand exactly what you're saying. Did she know how you felt?"

The microwave did it's little "ding," and she removed her cup. She then returned to the table and continued as she sat down. "I think she did. Say what you will about her, I never doubted her intelligence, just her sincerity."

"So you two never had *words* about it, or about anything else for that matter?"

"No, not really. Like I said, I'm sure she knew how I felt, but we never went at it. It was as though we both knew that once we started something like that, it wouldn't end well, and like a fight at a big party, it would suck in everyone around and neither one of us wanted that, for different reasons of course."

John studied her as he asked, "What about your not going to the wedding? Surely she must have said something about that?"

"No she didn't. That was part of the reason I began to realize her true nature. I mean, if *you* were going to marry a woman, for instance, and her children were not going to attend the wedding, wouldn't you feel compelled to say something? Wouldn't you be more than a little upset?"

He nodded. "Yeah, it would upset me, piss me off big time actually, excuse the French."

She smiled, "That's okay. I would think that would be a normal reaction and I had a little speech all prepared when the time came. Except, it never came. She never questioned me or my brother about it, and next time we met, it was as if everything was okay and it never happened. It was weird."

"Speaking of your brother, how was his relationship with her?" he asked.

She rolled her eyes. "That was a little more volatile."

"How so?"

"For a long time, it was obvious, at least to me, that he was as smitten with her as Dad was. Whenever she was around he would turn on the charm, big time. I even said something to him about it. He denied it of course. He *said* he didn't really like her either, but was trying to put on a good showing for my father's sake."

"But you didn't believe him."

"Of course not. He's my brother and we're very close. I know him and I know when he's on the hunt and he was definitely on the hunt."

"He's not married?"

Debra's face contorted as she replied, "Yes," she snapped, "he is. To a very lovely and charming woman much closer to *his* age. Her name is Tabitha." She rolled her eyes once again, "I don't know what it is about the men in my family."

"Did his wife know about his feelings?"

"What do you think?" she replied sarcastically, "Of course she knew. She's a woman, his wife for Christ sake and had received the *same* attention from him when *they* had met. Oh, he tried to be slick about it, but she knew."

"Was there any trouble between them because of it?"

"Oh yeah! Quite a bit. They kept it all shielded from Dad

of course. I'm convinced he knew nothing. But Tabitha and I talked about it a lot. She was furious. I was always afraid that one day she would snap and tear the woman's head off."

John felt a little jolt at that comment. "Really," he said. "Is she a violent person?"

Debra laughed. "She's Irish through and through and as fiery as they come. She's definitely got a temper. If the two of them squared off, you'd better believe my money would be on Tabitha. She loves my brother with all her heart and she would fight for him like a tigress defending her cubs. *I* wouldn't want to stand in her way."

John shook his head in wonderment. This case was getting curiouser and curiouser. He felt the beginning twinges of a headache. "Let's get back to your brother. Do you think anything ever happened between the two of them?"

The remnants of the previous laughter left her face entirely and turned sad. "I don't know for sure." She looked down at her teacup.

"What do you *think*?" John pressured.

"I think... I think yes. Just before she disappeared, I saw a distinct change in their relationship. My brother was calmer, much more reserved than he had been when she was around. It was the fleeting looks between them that really convinced me. It was like the chase was over and he'd gotten what he wanted. Now it was just a question of keeping it secret. If I didn't know my brother so well, I would have thought that things were back to normal with him. But every now and then, I would catch them looking at one another, the way lovers look at each other when they have a secret known only to them. There's no mistaking that look."

"And Tabitha?"

"She changed too. I could see a quiet, deep rooted anger taking hold. The loud, overt arguments were over, replaced by a stillness that was plain scary, because that's not her."

"What about after Sally disappeared? How did Tabitha and your brother react to that?"

"Tabitha's mood improved immediately. My brother... he hasn't been the same since. He's morose, quick to anger. After Sally was found, well, he's been really volatile since then. Nobody wants to be around him for fear of his vicious remarks about everything."

Now it was John's turn to gaze out the window. But he wasn't seeing anything in the backyard. He was thinking of his next question and whether or not he wanted to ask her about her brother's animosity toward him. His attitude may be a crucial piece of the puzzle and like all good investigators, he didn't like probing into critical areas until he had a good handle on the facts surrounding that area as best he could. Debra was his first interview and he had yet to develop a feel for the direction of this case. In the end, he turned back toward her and took the plunge.

"After calling you, I called your brother. Suffice it to say, his reaction toward me was less than warm. Any ideas as to why that would be?"

She sadly shook her head. "Like I told you, he's changed since Sally disappeared. He used to be a typical frat boy, laughing, drinking, the consummate jokester. All that has changed now. It's been long enough that I'm beginning to think it's permanent. Plus... oh, never mind."

"Please," John urged, "what were you going to say?"

"It was nothing, really."

He thought about it a moment and decided to let the matter drop. John could detect no discrepancies in Debra's story. In fact, he could find no sign of duplicity at all, so he decided to switch gears. "What about your father. Tell me about his relationship with Sally just prior to her disappearance. Any arguments, tension? Do you think he may have found out about Sally's affair with your brother?"

She shook her head. "Not that I could tell. He seemed to be a perfectly happy man."

"And after she disappeared?"

"He reacted as I would have expected him to." Debra replied. "He was devastated. The only... no, never mind."

John's eyes furrowed. There was beginning to be too much left on the field, too much left unsaid. "What?" he asked.

"It was nothing. Just a feeling, but I'm sure it didn't mean anything."

"Please, tell me," John urged. She was pulling this one too many times.

"It's just that... right after she disappeared, he was frantic to find her. He was on the phone constantly, calling whoever he could think of. Then, about two days later, he suddenly seemed to go directly into grieving mode. It was like he had already given up looking for her. That was when he told the police that she was having an affair with another, younger man. He felt that was where she had gone. At the time, I thought that it was odd, sudden, and made no sense. It didn't track with what I knew about her and her relationship with my brother or my father. But I really had no reason to doubt him."

There was silence for a while. She looked out the window and appeared to be deep in thought. Whether she was thinking about what she had just said or whether she was regretting what she had just said, John didn't know. He let her sit awhile before asking the question he was hesitant to ask. "Do you think there's any possibility that your father was somehow responsible for Sally's death?"

After asking the question, he studied her carefully, looking for a reaction that might tell him if her answer was truthful or not. She turned back to him and answered slowly, thoughtfully. "I don't think so. My Dad is a very intelligent, resourceful man, so it is possible for him to have carried something like that out. But like my brother, I'm very close to my father and I think I would have detected something wrong."

"What if it was a sudden decision? There would be nothing to detect in that case. What if he found out about the affair with your brother and killed her in a rage."

She suddenly looked as though she were fighting back tears, but stoically pushed forward with an answer. "You don't know my father. I don't think I've ever seen him suddenly lose his temper. I've seen him mad, of course, but not what I would call flying off the handle."

John decided to let the matter drop. He probably had already learned as much as he could from her. She didn't believe her father could kill in a rage. She was probably right, but then again, how could anyone know how a man would react to finding out that his wife was having an affair with his son?

"Thank you for your candor, Debra, and I think that will do it for now. I appreciate the time you've taken and I apologize for some of the questions I asked. Please keep in mind that I am looking at all angles. Most likely, none of your family was in any way involved in this."

"I understand," she replied. "And thank you for saying that."

They stood and walked toward the door. John still had one more question to ask, but he wanted to ask it as nonchalantly as possible. "Oh, by the way, did you or any of your family know Deputy Chief Ramsey?"

A stern look crossed her face. "Why do you ask?"

"No reason in particular. Like I said, I'm trying to cover all angles. I uncovered some information that may... and I stress *may*, indicate that Sally might have known him."

She laughed, but there was nothing funny about it. It was short and harsh. "Obviously you've just begun to look into that angle. Otherwise, you would have known that yes, we did know Deputy Chief Ramsey, knew him well in fact. Or I guess I should say, we thought we knew him well. His son, Bill, and my brother were on the same university swim team. He's been at my Dad's on numerous occasions for parties and such, never in a one on one situation." She said the last part, almost apologetically.

"No need to feel bad about it Debra. He fooled a lot of people and after all, he held a very respectable post."

She looked at him a moment with the obvious look of someone who is waging an internal battle. "John, since we're talking about Deputy Chief Ramsey, I suppose there is something else that you should know. It's what I started to tell you before. It concerns David. He... well... to be perfectly frank with you, he doesn't like you."

John's eyebrows furrowed in confusion. "What? Why? He doesn't even know me."

"You're right," she replied. "But he knows *of* you, through the Ramsey's. The Deputy Chief hated you and that carried on to his son and *that* carried on to David."

John's mind quickly processed this information. He was used to people not liking him, especially scum-bags like Ramsey. The feeling was mutual. But John's instincts were that this could be of considerable importance in this case. Suddenly, a scenario began to form. "Debra, what does David do for a living?"

"He's a psychiatrist. Why?"

"I was just wondering. That surprises me. I kind of thought he would be in the law field. What kind of work does he do?"

She was a bit baffled as to where all this was going and she had a feeling that none of it was good for her brother. "He wanted to be an attorney, but he was flunking out, so he switched his major to psychiatry. Now he works as a psychiatrist for the state penitentiary."

John pushed on, "And Ramsey's son, what does he do?"

"He does criminal defense work for Langstrom and Associates."

"Really? How has David's relationship been with Ramsey's son since all this went down?"

"I don't really know. David really hasn't been someone that people want to even be around, let alone talk to for any length of time."

John asked, "What's your general opinion of Ramsey's son?"

"I personally never liked him and I don't think my father does either. To our credit, neither my father nor I ever really trusted the Deputy Chief or his son. We didn't liked either one of them for that matter. That's why the Deputy Chief wasn't over more often. It was my brother who was all agog over him."

"Good instincts on your part. I can't think of anything else for now. If I do think of something, do you mind if I call you again?" John asked.

"No," she replied. "Call me anytime you want."

"Thanks." He opened the front door. Still facing her, he bid goodbye, turned and began walking out to his truck. Debra did not follow and he heard the door close quietly behind him.

As he was pulling away from the house, he thought about all that he had learned. And he had learned much more than he had expected to. The trouble was, none of it cleared up the overall picture. He had wanted a foundation from which he could build his case against Ramsey and find out who else might be working for Coeptus Guild. Not only did he not accomplish much toward that goal, he instead found that there were a lot more suspects in the murder of Sally Walton than he could have conceived of. In fact, all he succeeded in doing was to add a lot more pieces to the puzzle, and he strongly suspected that some of those pieces, were very twisted indeed.

CHAPTER

4

As he drove home, John mentally reviewed his interview with Debra. He tried to pick apart her story, but found no flaws that he could see. He conjured up images of her as she responded to his questions and scrutinized her appearance as she was answering. He could recall nothing in her demeanor that would suggest that she was lying. Of course, he had been wrong before, so he wasn't ready to completely buy into her story quite yet. How could he? There was just too much going on in that convoluted family to ignore any possibility. And to top it all off, they knew Ramsey well enough to have him over to their house on several occasions? That kind of closeness, however involuntary, made him nervous. The fact remained that if any one of the Walton's wanted some *"dirty work"* to be done, their previous sense that Ramsey was a seedy character would naturally lead them to him.

He thought about the Walton family and shook his head. It was yet another example of how a beautiful house with a white picket fence did nothing to alter the personalities of those inside. Most people thought that money would buy them happiness. John had handled enough police calls in the "upper crust" parts of town to know that it didn't. Like everyone else in the world, they loved, they hated, they lied, they conspired. They had secrets. And finally, they died, just like everyone else. In the end, all of the Walton's had reasons to want Sally dead. In fact, with the exception of Debra, good reasons.

He counted off his list of current suspects. Ramsey led the list. By association, his son would have to be thrown into the mix as well. David Walton and his wife, for entirely different reasons, were next. He didn't like the way David was acting, had been acting, according to Debra. The Judge was next and Debra was last. He could see no obvious reason for her to be involved. But there could be something there that he didn't know about yet and besides, the old adage, "Blood is thicker than water," had proven correct on many occasions. She could have killed just to help out the family. Who knew?

Wouldn't it be something if this had nothing to do with Coeptus Guild? It was just a coincidence? But John shoved that idea to the side quickly. He didn't believe in coincidences. Sally disappears the night before Ramsey tries to kill John and she has Ramsey's private cell phone number in her shoe. No way!

On the other hand, there were some powerful reasons for not throwing the Walton's out of the mix either. Perhaps there was some connection that went beyond inter-family squabbles. Like Coeptus Guild? The thought brought up some intriguing possibilities.

He turned his attention to the Coeptus Guild suspects. Deputy Chief Ramsey's involvement was a given. But what about his son? A defense attorney? And what of his buddy, David Walton? A psychiatrist for the state pen? Between the two of them, they had the perfect environments to recruit low life's for grunt work. John thought he could be reaching there, but he didn't think he was reaching too far.

Last, but certainly not least, who was the body recovered in the woods? Was he totally unrelated to this mess? Was he another innocent victim of Coeptus Guild? Or was he yet another peon that had out served his usefulness, possibly recruited by Walton or Ramsey's son? If so, perhaps a check of prison and parole records could yield an identification... and some much needed answers.

The puzzling thing to both bodies, was the uncanny timing with John's own run in with Coeptus Guild. It simply had to be more than mere coincidence. So what was the connection? Was it with him? He hadn't known any of them. If not him, then was Susan or the departed Emily the missing connection?

He shook his head. So many questions. So many possibilities. His meeting with Debra had made things as clear as the muddy Mississippi. He had thought he had a clear direction for this case. It was now obvious that all bets were off. He reached down and turned on his radio. He pushed the button that selected his I-Pod music player and then selected some Yanni. He drove the rest of the way home thinking only of... well, basically nothing.

He walked through the door of his house and was greeted

by an enthusiastic Mary Kate. Upon seeing him, she jumped up into his arms yelling, "Daddy!" After hugging him tightly for a moment, she began telling him about her day, barely pausing to take a breath in her haste to get all the news out. Her tale culminated by informing him that there was an "annoying" boy on the bus.

"Why is he annoying?" John asked.

"Because he keeps staring at me. I think he likes me. He's weird." She responded and then she ran off to play. John rolled his eyes. '*And so it starts,*' he thought.

He walked into his office and found Susan hammering away at her computer keyboard. She was a top notch programmer and was self employed. Most of what she did was so far over his head that he sometimes felt out of place with her, almost stupid. She currently was so into her work that she didn't realize he had entered the room. He studied her from the side for a moment.

As well as being exceptionally intelligent, she was exceptionally attractive as well, and with a figure to match. Her thick, long, dark hair had natural, gentle curls. As he watched, her bangs became entangled in one of her eyelashes and she unconsciously moved them to one side and away from her startling beautiful green eyes, before continuing with her work. She had never been married, but certainly not from a lack of suitors. Men had been busting down the door trying to get at her since puberty. A few had managed to get a relationship off the ground, none had succeeded in getting a ring around her finger for she carried some emotional baggage with her that had prevented her from marrying, or even maintaining any lasting relationships.

John knew that this was due to her distrust in men, stemming from her father's philandering ways when he was married to her mother. He had left Susan and her mother to be with a much younger woman. That hadn't worked out so well and though he had tried to make amends with Susan's mother, the damage had been done. Susan had never forgiven her father for what she had viewed as abandonment and for years, had refused to see him, speak to him, or even acknowledge his existence. That anger and feelings of betrayal had carried over to Susan's own relationships and now she sat, thirty nine years old and never married.

The one good event that had come from Susan's kidnapping by the Coeptus Guild, was that it had reunited her and Peter, Susan's father, she had learned that while she hadn't wanted anything to do with him, he had constantly kept tabs on her over the years. This vigilance had ultimately led to the discovery of the kidnapping plot and Susan's harrowing rescue. Some serious soul searching during her imprisonment had caused Susan to realize that she still loved her father. They had renewed their relationship and currently, in that respect anyway, all was right with the world.

Now, as John studied her, he was a torrent of emotions. Under normal circumstances, John would have found her to be irresistible, with her combination of good looks, intelligence, and common sense, she was right up his alley. But John carried his own baggage. The two biggest impediments to his acting on his latent desire to start a relationship were the memories of Emily Stone and Gregory Harris.

He just couldn't get Emily out of his mind. He wasn't sure why. He had only known her for three days, but in that time he had felt a closeness that he had never known before. She had just felt... right. Then, in a rapid fire series of events, she had betrayed him, saved him, and finally, suddenly, was taken from him. Her memory still haunted him in his dreams.

Gregory Harris was another matter. His memory was the antithesis of Emily's. His haunting took place during the day, when John was wide awake. Harris was a vicious, ex-military special forces soldier who sold his services to the highest bidder, which at the time, was Coeptus Guild. He had absolutely no qualms whatsoever about killing. Harris had kidnapped Susan Browning for the purposes of forcing her to work with Coeptus Guild and to reveal the highly effective hacking program that she had developed. He had taken her to a remote cabin in the north woods where John had found them and had succeeded in taking out all the captors but Harris, who subsequently had captured John.

He had accused John of being no different from himself, a cold blooded killer. But, Harris had said, John cloaked his impulses in the guise of respectability. In the end, Harris claimed, it all culminated with the same result. In an eerie precognition of the future, Harris went on to say that if he were to kill Emily Stone, John would in turn, gladly... no, happily kill Harris and take great satisfaction for having done it.

As it were, it all went down as Harris had unknowingly predicted. Harris did kill Emily and in turn, was killed by

John, in a particularly vicious manner. A knife to the neck, twisted back and forth before being removed. And as Harris predicted, John took great satisfaction in not only killing him, but watching him suffer as he died.

Harris's coup de graces came when, in his dying breath, he looked up at John, smiled and croaked out the words, "*I told you*," and died. John hadn't the time to give it much thought then. But during his recovery, he did begin to think about it and it disturbed him, greatly. Was Harris right? John had killed many times during his career as a cop and had always slept well at night. He justified it in his own mind by the comforting thought that he had had no choice. Kill or be killed. Kill or some innocent person would die. Simple matter really. He was the good guy in the white hat doing society a favor by eliminating those who tried to do harm to them. Finito. No further thought required.

The mathematics all balanced out and the world went on spinning. Except for one little fly in the ointment. That fly being Harris's prediction that John would feel elated at having killed him. That fly wouldn't go away, couldn't be forgotten. Like a bug floating in a bowl of soup, it tainted everything around it and made the previously appetizing, healthful soup, disgusting and unwanted.

Harris had died believing that he had proven to John that there was no difference between them other than the fact that John had chosen a different role to play the game with. In a chess game, one color is black, the other white. In checkers, one color is red, the other black. Does the color of the pieces make one player a better person than the other?

Does the color of the pieces make the desire to win or the satisfaction of winning any different? Where does the fine line between good and evil lie?

And so, John wrestled with these thoughts. Harris's smiling face haunted him during the day as Emily's smiling face haunted him in the night. Harris's face drove him to extreme physical and mental exertion so that he could forget. Those same exertions allowed his exhausted body to fall asleep at night. The mathematics once again balanced out and once again, the world went on spinning.

Except there was yet another fly in the ointment. This one not so unappetizing. More like finding an unexpected cherry on the top of an ice cream sundae. Susan. She was always there for him. She asked for nothing and gave everything in return. He shuddered to think what these past few months would have been like if she had not been around.

There was no denying that the sparks were there between the two of them. But they were twisted, muted, like looking at fireworks through the distorted glass at the bottom of a pop bottle. One more twisted piece of John's own life puzzle. Another piece that needed to be smoothed out and put in its proper place.

John had been too preoccupied with his demons to put much effort into straightening out that piece. It wasn't that he didn't recognize and fully appreciate what Sue had done, was still doing. It was more of a matter that he didn't want to go in that direction before he could handle it. He didn't need any added responsibilities at this juncture. However, he realized that taking on this new case involving Ramsey had been good for him on a number of different levels.

It took his mind off his images of Emily and Harris. It finally gave him an outlet to vent his frustrations. After all, no matter how much thinking he did, both of the causes for his torment were dead and there was nothing he could do or say to them to give him relief. It had to come from within. The fact that this case involved Coeptus Guild gave him the opportunity to deal with one more demon that was always lurking beneath the surface of the outward calm that he always displayed. *Anger.*

A deep rooted, black as night, *anger.* Anger at the Guild and the men behind that company that had caused him so much anguish and had taken so much from him. They had taken from other people as well and they should be justifiably punished for those crimes. But that was different. That wasn't him. That wasn't personal. This suppressed, unyielding anger worried him. What would he do when and if he actually came face to face with one of his tormentors? Would his world spin out of control? Was Harris right? Or would he keep his emotions in check and do the right and proper thing? Only time would tell.

Susan suddenly twitched in her chair and exclaimed, "Oh!"

John grinned, jolted out of his morose thoughts. "Sorry. Didn't mean to scare you. I just got home."

She let out a large breath and replied, "That's okay. I was so engrossed in my work that I didn't hear you come in. Is Nick with you? You know he mentioned something about them coming over tonight for dinner."

"No. I haven't talked to him all day. As a matter of fact, I have to call him anyway. I'll find out. How was your day? Even when I was here, I was pretty preoccupied."

She smiled. "That's okay. I think you needed to do something different for a change. How's it going anyway?" Susan had her own reasons for wanting to know how the case was progressing. She too would love to strike back at Coeptus Guild.

He walked over to a chair near Susan's and sat down. He briefly rubbed the back of his head and replied, "It's going okay, but it isn't as clear cut as I thought it was going to be. Ramsey's involvement notwithstanding, there's a lot going on here." He gave Sue a run-down of his conversation with Debra Walton.

When he was finished, she said, "Wow! Sounds like you could use help with some background checks." Because of her work on developing the ultimate hacking program, she had become an accomplished hacker in her own right. She would have to learn which databases to hack into for the information that would be useful to them, but once there, she could retrieve a treasure trove of information.

John felt a sinking feeling of apprehension course through his body as he replied, "I'm not sure that's a good idea. I don't know if I want you that close to this investigation, you know what they're capable of."

A look of sadness, tinged with disappointment, crossed her face. A moment later, the look changed to one of mounting anger as she replied, "Yes I *do* know what they're capable of and I also know this may be a chance to put some of those bastard's behind bars. I do not appreciate you taking away my opportunity in doing my part." Her voice rose as her own pent up frustrations began to release themselves. "I can't physically fight them. I can't shoot them. I'm not capable of striking back at them the way you can. But this," she motioned toward the computer sitting on her desk, "*this* I can do." Her face softened a little. "Please don't take this away from me. Don't you see? How poetic! I can use the very thing they lusted after against *them*!" And with a tone dripping of sarcasm, "It's just plain priceless."

John was taken aback. He had never seen this side of Sue before. He realized that in his self pitying mode, he had forgotten just how much they had mentally abused her as well. She was correct of course, he had no right to forbid her from taking revenge in the only way she knew how. He slowly smiled as he thought about it. It was indeed priceless.

His thoughts were shattered by a harsh, "What's so funny?" barked out by Sue.

"You're right!" he responded with a chuckle. "It is priceless. It's more than priceless in fact. It's hilarious."

Her face lightened and she began to chuckle too. John's chuckle turned to a full-fledged laugh for the second time that day. She followed suit. Soon the two of them were laughing until tears began to roll down their faces. Mary Kate ran into the room. "What's so funny? What are you laughing at now?" she asked.

John and Sue stopped laughing as they each began to think of an answer. They looked at one another and realized that neither of them could think of anything to tell her. They both broke into renewed laughter. Mary Kate looked at them as if they had lost their minds. But soon, she began laughing as well. She still wasn't sure what they were laughing at, but, she decided, it sure must be funny. Besides, it was funny just watching them!

Eventually, the laughter died down. Sue suddenly jumped to her feet, moved to John, impetuously plopped down in his lap and hugged him tightly. "Thank you." she whispered in his ear. He hugged her in return. It felt good, really good. He felt his defenses begin to crumble away and suddenly he wasn't sure if he was glad or not so glad that Mary Kate was in the room. He felt her presence and realized that she too had come over and had her arms around both of them.

Their reverie was broken when Mary Kate broke the hug and loudly asked, "What's for dinner? I'm hungry."

"I'm not sure." Sue responded as she backed her upper body away from John, but still remained on his lap. "Your Dad has to call Uncle Nick and see if he's still coming over." She looked at John.

Looking at his daughter, he said, "I'll call him in a minute. Now can you go do something while I talk to Sue?"

"Okay," she responded lightly and ran from the room.

John looked back at Sue and said, "You know, I think we may be losing it. That really wasn't very funny."

She looked at him with a strange mixture of amusement and sadness. "I know. I think it's probably a combination of things, with stress being the common denominator. Let's face it, this has been one long journey. Things really haven't been right for either one of us since the day I was taken."

He nodded his head in agreement. "On the bright side of things, this was twice we've had a good laugh in the same day. I think that may mean we're finally coming out the other side."

"I think so too." she said and gave him another quick hug. He hugged back and it felt good. It felt right.

John continued, "As far as your helping me, let's see what Nick has to say about all this and how much he can help us. I'd like to try to get as much of this information as possible through the front door. You understand?" She nodded and began to get off his lap while saying, "I understand completely. Why don't you call him now?"

John's arms unexpectedly gripped tight and prevented her from sliding off his lap. She looked at him in anticipation, hoping she knew what was coming next. It did. The kiss, tentative at first, grew harder and more demanding. She responded in kind. Their tongues became implements of passion. Suddenly, with a slight moan, Sue broke away and stood up. With a rueful smile on her face she announced, "We both have things to do Mr. Harvard. I think it's time we get at them. We can discuss this further at a later time."

"Yes." he said with a short, amusing laugh, "I suppose we can."

"I'm going to check out the possibilities for dinner. Let me know as soon as you can because I have to admit, I'm famished as well," and with that, she walked from the room.

John picked up the phone and dialed Nick's cell. "Hello," came the response from the other end when the call was answered.

"Hey Nick. How's it going over there?"

"Not good, but I can't really talk about it right now. You?"

John went through his interview with Debra Walton once again. When he finished, he said, "I'd like to know who all the players are on this. We've got nothing on the guy in the woods. I'm leaning toward David Walton as a possible player here. Do you think you could check out any releases and parole violations since last summer? If the guy in the woods is a parolee, he obviously has missed his check in."

"Yeah," Nick sighed and answered a little glumly. He lowered his voice. "John, I don't see anything obvious, but my guts are screaming at me right now. It's getting to the point that I'm a little leery about looking over the next hill. I think I'm beginning to know how Custer felt at the Little Big Horn. Somethings brewing. I can just feel it."

Like all cops, be they ex or current, Nick and John were both firm believers in gut instinct. If Nick felt like, "Thar's injuns in them thar woods." Then there probably were. It added a sense of urgency to their efforts.

"Okay," John replied. "Let me know if there's anything I can do. On a more upbeat note, Sue wants to know if you and Janie are coming over tonight?"

"Ha!" said Nick. "You're going to have beer, right?"

"Do you think I would invite Janie over and not have beer?"

"Alright, it would do me good to get out and have a few,

though I think I'll stick with that sissy wine you and Sue drink. My gut's getting a little out of hand. It'll do Janie good to come over too. You know how she's been since the last one left the nest."

Nick and Janie had three kids and the youngest had just gone off to college. For the first time in a long while, it was just the two of them. Janie, who lived for her kids, was having some difficulty with the transition, and Mary Kate had become her pseudo child.

"Good." John said. "What time?"

"If you don't mind," answered Nick, "How about six? *Some* of us have to work in the morning."

"Asshole!" retorted John humorously. "See you then," and hung up.

Nick and Janie, as always, were prompt. They opened the front door and let themselves in, right at six o'clock. "Aunt Janie!" Mary Kate squealed as she ran across the room and jumped into her arms.

"Oh, you precious little thing, you." Janie exclaimed and squeezed Mary Kate tight. Sue joined them from the kitchen and the two of them struck up an instant conversation.

Nick, got right to the point. "Where's my wine?" he said in a loud, serious voice. Then he laughed. He carried with him a manila folder.

"Come on. I'll get it," answered John, and the two men walked into the kitchen.

As John was uncorking the bottle, Nick commented, "I think we hit pay dirt on your hunch." He lifted the folder for emphasis. "I have a few names in here for you to look at, but there's one parolee whose last check in was the day before your shootout. He hasn't checked in since then."

John handed Nick his wine and took the folder from him as he asked, "What's his name?"

"William Raymond Jenkins, AKA, Billyray. Forty two years old. He's been in trouble with the law since he was a juvenile, mostly burglary's and strong arm stuff. He's from Alabama. He came up here because the heat down there was getting too intense and I don't mean temperature wise. I made some calls and found out that they were trying to link him and the gang he was running with to a series of armored car heists. He got out just in time because the police were waiting for them on the very next job they did. The thing is, several of the guards on these robberies were shot to death and the police think it was Billyray. None of his cohorts cracked, cops think they were more terrified of Billyray than them, so they had nothing on him.

"Shortly after moving up here, he pulled an armed robbery at a liquor store and shot the attendant. Fortunately for Billyray, after surviving a coma for a few weeks, the man survived. Now, ready for the icing on the cake?"

John, who had just finished pouring the wine, looked up and gave him a questioning stare. Nick smiled and said, "David Walton was his staff psychiatrist, spent a lot of time with him. He testified at Jenkins' parole hearing and gave him a full-fledged backing."

John nodded grimly, but said nothing. He picked up the file and studied a mug shot of Jenkins. If ever there was a stereotypical picture of a thug, this was it. Jenkins had one of those faces that makes a mother collect her children when they see him. Women move to the other side of the street. Hell, even men would avoid looking at him directly. There was nothing inviting or friendly about him. A prospective employer would take one look at him and mentally rule him out of any job opening available, even before Jenkins uttered a word. To John, it was mainly in his eyes. They were cold, hard, mean, emotionless.

Though John normally took a hardcore view of criminals, his belief was life was what you made of it, hard fathers and uncaring mothers be damned. Sometimes one had to wonder what made men like Billyray. They were so devoid of normal human emotions, so bereft of normal reactions to everyday stimuli that one had to ask if there wasn't something else at work. Genetics? Chemical imbalance? A blow to the head as an infant that shook something loose? What? Or could it be that his conditions as a child were so absolutely horrible that this was what it produced?

Fortunately for the world, there weren't too many Billyray's. He went beyond a normal serial killer. Most serial killers at least have passion for what they do. Sexual, sadist, revenge, whatever. But the Billyray's of this world have no passion, have no apparent feelings. They kill only because it suits them at the time. Or they don't kill, because it suits them at the time. And when they do kill, it's usually without anger. They just felt it needed to be done, that's all. Then they go about their business with as much thought about what they had done as a normal person would after feeding a parking meter.

He glanced over some of Billyray's record and looked up at Nick. "I can't believe that any competent psychiatrist would even think of letting an animal like this back out onto the street."

"Unless he was needed." Nick rejoined. "Which lends a lot of credence to your theory about David Walton."

John was about to answer when the three girls came into the room. "Where's my beer, sweetheart?" Janie announced loudly to Nick. Nick laughed and moved to the refrigerator.

John threw some steaks on the grill and the evening progressed in a most pleasant way. There was no discussion about any of their troubles. For once, it was almost like they were all normal people dealing with normal day to day issues and routines. As the evening drew to a close, John and Nick went off to John's office and the women began to clean up.

They sat down at the desk and as he reopened the file Nick had given him, he said, "I think you should let the County boys in on this now. They're going to have to compare dental records to see if the guy in the woods was Billyray."

"And what reason am I going to give for looking at the parolees to begin with?" countered Nick. "I don't think it's a good idea to be accusing a judge's son of anything at this point. I don't think my political position is strong enough to withstand the heat. I'll do it if you think I should, but I don't believe it would add anything significant to the investigation yet. I think try to figure out another way to confirm it's him before we even consider bringing Walton's name into it."

"I agree," said John. "As far as what you were doing snooping around parolee records, just tell them it was a hunch, that's all. They're going to think it was a hell of a hunch and it may cause all sorts of speculation, but there's not much to be done about it. We have to make a comparison and there's no quiet way of doing that."

Nick nodded. John continued to browse through the file, looking at other names as well. After a while, he closed the file and put it on his desk. He looked at Nick and said, "You know, we're going after Billyray because he's the most obvious choice. But there are a few other names in there," he nodded toward the file, "that could just as easily be mixed up in this. I see that there are about eight that have missed the check-ins with their parole officers, six of those have David Walton listed as their counselor. It could be any of those."

"Yeah, but if I give them all of those names at once, it wouldn't take much to place David Walton as the common thread. The lead investigator from the County is sharp. I don't think he would overlook it. And we already agreed that we don't want to go there yet."

John sighed. "Yeah, I know. I just think we should keep an open mind. I'm not a betting man, but I'd be willing to wager a lot of money that one of those men on that list is the guy in the grave. I just wouldn't be willing to bet it's Billyray quite yet. I think it most likely is, just don't want to get blinders on the situation."

They could hear Janie and Sue approaching. It was obvious they were ready to call it an evening. "Agreed." said Nick as he stood up. "I'll let them know about Billyray first thing in the morning. I'll keep you posted."

The Giovanni's had left. Mary Kate was down and John was sitting with Sue in his office, each with a glass of wine. He was explaining to her the contents of the file and his conversations with Nick. She opened the file as he was talking and began looking at the information on Billyray.

"It's got to be him, John," she said.

"Why? Because he looks the part? Because of his record of violence? Most of the guys on Nick's list have a record of violence. Granted, not as violent as Billyray, but violent all the same. Even the guys that don't have a violent past could be the one. There's nothing to say that even a burglar couldn't get tied up in all this. It depends on which skill set they were looking for. Always keep in mind, Sue, that an investigator *must* keep an open mind.

"Our job is to follow the trail, through interviews, evidence, and facts to the ultimate conclusion. The biggest mistake an investigator can make is to lock onto a suspect and make everything else fit the circumstances that you want. Think about it. Besides his looks and his background, what differentiates him from the rest? Remember, courts don't allow you to bring up a suspect's criminal background for a reason, it has nothing to do with the current case."

"Well then... nothing. I guess," she said quietly.

"Exactly," John responded. "So with that in mind, I think we should progress as though any one of these guys could be the one. Do you think you could start doing some backgrounds on these guys? Maybe you can come up with something that would at least confirm if they are alive. Obviously if they are, then they're not our guy."

"But wouldn't the state already have done that? After all, they have missed their meetings with their parole officers. Wouldn't they have done all this in an attempt to find them?"

John snorted. "In theory, you're one hundred percent correct. Reality, however, is a different matter. Most bureaucratic agencies are bogged down through a combination of incompetence and understaffing. Even ruling those out, sometimes a perfectly competent investigator can just plain miss something. The other factor is time. When a person first goes missing, for whatever reason, there is a flurry of activity to find them. After a period of time, different for different cases and reasons, the initial furor dies down and the file gets shoved to the side. New things happen that don't get caught because no one is looking at them.

"Take Billyray as a hypothetical example. Say Billyray is still alive. When he first went missing, everyone went nuts trying to find him, doing computer checks, interviewing known associates, etc. But he's careful and they find nothing. After a couple of months, he's off the main burner. Now, it's fairly easy for a person to remain vigilant in the short term, It's a much more difficult thing to do over time. If, say *six* months later, they were to talk to say, the neighbor who lives next door to his mother, they would find that he saw Billyray a month ago when he came to visit his mother. You see? The information that wasn't there when you were originally looking is there now, you just have to find it."

Sue nodded. "I understand. Alright. I'll start looking first thing in the morning." She didn't tell him that she already had a leg up on her efforts. Emily Stone had been an expert in hacking into information systems. Since Emily had worked for Sue's father, it had been an easy matter for her to go through Emily's computer and notes after her death to retrieve the information she would need for this little foray into the detective world. She had foreseen the day that John might want her help and had taken steps to make sure she was ready. She didn't see the need to tell him this and bring up Emily's name, possibly sending John spiraling back downward and reversing the progress that she herself had made with him.

Instead, she stood up and said quietly, "I think it's time to turn in."

She left her carefully chosen words hanging in the dark, quiet air of the office. She waited to see what his response would be.

He stood up, moved over to her and took her in his arms. He held her quietly for a while, then gently kissed her. He broke the kiss and moved slightly away. Softly, he said, "Okay, I'll see you in the morning. I want to go over this file one more time and then I'll turn in."

They looked into each other's eyes for what seem like hours. Then, she smiled, "Just don't stay up all night. You don't know what's going to happen tomorrow and you've told me before that sometimes a case breaks and you don't sleep for hours, if not days."

He grinned in return. "Don't worry, Sue, I won't. Wouldn't want you mad at me again, would I?"

"No, you wouldn't," she returned lightly. "Good night, see you tomorrow," and with that she strode from the room. She was smiling as she walked to her bedroom. They, had made great progress today, in every way she could think of. She had already known that John was a man she could most likely spend her life with. But the person she saw emerging today was even better than the one she had lived with in the past few months. He was just... lighter. His mood, his step, his humor, everything was better. She just hoped that this case wouldn't take a turn for the worse and reverse all of the progress that had been made since leaving the hospital, both for John personally and for her budding relationship with him.

As she undressed and climbed into bed, she reviewed the day's events in utter amazement. So much had happened since she sat drinking her coffee and watching John run around the lake this morning. And they had kissed! Something that she had not foreseen happening for some time to come. Oh wait until she told her mother!

She smiled even broader and then began to think of how she would go about retrieving the information tomorrow and the possible outcomes. After a while though, she found she was having trouble keeping her mind on course. She kept thinking about the feeling she got when John held her. It was a pleasant thought. And one that stayed with her as she drifted off to sleep.

CHAPTER

5

John watched as Gregory Harris raised his arm, at the same time cocking his forearm back. He held a larger than life knife in that hand as he held Susan Browning in the other. John began pulling his gun from its holster. But for some inexplicable reason, he was moving slowly, much too slowly to prevent what he knew was going to happen next. It was as if he were trying to move while he was up to his neck in water. To his horror, Harris's arm suffered no such restrictions and moved rapidly downward, driving the knife into Susan's neck. He twisted it and then viciously yanked the knife out. Her life's blood immediately began to rhythmically spurt in a red geyser that splattered onto a nearby wall with an exaggerated, sickening sound. She looked at John with panic in her eyes. "Why didn't you save me?" she moaned as she fell to the ground. All the while, John fought the unseen force that was slowing his gun as he attempted to bring it into action.

Harris stood above her, grinning and looking at John. As he stared into John's eyes, his knife arced downward once again and sliced Sue's face from her mouth to her ear. She screamed. John yelled, "No!"

His gun was finally pointed at Harris. He fired and he watched as Harris's body shuddered, but didn't fall. He fired again, and again. He continued until his clip was empty. Eight hollow point shots from a .45 ACP, had hit Harris in the chest. But Harris continued to smile. And his vicious knife continued its demonic work as Susan screamed with each strike.

"You see, doesn't really matter in the end. You can't save her, anymore than you could save that other traitorous bitch. Feels good though, doesn't it?" asked Harris in a maniacal voice. "Go ahead, reload. Do it again. You'll feel better. You'll see."

"Yeah, he's right," said a southern drawl voice unexpectedly from the side. John jerked his head in the direction of this new voice and saw "Billyray" Jenkins, the vicious ex-con who had disappeared. "Y'all need to listen to him," Billyray continued softly. "I personally don't get off the way he does, but you gotta admit, he needs to be fuckin' killed. Y'all know you can do it. After all, yer one of us."

"Ya know, Billyray," Harris looked at Jenkins and said, "you're not supposed to be here yet, but I can use your help. He..." he motioned toward John, "he still thinks he's better than us. But I think he's ripe for the picking. Just needs a little guidance to make him understand." He looked down at Susan. "I think I'll cut her teats off. We can hollow 'em out and use 'em as drinkin' gourds."

Billyray smiled. "Yeah Greg. That'd be fuckin' cool." He nodded toward John as he egged both of them on. "I don't think y'all have to worry about the pussy here stoppin' ya."

John looked at Susan, who was on her knees, leaning against Harris. She was too weak to talk, but her eyes implored him to make the pain stop. John felt his anger reach blinding, unimaginable heights. He quickly reloaded, the unseen force had mysteriously evaporated. He emptied another clip into Harris. This time Harris responded with an obvious look of pain. He didn't say anything, but looked at John in surprise. "Yeah man," said Billyray. "See, he can be fuckin' killed. Use that hate. Do it again. I can tell y'all are fuckin' liken it. It'll work better this time. The more pleasure y'all feel, the better it'll fuckin' work."

Billyray was right. He *was* liking the pain he saw on Harris's face. The bastard deserved it. He reloaded and was bringing his gun to bear once again when yet another voice stopped him cold.

"Stop!" Suddenly, Emily Stone materialized next to Harris. John's heart skipped a beat when he saw her. "Don't you see?" she asked. "He's trying to make you cross the line John. Because there *is* a line. I don't care what they say." She motioned to Harris and Billyray. "You're not like them... now. But if you do what they ask, if you let the hate drive you, if you don't put the pleasure you're feeling in perspective, then... then you *will* be like them. You're better than that, John. That's why I was falling in love with you. You're a good person. I can't be with you now. But she," she motioned with her hand toward the disfigured Susan, "she can be with you. You saved her John. There was nothing you could do about me. You know how it is. People make choices. Most of the time, it's like you said, they put themselves into harm's way. I did... and I paid the price. Susan had no choice and you saved her. Now you're the one with a choice. Are you going to make the right choice, John?"

"She needs to fucking go," said Billyray calmly. He suddenly pulled his own gun and steadily, methodically began shooting at Emily.

John stood in shock and wonderment as Emily smiled. "You know you can't hurt me," she said to Billyray. "I'm beyond that now. She turned back to John. "But *you*, John. You *can* hurt me. I gave my life for you. Show me that my life was a good trade for yours."

Tears were forming at the corners of John's eyes. He slowly lowered his gun and holstered it. "Noooo!" shouted Harris and Billyray in unison.

Emily smiled. "Thank you," she uttered softly.

"Emily," John said shakily. But Emily said nothing. In fact, the entire scene, with the exception of John himself, was morphing into an old time still photograph. Like a still frame from a movie. No one was moving. Harris's and Billyray's lips were still puckered as they shouted their, "Nooo." He didn't want her to go. He wanted to talk to her. He wanted to hold her. "Emily!" he shouted and then again in progressively softer tones, "Emily. Emily..."

"...Emily, Emily." The first rays of the early morning

sun cascaded over John as he lay in bed. He moved his hand to his face and found tears streaming toward his ears. He wiped them off. "Jesus! That was really fucked up. It had been so *real*."

He sat up in bed and thought about his dream. After a moment, he muttered to himself, "Jesus," he said again. "I am so screwed up." He got up and began to dress, putting on sweatpants and a sweatshirt. He replayed the whole thing in his mind once again, while he was putting on his running shoes. As with most dreams, this one was fading rapidly. He realized that one comment made by Harris struck him as odd. "*Ya know Billyray, you're not supposed to be here yet.*" Harris had said. *Yet?* What did he mean by *Yet?*

John shook his head and laughed softly to himself. '*Christ,*' he thought. '*I think I need to see a shrink. It's only a fucking dream.*' Still, as he finished tying his shoes and walked into the kitchen, the dream comment stuck in his mind.

John was a big believer in gut instinct. It had served him well many times in the past. He also knew that the scientific rationale for something as vague and mysterious as gut instinct, was that it was really made up of subconscious clues and concerns that the mind receives, interprets, and returns to the conscious brain in the form of an urge to take some sort of action.

The rational part of John's brain told him that his dream was a conglomeration of those subconscious clues and concerns. That all made perfect sense. So why was he having so much trouble accepting that and moving on? He had no reason to think that the mystery body in the grave in the woods was anyone other than Billyray. Everything pointed to the fact that, logically, it was Billyray. Once again, it all made perfect sense. But it stuck in his craw, like a popcorn kernel between the teeth that you couldn't quite get to.

He walked into the kitchen and found Susan making breakfast for Mary Kate, who was sitting at the counter watching TV. "Good morning everybody," he said cheerily as he approached them.

Mary Kate tore her eyes away from the TV long enough to give a, "Good morning Daddy," that almost sounded sincere.

Susan turned and with a huge smile on her face, replied, "Good morning. Did you sleep well?" She didn't ask him if he wanted anything. When she saw his running clothes, she knew the answer.

"Yeah, pretty good. Can you go over those names I showed you last night? See if you can dig up anything on them today?"

"Sure. I'll start with that Billyray guy," she answered, a little surprised at this request. Last night he had said he wanted to wait. But she decided not to question it.

For John's part, he must have given some sort of visual cue to her starting with Billyray, because the smile dropped from her lips and she added, "What's wrong? You don't want me to start with him?"

"It's just that I have a feeling that Billyray may not be the guy in the gra... err," he glanced at Mary Kate and then continued. "...the guy in the woods. I think Billyray's alive and well," he replied.

She frowned. "Why do you think that? I know you said last night that you didn't want me to get tunnel vision, but I thought you and Nick agreed that it was most likely him."

He really didn't want to tell her about his dream. She'd think he was just plain goofy. She was a programmer who dealt in rational, well thought out strategies, a left brain thinker to the max. Working on a hunch based on a dream didn't exactly fall within those parameters, even though he was convinced the dream was merely an expression of his own inner thoughts and fears.

So he compromised by answering, "I think Billyray is too street smart, too elusive to get hit in the back of the head in the woods." He glanced over at Mary Kate. He was still couching his words for her sake. She appeared, however, to be engrossed in her TV show and not paying the least bit of attention to their conversation. He continued, "I doubt he's a hiker or a nature lover. If he went out there with someone, he'd have to know something was up and he would know better than to let anyone get behind him. He doesn't strike me as a person who would meekly submit. I might be wrong, but I think he's alive."

"Then do you have any ideas about who the guy in the woods might be? Do you still think he's an ex-con?" she asked.

"No I don't and yeah, I do. I think we're on the right track there and I do think Billyray's in it up to his eyeballs. He's just too perfect a fit to not be a '*handyman*' for Coeptus Guild. He's smart, tough, and with absolutely no morals what so ever."

"Okay. I'll get started on it as soon as Mary Kate gets off to school," Sue responded.

"Thanks. We'll talk more when I get back," he walked over to Mary Kate and gave her a kiss and a hug. "You have a good day at school, Angel."

She tore her eyes from the television and hugged him back. "I will. I love you, Daddy."

"I love you too, Angel," and with that, he walked out the back door and headed down to the lake.

The head of John Livingston Harvard showed up crystal clear in the 10X42 Leupoid Ultra Mark IV sniper sight. It was mounted on a Remington Model 700BDL rifle, both of which were part of the U.S. Military's M24 sniper system. This particular rifle had been chambered to hold Winchester's powerful .300 magnum round, that kicked *worse* than a mule and was definitely *not* for the faint of heart.

The sniper had loaded the gun with his preferred .300 magnum round, a Speer, 200 grain bullet, that stepped out at just a hair under 3,000 feet per second. Compare that to a .45 ACP handgun round that left the barrel at approximately 800 feet per second. That meant the bullet from the sniper's rifle traveled at supersonic speeds and *that* ensured that it would arrive at the target even *before* the sound made by the rifle blast. It surely was a case of the proverbial, "*He never knew what hit him.*"

Though the system was military, the sniper was not, nor had he ever been. He was, however, a very good shot. He'd grown up in the Bayous of Louisiana and had held a rifle in his hands since he was a young boy. He and his daddy had hunted almost daily, providing much needed meat for the dinner table. As is so often the case with poor families in their predicament, coming home empty handed often meant going without dinner and that provided quite the incentive for accurate shooting.

The sniper's employers had provided him with this weapon and after a few days of practice, he decided that it was an exceptional gun indeed. He loved to shoot it and had a sore, black and blue shoulder to prove it. The rifle had its own built in recoil suppression system, but he found that it was inadequate for the constant firing he was doing while practicing. The sniper could not get enough of the weapon and he had resorted to using towels placed between the butt of the rifle and his shoulder as an additional cushion.

He eventually, reluctantly, conceded defeat and after a thorough cleaning, put the weapon back in its case. The muscles in his shoulder had periodically spasmed for days afterward and it was some time before he practiced again.

Now, he used the scope to follow John Harvard as he walked down his deck and began his daily run around the lake. This was the sniper's third day here. He had seen Chief Giovanni come and go and had duly reported it to his employers. He had lain perfectly hidden, reporting everything he saw. Watching Harvard and his other targets. The woman and the little girl.

His employer's had told him that *they*, the woman and the girl, were his primary targets. He would receive an order and he would then take out the woman first. After confirming with his employers that the woman was dead, he may, or may not, receive another order to take out the little girl.

His employer's had also told him to be cautious. Very, very cautious. Harvard was extremely dangerous, they had said, and not to be trifled with lightly. The sniper felt safe in his hidden liar, on a hillside some two hundred yards away. From this distance, Harvard didn't look very menacing to him, although, he conceded, the man was in shape. And he practiced that kung fu shit all the time.

The sniper himself was wiry, lean, tough, though he had never worked out a day in his life. A lifetime of traipsing through the bayou had toughened him. He'd never had any formal fight training either, but fights on the bayou were usually no holds barred, vicious affairs that sometimes ended up with only one man walking away, leaving the other man down, permanently... gator bait.

He'd been in bar fights where his opponents tried that kung fu, karate stuff on him and he'd personally found it to be all show with little substance. They often tried those spinning kicks on him, turning their backs while they spun. The sniper would take the opportunity to punch them in the kidneys for their efforts and that would be that. There were no rules here, other than survival.

The sniper shifted his scope from Harvard to the kitchen window in the house. His finger caressed the trigger as he sighted in on the woman. This would be easy. He shifted again and zeroed in on the little girl. He smiled. Like shooting fish in a barrel.

The sniper had no compunctions about shooting the woman or the little girl for that matter. Life simply didn't matter to him. His own or anybody else's. Men often thought of the sniper as brave, having "balls." But to be brave meant conquering fear. The sniper had no fear. Like a reptile, he was driven to attack or retreat, based on sheer instinct. Emotions were not part of the equation. He usually had no feelings about anything. Oh, he felt pleasure, like fucking. Woman, man, even an occasional animal, made no difference to him, just the final release. Or firing the weapon he now held in his hands, that was pleasurable too. Watching his target fall. Knowing he had the skill to kill from a great distance. It was all good.

He also felt displeasure. And the one thing the sniper didn't like, was cold. It was too fucking cold up here. Why would anyone choose to live in this place in the winter? And it wasn't even winter yet. Christ! He hoped his employers would give him some jobs back down south so he could get away from this god forsaken land before it got really cold.

He was hungry. He put the stock of the tripod mounted rifle on the ground and retrieved some beef jerky from his pack. He watched John Harvard run as he was eating. Yep. Just another day at the office. "Gotta get this fuckin' show on the road," he muttered softly. He sat there chewing his beef jerky and waited for his cell phone to vibrate, waited for the order to begin the carnage.

❖ ❖ ❖

John finished his run, had breakfast, and was now standing in the shower, letting the hot water cascade over him, contemplating his next move. He did his best thinking in the shower. He didn't know why, but it worked.

This puzzling case had way more pieces than normal. If Billyray wasn't the man buried in the woods, then who the hell was he? John was certain that the man was another ex-con. He thought about the possibility that he had just uncovered a major source of low tier recruitment for Coeptus Guild. If that was so, then he wanted to proceed with prudence.

Excitement began to manifest itself deep within him. This could be a chance to follow the chain back up to a major player, something even the vaunted F.B.I. had been unable to do. They had been trying to catch smoke and follow it back to the source. But every time, they found that all they had found was an isolated puff, with no apparent origin. John begrudgingly admitted to himself that evil as Coeptus Guild was, they were very good at what they did. To catch them would mean to have a little luck, maybe even a lot of luck.

He shut the water off and got out of the shower. A few minutes later he was dressed and on the phone in his office, talking to Nick Giovanni.

"How's it going Nick?" he asked.

"Man, do I have a lot to tell you." Nick continued in a somber, press release type tone. "First off, you were right. There was some human debris on Ramsey's gun. They did a DNA analysis on it when they first took it in to the lab.

However, they didn't run it against anything because at the time, they had a huge backlog and they figured the blood and stuff was yours anyway."

"It happens," said John. "A little sloppy on procedures, but I can understand their thinking. So have they run it now?"

"Yeah, they sure as hell did. I asked the lead detective to look into it after you and I talked and he in turn ordered up the test. You ready for this? The debris at the end of Ramsey's gun belongs to the dead guy in the woods."

"What?" To say that John was surprised would be an understatement. Astounded would be a more apt description. He continued. "That doesn't make sense. That would mean that Ramsey killed *two* people before he came after me? I don't like this Nick. Something's off here. Was there anyone else's blood on there?"

"Oh, after that little discovery, they went over that gun with a fine tooth comb. The only other blood on there was yours."

"Shit!" John retorted. "I'll say it again. I don't like it."

"Well, Ramsey was unaccounted for, for quite awhile. He…"

"Yes, I know that," John butted in. "But why all the clean up?" He was speaking in a rapid, agitated tone. "One of the things that bugs me about this, is what do the judge's wife and the guy in the field have to do with me and Sue? That whole thing with us was a major disaster for Coeptus Guild. All of their attention should have been focused on us. Killing Sally Walton and the other guy is kind of like you responding to an Armed Robbery in progress and deciding to stop and give somebody a traffic ticket on your way there. It just doesn't make sense. Why were Sally Walton and the mystery guy in the field so important that they had to make a move when the roof was falling in around them?"

Neither one of them spoke as they thought this out for themselves. After some time, Nick continued. "Look, Ramsey was a looney-toon. You know that sometimes there's no explaining the actions of a person like him."

John was getting frustrated that he wasn't getting his point across. With an uncharacteristic attitude of exasperation, he replied. "Nick, I know that Ramsey's elevator didn't go all the way to the top. But the man had a good instinct for survival. He knew that there was a good chance that the lid was about to come off Coeptus Guild, exposing him as well as the other bits in the stew. I understand why he felt compelled to rush up to the cabin to make sure the lid stayed on. I suspect that if things had gone a little differently, *he* would have tried to kill Harris in order to keep things contained.

"But *that* brings us back around to my original point. Keeping things contained should have involved all the players at the *cabin*." He raised his voice to almost a shout and continued, with a slight hesitation between his words for emphasis. "What... Does... Sally Walton... And... The... Guy... In... The... Woods... Have... To... Do... With... That... Containment?"

The air hung heavy between them over the phone once again. John and Nick had been friends and coworkers for a long time. They almost always thought along the same lines. Like an old married couple, more often than not, they finished each other sentences. John was irked that Nick didn't seem to be getting the point.

Nick cleared his throat and said. "Okay John, I see your point. I think there's something else you should know about and this too doesn't make sense."

"Sorry about that Nick." John replied quietly. "You know how I try to make sense of everything. Maybe you're right. Maybe I'm just trying to make sense of a senseless act. What's the other thing you want to tell me?"

Nick said, "The City Council has asked that the County Crime Scene Unit return to the corn field where they found Sally Walton and look for the bullet again."

"What?" John's eyes rolled up. What other surprises was this case going to throw at them? "What business does the City Council have to make a request like that? And don't they know that anything they find now will be suspect? The chain of evidence is shot. The scene hasn't been secure for how many days?"

When a crime occurs, the first thing the police must do is to protect the scene so that it remains in a sort of time capsule. It is imperative that nothing changes so that the police can accurately reconstruct what occurred there. For example, a policeman carelessly tossing a cigarette but into an ashtray at the scene, could send the police technicians off on a wild goose chase, thinking that the perpetrator may have left the butt there.

In another example, a bloody glove that was recovered in

a place not under police control, would lead a defense attorney to question whether or not the glove had been "planted" there by someone else, after the crime occurred. The only way to discount this would have been to have the police keep a watchful eye over the area to make certain that nothing was disturbed.

The corn field where Sally Walton was found had been vacant for several days. The police had done a thorough search of the area, looking for the evasive bullet. While it was possible that they had missed it, it wasn't likely, bringing in to question the possibility of crime scene tampering.

Nick continued, "I agree with you. This is an extremely unusual request and you know they have no business making it. That's why I'm worried."

"There's definitely a rat in the pantry Nick. Who's pushing this? Do you know?"

"No, I don't. I'm trying to find out, but as of right now, I'm kind of persona non grata so it's making it difficult. At any rate, their wish was granted and the county boys are out there as we speak."

"That was fast."

"Yep. Look, my other line is ringing. I'll keep you posted. Later."

John hung up the phone and sat back in his chair as he thought about what he had just heard. Twisted pieces. So many pieces of this puzzle were warped almost beyond recognition. It was good news that the DNA from the guy in the woods matched some of the blood on Ramsey's gun, but it muddied the waters a little more because he knew that the time of *Walton's* death coincided perfectly with the time period that Ramsey had tried to kill John. Therefore, he half expected that the blood would not match the guy in the woods but the possibility of blow back had been too strong to ignore. So Ramsey *had* killed the guy in the woods. Maybe he didn't kill Walton. He kept an open mind about it, but it was too much of a coincidence, with his number in her shoe and all, for him to rule out the possibility that he'd killed twice before coming after John. Why? What was so important that he suddenly had to go on a killing spree? The depth of the mysteries of Coeptus Guild only got deeper.

But now the *City Council* wanted the crime scene guys to look for the bullet that killed her? Again? After so much time had elapsed? Why? The great, fictional detective, Sherlock Holmes, once said, "When you have eliminated all other possibilities, whatever remains, however improbable, must be the answer." A work of fiction. True. But John was a firm believer in that statement. It was certainly a truism that no competent investigator could ignore. To John, there was only one logical conclusion to be made. At least one person on that Council was working for Coeptus Guild.

Sherlock would have enjoyed this case. John wished the fictional character was with him now. He was getting a bad feeling about this series of events. Something was up. Something big. To make matters worse, he had the feeling that he and Nick didn't have much time. Whatever was going to occur would happen very soon. Coeptus Guild's plans were about to come to fruition. John just knew it. He and Sherlock had to get this puzzle put together and they had to do it fast. Twisted pieces notwithstanding.

CHAPTER

6

John was sitting in his office with his laptop computer. He had been making notes on the case, studying the files Nick had given him, and reviewing his interview with Debra Walton. Then he had brought up the city's website and was currently in the process of going over the biographies of each of the council members. There were twelve. Each short bio had a photograph attached.

When he had first brought up the site, he had started by studying each of the accompanying pictures. He was trying to discern, by merely looking into the eyes of their still photographs, who would be the object of his investigation. He was a big believer in eyes. They could speak a language of their own. In most cases, a truer, more telling story than the one spoken by easily controlled lips. But, he learned nothing. All had smiling, happy eyes with no hint of a hidden story. "Typical politicians," he muttered quietly to himself.

There were seven men and five women. He began to read the short histories next to the photos. As would be expected, they came from varying backgrounds. One of the men was a school teacher. Another came from the construction business. Two of the other men were in the trucking and concrete business, respectively. Two were self employed, no specifics as to what their businesses were. The last man was an attorney. '*That would fit right into this case,*' he mused.

One of the women was a housewife. Two of the other women were in sales. One, a pretty Asian woman, was a programmer. Knowing Coeptus Guild's propensity for programmers, '*That,*' he thought, '*could be interesting as well.*' The last woman was a self employed "headhunter," catering to higher end jobs, CEO's and such.

All in all, it was quite a diverse group running the city. Which one, he wondered, was padding their pockets with a little extra cash? Hell, for that matter, who said there was only one?

The phone rang. He was going to ignore it, but he saw that it was the police department displayed on the Caller ID. He picked it up.

Assuming that it was Nick, he smiled and immediately said, "Whhaat ju want, *señior?*" he drawled in a bad, pseudo Mexican accent.

Nick's response was anything but jocular. "They found a bullet," he said tersely.

John sat up and exclaimed, "What! Already?" He looked at the clock on the wall and was dismayed to find that almost three hours had elapsed since he had talked to Nick. Still, that was awfully fast to find something as small as a bullet after they had thoroughly searched the area before. He said as much to Nick.

"Yeah, well, they apparently extended their search area,"

he replied. "Now that the corn is all gone, it was much easier to do. They found it about a hundred yards away."

This was definitely plausible, but it still didn't sit right with John and judging from Nick's voice, with him either.

"Have they matched it up to Ramsey's gun yet?" John asked.

"They're working on it now. All I know at this point is that that the class characteristics are consistent with a .38 Chief's Special."

Class characteristics were general characteristics that all .38 Chief Specials would have in common. For instance, the bullet was a .38. It had the correct number of "lands and grooves," and the grooves had the correct directional twist, such as left or right. Those grooves on the bullet were determined by the rifling in the barrel of the gun. One other major point the firearm examiner would make would be the degree of twist on the bullet. If all of those points matched up, then the examiner could say that the bullet *could* have come a .38 Chief's Special.

To say that the bullet *did* come from a *particular* weapon, the examiner would look at the bullet under a microscope to determine *individual* characteristics. He would look for scratches on the bullet caused by the barrel of the gun or in some cases, those caused by a silencer. These scratches, called "striations," are unique to each gun, like a fingerprint for that gun.

The individual characteristics from the bullet in the field would be compared to a test bullet fired from Ramsey's gun. It they matched, then there would be no doubt that the gun fired the bullet recovered from the field.

John spoke up. "I don't get it."

"Yeah, I know," said Nick. "Why would someone on the council go to all this trouble to confirm that Ramsey was the shooter? I wasn't responsible for him back then. Hell, technically, he was *my* boss. So where's the benefit?"

"Right. It doesn't make sense." There was a brief lull in the conversation and then John continued. "Unless they're going to try and show that you muffed the investigation and it needed the county boys to come in and wrap it up for you, either due to incompetence on your part or a cover up on your part to protect the department from further embarrassment."

"Seems pretty lame for so much effort, don't you think?" Nick responded.

"Too lame," said John. "I'm waiting for the other shoe to drop."

"Maybe we're just reading too much into this John. We've made Coeptus Guild out to be some huge, mystical creation endowed with a large amount of omnipotence. After all, they're just guys, like you and me and as the saying goes, they put their underwear on the same way we do. Like any large entity, I'm sure they have their top notch, on the ball guys and then they have their *also ran's*. Maybe this operation is being run by some of the *also ran's*."

"Maybe," John reluctantly agreed. "It's just that between what I know of them and what the F.B.I. has encountered, these guys don't make many mistakes. I've seen nothing but all pro all the way."

"Look, we don't even know for sure that they're involved in this. It could be this all boils down to a bunch of power hungry council persons."

"Point taken. Speaking of them, I was just looking over their profiles when you called. I've found a couple that I think bear further looking into. They're a good place to start anyway."

"Well, let me know. I've got to run. The lead investigator from the county will be here soon to discuss the case and I have a couple of things I want to do first."

"I thought you were on the outside on this one? I didn't think they were telling you much about it lately."

"It did surprise me when he called a little while ago," said Nick. "He said there were a couple of things he wanted to discuss with me about the case."

"Good. I was thinking of calling him today anyway to see what he might tell *me* about the case. Now you can fill me in instead."

"I'll call you as soon as he leaves," Nick replied.

"Okay. Later Nick."

After hanging up, John opened the file and found Judge Walton's work phone. He wasn't sure if the Judge would be in his chambers, but John had decided that he was the best person to talk to next.

He was in luck. The judge answered. John identified himself and asked if he might talk to him for a few minutes, preferably, in person.

"What do you have to do with this case?" The judge asked in a tone reserved for attorneys that were caught trying to put one over on him. It made John feel uneasy. He wasn't used to having judges use that tone with him. After all, he was one of the good guys.

"The Chief has asked me to look into some things on this case," he replied. "He wants a fresh view from someone outside the department, with no interest in the case, at least as far as the department goes."

"Well, that's not exactly true, is it?" the Judge replied in the same tone. "After all, you used to work for the police department and I do believe the Chief is your ex-partner and good friend. Not only that, but Ramsey tried to kill you and I do believe that he is the number one suspect at this point. So you're not exactly impartial, are you?"

John briefly wondered how the judge already knew that Ramsey was their main suspect and pushed on. "No, you're right Judge. But the fact of the matter is that up to now, I really have had nothing to do with all the investigations that have been going on since Ramsey's death. Look Judge, I have a proven track record when it comes to solving cases. Isn't finding the person who murdered your wife the most important thing here? All I'm trying..."

The Judge interrupted. "The Sheriff's office is investigating it and from what I can tell, they're doing a fine job." There was a moment of silence before he continued with an accusatory tone. "Are you saying they're bungling the job? After all, they found Ramsey's phone number with her. It seems like a pretty open and shut case. I just don't get why you're involved here."

John took a deep breath. This wasn't going well. He

thought back to the brief talk with the Judge's son. He was beginning to think that being obstinate was in the genes. "I think the Sheriff's office is doing a fine job. But they're looking at this as a single incident. I'm sure you're aware of Ramsey's involvement in, shall we say, extracurricular activities. I'd like to find out why Ramsey would want to do harm to your wife. As a Judge, I would think you would want the same thing. And besides, what does it matter how many people or even who looks into this? The more the merrier I say. If we all come to the same conclusion, doesn't that solidify the results?"

The judge's tone now switched to one of anger. "Are you trying to implicate my wife in Ramsey's illegal doings? How dare you!"

John raised his voice a notch. He wasn't getting angry, just exasperated. "Judge, I'm sorry if I came across that way. But think about it. Whether you like it or not, when this all comes out, other people are going to think that. I'm open minded. I have no preconceived notions about your wife's relationship with Ramsey. There may be a perfectly logical, legal, explanation as to why Ramsey's private cell phone number was found in her shoe. I'd like to find out what that reason is because, as you so eloquently pointed out, I have a personal interest in this case."

The first hopeful sign that the tide had turned in John's favor, was the fact that the Judge didn't respond immediately. In fact, there was an uncomfortable length of silence. John was just about to begin his argument anew when the Judge finally spoke, He was obviously still angry, but quieter and even slightly contrite.

"Alright. I see your point. I'm sorry that I lost my temper. But I just found out that my wife was murdered and stuck in a makeshift grave in a cornfield. I'm used to *hearing* cases like that, not being *involved* in them. When would you like to see me?"

John was relieved. "Today, if possible."

"Unless you can be here in thirty minutes, that's not possible."

"I'll be there." John replied. He didn't want to give the Judge time to change his mind. He had him on the ropes, do the interview now.

"I'll see you then," and the Judge hung up.

John put the phone down and turned back to his computer. He printed out the page from the internet showing the bios of the council members. He went to find Sue and found her in her bedroom folding clothes. She smiled when she saw him.

"Judging from that look and those papers in your hand, you have something you want me to do," she said lightly.

"Yeah," he replied. "I just went through the city's website and pulled up the bios on the council members. I'd like you to do some searching on the computer and see what you can come up with. I want you to look into property records, vehicles, anything that might tell us if they are living above their means. I also want you to look into any professional licenses they may have and anything else that might tell us who they really are. I don't expect you to find much, at least nothing obvious. They are politicians after all, and if there was anything glaringly wrong, they wouldn't be where they are."

"You're probably right there," she said. "Say what you want about the press, but there's nothing better to get their journalistic juices flowing than to uncover a dirty politician. Is there anyone in particular that strikes you? Someone you want me to concentrate on?"

He debated whether or not to tell her. She was new to this and he did not want her getting tunnel vision. He decided to trust her on the matter. "Actually, there are two, but I don't want you to concentrate on them at the expense of a thorough inspection of the others."

"I won't," she answered as she took the papers from him. "Which ones and why?"

"I'm particularly interested in the lawyer and the Asian girl who has her own programming business," he said. He started to explain why, but she interrupted him.

"Wow! We know how Coeptus Guild loves geeks, and the attorney would certainly fit this case."

She was quick, he thought. Somehow, it didn't surprise him. She had a good combination of intelligence and street smarts. Granted, her sheltered upbringing hadn't provided her with the intimate knowledge of the seedier aspects of life, but she knew enough about them that her analytical mind was quick to grasp the importance of those two jobs as they pertained to this case.

"Good," said John. "Let me know what you find and as we talked about before, try to keep things on the up and up, for now at least. Anything you want that isn't perfectly legal, let me know and I'll ask Nick to get it. Now, unless you have more questions, I'm in a hurry. I have to get to the courthouse and meet with Judge Walton."

Sue lifted her face to his. The look on her face told him that she was no longer thinking about the case. After a moment of indecision, he leaned down and kissed her, lightly, on the lips. He broke away, but kept his face close to hers, reading her.

"Is that all I get?" she asked demurely.

He leaned down and kissed her again, with mounting force, with rising passion. She responded in kind.

After a moment, she backed up and pushed him away with her free hand. "Go," she laughed teasingly. "I don't want to be responsible for you missing your appointment."

He looked at her a moment. Both realized that their relationship had now officially gone to the next level. He knew that she welcomed it. Did he? *Yes*, he thought, yes, he was ready as well. "I gotta go. I'll talk to you later." He turned and walked to the garage.

A bailiff escorted John to Judge Walton's chamber. The bailiff knocked and the Judge responded with a gruff, "Come in."

The bailiff opened the door and stepped inside, blocking John's entry at the same time. "Mr. Harvard is here to see you, sir," he announced.

John heard the Judge, "Let him in and then you can go."

"Yes Judge," the bailiff replied and stood clear to let John enter. After he had done so, the bailiff stepped out and quietly closed the door.

"Sit down Mr. Harvard. Now, what do you want to ask me that the police haven't already asked?"

John took a seat in a very comfortable stuffed leather chair. The chamber held a pleasant aroma of furniture oil, books, and a hint of cigar. He scanned the tastefully decorated room and decided that it would be very intimidating to outsiders. If the Judge was a suspect in this, or any other case, this would NOT be the place to conduct an interview with him. He would feel very comfortable here and in charge. But since the Judge was not a suspect, that wasn't a problem. In fact, it could work to John's advantage by putting the Judge at ease and make him more talkative.

With that thought in mind, he noticed several pictures of the Judge. A large 8X10 of the Judge and a very beautiful woman, hung on the wall. He recognized the woman as Sally Walton.

He also saw pictures of Debra Walton and a young man. Judging from the uncanny resemblance to the Judge, it had to be his son, David. He looked like a handsome, preppy, no nonsense kind of guy that would have no problem in the girl department. He thought of the possible/probable affair between him and Sally Walton. He could certainly see why she would be attracted to him.

He turned back to the Judge and complemented him on his surroundings and on his family. The Judge thanked him. "If you're trying to butter me up, don't bother. I've been around cops and prosecutors my whole life, I know the drill."

"Fair enough," John replied. "I was only half buttering you up, by the way. These really are nice chambers and you really do have a beautiful family. But since you want to get down to business, let's start by telling me about what you know of Ramsey."

The Judge seemed a little surprised at the question. "I didn't know much. I knew of him of course and I'm sure that sooner or later, you will find out that he attended some social functions at my house. That was mainly due to his son's relationship with my son, David, they're best friends."

"And what did you think of Deputy Chief Ramsey?"

"I didn't like him. I thought that he was a rather boorish man of questionable integrity, a fact that was obviously later borne out. He had no business being a cop and I can't believe that he rose as high as he did without being discovered."

"Don't feel bad Judge. He had a lot of people fooled. The one thing you couldn't accuse him of was being stupid."

"From what I hear, he never fooled you," said the Judge as he looked intently into John's eyes. John was beginning to get the feeling that the Judge was interviewing him, as well.

John brushed it off. "Well, I had the unfortunate luxury of working with him for many years. I got to see him in situations that most people wouldn't have. I had inside information that led to my conclusions concerning his character."

"What kind of information?" asked the Judge sternly.

The Judge was turning this around again. John guessed that it was to be expected. As the Judge had said, he'd spent his entire adult life working with criminals, cops, and prosecutors. It was only natural that he would want to ask these questions. "We're getting off the track here, Judge, and you indicated that I only have a limited amount of time. So let's get back to the point. What did Mrs. Walton think of Ramsey?"

"She thought the same thing I did. It was really quite amazing how alike the two of us thought about everything from place settings at the dinner table to political views. Every time the subject of Ramsey came up, we always discussed what a contemptible person he was."

"Let's switch gears here a minute," said John.

"More interview tactics, Mr. Harvard?" asked the Judge with a knowing smile.

"No, I'm just asking questions as they come to me," lied John.

"Then may I say," the Judge responded, "your thoughts are rather chaotic."

John smiled and rolled his eyes. "I do the best I can. What was your relationship with your wife like, just prior to her disappearance?" He watched the Judge intently, while trying to appear as nonchalant as he could. He wanted to see if he could detect some clue as to whether he was aware of his wife's involvement with his son.

The Judge turned and looked at the picture of him and his wife. He studied it a moment and John could see tears welling up in the old man's eyes. But he stoically held them back and answered John's question, while still looking at the photograph. "I know everyone said that she was too young for me. Maybe, in retrospect, she was. But we were alike in so many ways. I really, truly, felt that she was my soul mate and I couldn't imagine not being with her.

"To answer your question, Mr. Harvard, at the time she disappeared, I thought everything was fine. I had no inkling that she wasn't just as happy with our lives together as I was."

"So what changed your opinion of that?" John asked softly.

"Starting a couple of weeks before she went missing, I noticed that her time was unaccounted for on several occasions. Before that, we talked to each other constantly. Each of us always knew where the other person was. I wasn't particularly concerned about it. Curious where she was perhaps, but nothing more than that, certainly not suspicious.

"Then, after she was gone, the police started looking through the house, our phone records, everything. They came to me with some phone numbers that they couldn't track. They said the phone numbers were from one of those throw away phones that criminals like to use. There were also, on at least two occasions, calls made to the police department, directly to the Chief's secretary. We don't know who my wife talked to and the secretary apparently didn't remember getting them."

"I wonder why she would call the Chief's secretary?" said John, more to himself than to the Judge. "It's unfortunate. If she had called the main dispatch, like most people do, there would be a recording of the call. But maybe, that's why she didn't."

"Yes," said the Judge. "And why would that be? The Chief said that he had never talked to her and the investigators believe him. So that means she was calling the secretary so that she could be transferred to the person she really wanted to talk to. If she was on the up and up, why would she go through back channels to avoid being recorded?"

"Okay," said John. "We've established that something was out of whack. Why do you make the jump to an affair? You told the investigators that you thought she had run off with a younger man. Ramsey's phone number was with her. Why don't you think that she was calling Ramsey at work?"

"Why? Why would she? She had Ramsey's private cell phone number. Why risk being discovered by calling the Chief's secretary and asking to be transferred? It doesn't make sense… and… there is one more thing."

John looked at him expectantly, but didn't ask the question. The Judge answered on his own. "On at least two occasions, I smelled a man's cologne on her. Both times I had come home unexpectedly and found her getting ready to take a shower. She said she had just come from the gym and wanted to shower the sweat off. Again, at the time, blindly, I just assumed that there had been a man around her that had gone a little overboard on the cologne. It wasn't until the police started asking me detailed questions and the matter of the phone calls came up, that I started to put things together."

The Judge was barely holding himself together now. His body was trembling with the effort. John was uncomfortable doing so, but he had to delve a little deeper. "So maybe it was Ramsey? And maybe he killed her because she told him she wanted to break it off."

"No. It wouldn't be Ramsey. She may have been a cheater, but I still think I knew her pretty well. She hated Ramsey, loathed him. She certainly wouldn't have fucked him."

John's body jolted at the unexpected vulgarity. He gave the Judge some time and pressed on. "Then why do you think it was a younger man?"

The Judge looked up at him from a drooped head. "Look at me Harvard. I'm old, yes, but I know I'm still good looking and I am in top notch shape, better than most thirty year olds, and I definitely don't need any Viagra. I'm a Judge and I have quite a bit of money. I have a great pension and an even better life insurance policy. I don't mean to toot my own horn, but I also know I have a personality to match. Now, unless you disagree with some part of that, what earthly reason would she have for cheating on me unless it was for some younger meat?"

John said nothing, but nodded his head in agreement.

"No Mr. Harvard. I think she was having an affair with a younger man and I think it was with somebody from your old department."

Most of this fit with Debra Walton's suspicions that Sally and her brother were getting it on. Except the phone calls to the department. He asked the Judge, "Did you, by any chance, recognize the cologne? Have you maybe smelled it on someone before?" If David Walton wore cologne, the Judge would surely recognize the scent.

Judge Walton shook his head. "No, I don't remember smelling it before or since."

John sat, collected his thoughts, and asked. "Why do you think Mrs. Walton had Ramsey's phone number with her? If not for an affair, then what?"

The Judge started to answer, "I…" The intercom on his phone rang. He picked it up. "Yes, I told you I'm not to be disturbed." He listened for a moment and then said irritably, "Fine, I'll get it."

He looked at John and said, "I have to get this. It may have something to do with what we're talking about. Then he punched a button on his phone and said, "Judge Walton."

John watched the Judge's face as he listened to the caller and wondered, who had called? Judge Walton's expression went from one of aggravation, to a complete deadpan. He said nothing until the end when he said, "Fine. Thank you for calling and please keep me informed." He hung up very slowly and looked at John.

Before John could ask, the Judge rose and said quietly, but firmly, "This interview is over Mr. Harvard. You will leave my chamber immediately."

Startled, John rose to his feet and asked in shock, "What? Why? What's going on? What was that phone call?"

Instead of answering, the Judge reached under his desk. Almost instantly the door of his chamber flew open and one excited looking bailiff ran in, one hand on his gun butt.

"What's wrong Judge?" he asked, looking warily at John. John also noticed that the bailiff moved to a position that would put the Judge out of the line of fire if he had to draw his weapon.

John was in total dismay. "What...?" was all he said before the Judge answered him.

"That was Frank Carlotta, the lead investigator for the Sheriff's office. He just informed me that Chief Giovanni, your friend and ex-partner, has just been arrested for the murder of my wife."

CHAPTER

7

John barely remembered the walk back to his car. He got in and sat in stunned silence. He fought to gain control of his spinning head. This didn't make sense! He had known Nick for many years. He didn't know what evidence they had, but something was terribly wrong. He had sensed that the Coeptus Guild was about to bring the hammer down, but this was far beyond his wildest imaginations. How had they done it? He didn't have to wait long to find out.

His cell phone rang. At first, he wasn't going to answer. He was still getting his mind in order after the knock-out blow about Nick. Then he looked down and noticed that the caller ID showed it was from the county jail. In a fog, he picked up the phone and connected the call. An obviously shaken Nick Giovanni was on the other end.

"John?" he said.

"Nick, what the hell is going on?"

"I... I don't know. The bullet they recovered from the field this morning... they say it came from my gun."

"What?" John retorted. "You don't have a model 640. You..."

"Actually," Nick interrupted, "I do."

"What are you talking about? I've never seen it."

"I bought it when I first became a cop. I thought it was cool. But I always had trouble qualifying with it at the range, so eventually I bought a .380 to replace it. I never sold it though and it's been years since I've even touched it."

Cops at Nick's department, as with a lot of police departments, bought their own weapons, both on duty guns and off duty guns. The on duty guns were restricted only by the caliber of the weapon and that was done to ensure that if some sort of gun battle erupted, a fellow officer could loan you ammunition if it was needed or vice versa. But regardless of what gun was owned, the officer had to qualify with it at the department's gun range, which meant going through a course of fire and obtaining a minimum score. If the officer could not shoot that basic qualifying score, he was not authorized to carry the gun, on or off duty. To do so, would risk not only departmental action, but civil action as well if the gun were ever used.

Nick continued, "That's not all, John."

Numb, John asked, "What else, Nick?"

"They asked me if I knew Sally Walton and did I ever talk to her. I told them no. Then they told me that they have department phone records that show that I talked to Sally Walton twice just before she disappeared. John, I have never met, nor talked to Sally Walton in my life."

For a fleeting instant, John actually wondered if there was any chance that Nick was lying to him. John recalled his recent conversation with Judge Walton. *"I think she was having an affair with a younger man and I think it was with some-body from your old department,"* he had said. Nick wasn't exactly young, but he was much closer to Sally Walton's age than the Judge was. He also remembered the Judge telling him about the phone calls to the Chief's secretary. He had to admit, that if *he* was the lead investigator on this case, he would have to agree that it was a good arrest. The evidence was pretty damn good and if he hadn't known Nick so well, for so long, he would have to conclude that they had the right man. As it stood now, he doubted the State's Attorney would have any trouble convicting him.

"How'd they track the calls? I was just told that they went to the Chief's secretary and then on from there. Those calls aren't tracked."

"Apparently they are now," Nick answered. "We put a new system in about a year ago that I guess tracks everything that comes in from the outside. Only the radio room calls have matching voice recordings but the connections for other lines are documented."

"Nick, where is the gun now?" John asked.

"They have it. Based on the phone calls, they got a search warrant for my home and found it. John, now they think that I was tied up with Ramsey too. They're accusing me of killing Ramsey because he was a loose cannon and needed to be silenced."

"Jesus Christ! They've got themselves a nice, neat little package now, don't they?"

It was a rhetorical question and was taken as such. The gun and the phone calls. Wow! That would be tough to overcome. He thought about the phone calls. They couldn't track them then, but now they're able to track them to Nick, who was a Captain in charge of the Crime Lab at the time? The whole thing stunk to high heaven.

"John, they're telling me that my time is up. I don't have an attorney yet. Can you find one for me? Also, I guess I need to officially retain your services. Between you and an attorney, I'll have to ask you to wait until I sell my house to get paid. I…"

"Forget it, Nick. You're the best friend I've ever had and I'm not charging you a dime. Like I told you before, Sue's father paid me enough that I won't have to worry about money for a long time. Money isn't an issue, Nick. We just have to figure out how they did this and bring it to light. What about this lead investigator for the county, is he straight or do you think he's in on it?"

"I don't know for sure, John, but my guess would be he's a straight arrow. I've known him off and on for years. Never hung out with him or anything. Seems pretty likable. As a matter fact, he's a lot like you and even has a similar reputation. You know, kind of an asshole, but one that nobody would want after them."

John could almost see Nick grinning over the phone. "Glad to see that your sense of humor hasn't completely left you, Nick."

"Yeah, well, I gotta tell you buddy, I'm scared shitless. I've seen a lot of assholes crumble in this lock up and now I know why. When you hear that steel door thud shut behind you, you realize that this is for real. You're not going home.

You're not watching Survivor tonight. You're not having a beer tonight. Your wife is going to sleep without you tonight. Your life is over. You can't believe you're in here and at the same time, you can't believe you can ever get out. It's... *Yeah, I'm almost off*," he shouted to an unknown observer. "John, I gotta hang up. Keep me posted."

"Don't worry, Nick, I'll get this figured out. You hang in there buddy."

After sitting in the courthouse parking lot a little longer, he started the car and drove toward his house. His phone rang again. This time it was an obviously distraught Sue.

"My God, John, have you heard about Nick? It's all over the news."

"Yeah I have, Sue. I just got off the phone with him."

"He didn't do it, right? Oh God, please tell me he didn't do it."

"No Sue, he didn't do it. But Coeptus Guild has out done themselves on this one. They've got some pretty damn good evidence. Even if we can keep him out of prison, his career is over unless I can prove beyond a doubt that he was set up."

"Can you do that John?" For the first time, he could tell just how upset Sue really was. She was close to tears.

"Hey," he said gently. "Don't worry about it. We'll figure something out. Alright, they surprised us with a jab out of nowhere. But we're not down and now we know where they're coming from. What we have to do is regroup and think this thing through. Okay?"

Quietly, she responded. "Okay. What do you want me to

do? I finished with my searches on the council members, at least as far as I can go through the front door."

"Well, first of all," John said, "do you, or your father know of a good criminal attorney. Nick's going to put his house up for sale…"

"Yes! My Dad knows a great one and I don't want to speak for him, but I suspect that Nick won't have to worry about selling his house. My father and I owe Nick a great deal. If he and the S.W.A.T. team hadn't shown up when they did, not only would you be dead, but I certainly would be as well. Don't think that my father doesn't know that."

"Good. That'd be great. Okay, next, as far as the front door on your searches, go, all bets are off. I don't care if you have to hack the computer system of the Pentagon. We need information! Also, the file Nick gave me on this case is sitting on my desk. In there you will find the name of the lead investigator, a Sergeant Carlotta. See what you can find out about him. Nick thinks he's straight, so I'm thinking of contacting him. But I want to know the size of his underwear before I do."

"Done," Sue responded. "John, there's someone at the door. I'll see you when you get here."

She hung up and John put the phone down. Well, this day certainly hadn't gone as planned. Though the shock was wearing off, he was still having trouble believing what had just transpired. How had they managed it? For this to have happened, they would have had to have obtained Nick's gun, fire it, plant the bullet in the field, and then return the gun to Nick's house. And that was not even counting the fact that the City Council had to put pressure on the police to return to the crime scene to look for the bullet again.

Then, they would have had to somehow alter the Department's phone logs to show that the calls made to the Chief's secretary were forwarded on to Nick. There had to be a lot of players in on this. John smiled. For if there was one thing he knew, it was that the best way to keep a secret, was to have only one person aware of it. Anything more than that, well, suffice it to say, John was confident that this little secret wouldn't be a secret much longer.

The sniper watched as an unmarked police car approached Harvard's house. He knew it was a police car because it had all the markings. It was a plain color. It had four doors. It had black wall tires. It had antennas where a normal car wouldn't have antennas. And most importantly of all, the driver was a cop.

The sniper could tell. He could *smell* him even from this distance. The way he walked. The way his eyes were always moving around, even as he drove. No, the sniper was all too familiar with cops to not be able to pick one out, even if they were clad only in underwear. He watched through his scope as the car stopped on the driveway. The cop got out, looked around, and then walked toward the front door, out of the sniper's view. He rested the butt of his rifle on the ground and wondered who the cop was. It wasn't that Police Chief that had been there before and it wasn't anybody in the photographs he'd been given. He looked down at his cell phone and wondered when he would receive *the* call.

John pulled into his driveway and drove toward his house. The driveway was long, winding and heavily wooded on both sides. He normally enjoyed the approach and used it to calm himself, if needed. He rounded the last curve and was alarmed to find an unmarked squad car already there. His mind raced. Had they gone so far as to implicate *him* in this whole mess? *That* would certainly complicate matters. Hard to perform an investigation from inside a jail.

He briefly considered leaving, but decided against it. Who was here and what did they want?

He parked in the garage and walked into the house. He heard voices in the kitchen. One belonged to a man. The man was sitting at the counter talking to Sue when he walked in. The man looked toward John as he entered and got up. As he rose from his chair, his coat fell open, revealing a Sheriff's Department badge hanging off his belt. For a moment, each man stood, without talking, sizing up their counterpart.

John placed the deputy to be in his early forties, approximately five feet ten inches tall, with a slender build. He had thick black hair that was parted to one side. An unruly cowlick rose from the rear of his head, while another lock of hair hung over one of his piercing blue eyes.

John studied the man's eyes. They showed intelligence.

They showed hardness. They showed compassion. Most importantly for John, they showed no sign of deceit. John took note of the fact that the deputy didn't speak, but was studying him as well. He liked that. In fact, he hoped that his initial assessment of the man was correct because he thought he could like this man.

"And you would be?" John finally asked.

"I think you know," the deputy replied.

"Alright. Then why are you here?"

"Because," the deputy answered, "this case stinks like rotten fish at an outdoor market."

"Not all stinking fish is bad you know. Sometimes good fish just smell bad."

"Yes," countered the deputy, "and sometimes people throw out bad smelling fish, only to find that the smell didn't come from the fish they threw out."

John grinned. So did the deputy.

"Oh, will you two stop it," said Sue. She had been watching the exchange in growing disbelief. "You're both two peas from the same pod. Christ, it's like I'm looking at a double exposure. John, this is Frank Carlotta. He's the Detective Sergeant who's in charge of Nick's case."

"Just so there is no mistaking your intentions..." John began.

"I think Chief Giovanni is being set up."

"Then why did you arrest him?" John asked.

"You know why. If you had been in my shoes, you would have done the same thing. All the evidence points to him. What I think on a personal level doesn't mean squat without proof."

"So why are you here?" John queried.

"Because you're his friend. Because you're very familiar with the group that I think set this up. And, like you, I don't know who I can trust in *my* own department. And lastly, because if you're half as good as your reputation, you're very, very good and I'm going to need some help on this one."

"Does Nick know you're doing this?"

"No," Frank said. "As far as he knows, I'm popping a bottle of champaign tonight with everybody else, celebrating a sensational arrest."

John nodded. "Let's go in my office."

"I'd like to come," Sue interjected.

Frank looked at her with a questioning stare. John said, "That's fine, Sue. Where's Mary Kate?"

"She's at a friend's house. She won't be home for another hour."

Frank spoke up, "I don't mean to be rude, Susan, but this..."

"It's alright Frank." Nick said. "I would like her to be there. I'm sure you know that she's had personal dealings with Coeptus Guild. However, above and beyond that, she's very good at getting information over the computer and that, I think will stand us in good stead."

Frank shrugged his shoulders. "Okay. If you say so."

They walked into John's office together and sat down. "Okay," started John. "Why don't we begin with you telling us what you know. Coming here is really putting your neck out on the line. So I would like to know what made you take such a drastic action."

Frank didn't answer immediately. Instead, he studied John for a while. Then he said. "You still don't really trust me do you?"

John shrugged. "Would you?"

Frank nodded and then continued. "Not too long after you were shot, my Sheriff called me into his office. He said that several people had voiced concerns to him about corruption in your department. Since the County Sheriff is the person ultimately responsible for the well being of citizens within the county, it falls upon him to investigate any possible corruption within a city police department if it is felt that they can't handle it themselves."

Though John already knew the real answer to the question he was about to ask, he wanted to find out what Frank knew, or suspected. "What about you, did you feel that Nick couldn't handle it?"

Frank shook his head. "It wasn't a matter of his investigative skills, nor the skills of the people he put in charge. It was a matter, at least at first, of their loyalties." He looked at John and saw that his face was expressionless. Frank realized that this was a crucial point in gaining John's trust.

"Look, I was doing my job. I didn't really know any of your guys, including the past and present Chief. Sure, I'd worked with several of them, including Ramsey, on various cases. But working with them on some cases didn't mean I *knew* them. I'd never had any reason to suspect that they were anything other than hard working cops. I'd heard the rumors about Ramsey, but you know how rumors are. I personally had never seen any sign of him being anything other than true blue. I was as shocked as anyone else when I heard what had happened last spring."

"So what changed your mind?" John asked sternly.

"Well, my own probes into their backgrounds, starting with Chief Giovanni, turned up with absolutely nothing to indicate they were on the take. If they were, they sure hid it well. Hell, a couple of the guys, I don't know how they make ends meet each month. Not only that, but their own work on finding anyone else from your department that may be involved, was exemplary. I could find nothing wrong with it."

Frank looked at Susan. She was nodding her head and he could tell that she believed in him. John was another matter. He couldn't tell anything about his inner thoughts. John's face was as deadpan as a solid block of stone, revealing nothing of his reflections on Frank's story. Frank realized that John was as good as they said. Certainly his interrogation technique thus far was beyond reproach. And Frank had no doubts that this had turned into an interrogation. He forged ahead.

"I began to get suspicious... let me rephrase that. I wouldn't even say suspicious, more like feelings really... nagging doubts about the real reason for me having this investigation in the first place. They started after they wouldn't let the matter drop. I continually fed my findings back to the Sheriff. Each time I walked into this office and reported what I had found, I fully expected to walk out of there with my investigation complete. And each time, I was told to keep on probing. I began to seriously question what his motives were. It didn't make sense to keep on with it."

John finally spoke with a short, terse question. "Why do you think the Sheriff wouldn't let it drop?"

"I don't know. I've known him for a long time. I've even wondered if he is involved in all this. At this point, I don't think so. But as you and I both know it's difficult for one person to really know another, to know his or her true feelings and thoughts... what their *true* intentions are."

"Yes," said John tersely. "That's certainly *very* true. Isn't it?"

He ignored John's innuendo and stared into his eyes intently. The two of them remained with eyes locked for some time. Eventually, with eyes still locked, Frank slowly nodded and said, "Yes. Yes it is."

Frank tore his eyes away and looked at Susan. He could tell that for the first time she realized what was going on between him and John. Doubt was beginning to creep across her face. With growing frustration, he looked back at John and continued.

"Anyway, that about brings you up to speed until the point where the bodies were found. Once they came into the picture, I began to form a case around Ramsey being the shooter, based on the fact that his personal cell phone number had been found in her shoe. I was hoping that perhaps this stuff could finally be laid to rest. Everything fit. Then the fly in the ointment."

He scanned the faces of John and Susan before continuing. "The Sheriff called me into his office. He was obviously disturbed, bordering on barely controlled rage. He informed me that he had received a call from your city council, urging him, in the strongest of terms, to reexamine the crime scene where the Judge's wife had been found. Specifically, to make another attempt to find the bullet.

Now, he doesn't report to them. They have absolutely no control over his actions. So I can only assume at this point, that he acquiesced to their request for the sake of political peace. It was certainly a slap in his face, someone was, in reality, questioning our competence. Regardless, he ordered me to conduct another search. You know the results."

John spoke, while maintaining the same relentless stare. "You still haven't explained why you decided that something was wrong. Why you decided that not only is Nick being set up, but why you have decided to trust me, his best friend."

Now Frank began to get nervous. The man wouldn't let up. He feared that he was going to have to reveal something that he had promised he wouldn't. "I'm going on gut instinct here. Things just aren't adding up."

John spoke up again, shaking his head. "I'm still having trouble with it. You're taking a step that could end your career. Just on a hunch?" He shook his head again. "I don't think so. If that's all you have to go on, you're either a very brave man, very committed to his instincts, or a very stupid one. There's a lot at stake here and I don't think I want to take a chance on you being the latter. I'm going to ask you one more time, why are you here?"

Frank sighed and looked around the room. He rubbed his face and chin with one hand. "Shit," he said softly. He glanced at Susan and saw a look of total distrust. Somehow, it hurt him to see the look. He liked her.

He turned back to John. '*Bastard,*' he thought. He reached into his coat pocket and retrieved two cell phones. He threw them on the desk near John. For the first time, John's hard stare broke, replaced by one of pure curiosity. Frank grinned in spite of himself. '*Got you on that one asshole,*' he thought.

"What the…" John began, but stopped before he finished the sentence.

Frank's smile grew wider, but at the same time sadder. "You think I had a lot on the line before?" he questioned. "Now I really have it out on the line, but this time, much closer to home."

"Alright, you have my attention. What gives?" The steely flint was gone from John's voice, replaced by one of a more inquisitive nature.

"Good," said Frank. "Now, I must ask you to keep what I'm about to tell you completely to yourselves. What is said in this room must remain in this room."

John's voice hardened, but only slightly. "You're really in no position to make such a request."

Frank stood up and retrieved the phones. He looked down at John and said, "If I don't get your agreement on this, then I'm out of here. I'll do what I can to find out what's going on, but without your help, I doubt I'll be successful. Not only that, but I doubt you'll have much luck on your own, either."

John remained seated. "Why are these phones so important?" He thought for a moment then continued. "You indicated that those," he motioned toward the phones, "have some sort of personal involvement with you. What did you mean?"

Frank said, "I'm not saying anything more until I have your word." He looked over at Susan, "And yours as well."

John studied Frank for a moment. It was obvious that whatever this was, it meant a lot to Frank, personally. It would be highly unusual for a criminal to involve someone or something that personal in a situation like this. John decided. "Okay," he said. "I give you my word."

Frank looked over at Susan. "And you?"

She nodded. "Yes. If John is willing to give you his word, you have mine, too."

Frank put the phones back on the desk. "One more thing," he said. "Have you ever swept this room for bugs? And if so, when was the last time?"

John shrugged. "I haven't done it for a few months. I do have detectors that pick them up in this room. That's one of the reasons why I wanted us to come in here. If you were wired, I would have known it the instant you walked through that door."

"Okay," said Frank. "But I'd still feel better if you turned a radio on."

"Fine," said John. He reached into his drawer and retrieved a remote control. A moment later, music filled the room He browsed through the stations until he found one with a male singer with lots of background accompaniment.

Susan looked at both of them in complete bewilderment. "Okaaay," she said slowly.

John grinned and stood up. "Let's move over in the corner and I'll explain." He looked at Frank. "It's probably best that we move away from the desk anyway. This comment obviously confused Susan further.

After all three had moved away from the desk, John explained. "A 'bug' is an eavesdropping device. Usually a tiny microphone placed in a strategic location that would allow a listener to hear everything going on in a room. Now I could spend all day talking about the various types and the problems associated with each, but for right now, all that matters is that most of them have a flaw, that being that the microphone picks up everything, including the radio. The problem is, even though the human brain can sort out the difference between a radio and a live person talking, a microphone can't."

Susan didn't look like things were getting much clearer. John explained further by asking, "Do you have any problem hearing and understanding what I'm saying right now?"

She shook her head and John continued. "Good. That's because even though your ears, or your internal microphones, if you will, hear everything that an artificial mic hears, your brain is able to sort out the hailstorm of noise and let you cue in on whatever it is that you want to listen to. An artificial mic doesn't have that advantage. Therefore, someone else listening in will mainly hear the loud music, with the sound of the instruments being the loudest. They can probably hear that someone is talking, but they won't be able to hear what is being said."

"But they have computer programs that can filter out the extraneous noise," Susan said. "And why are we here in the corner?"

"To answer your first question," John replied, "yes, they do have computer programs of varying efficiency. But they don't have a program that can equal the human brain when it comes to sorting that stuff out. The answer to your second question is that if someone planted a bug in this room, it would most likely be centered around someone talking at the desk, not over here. Not only that," he pointed upward, "but one of the speakers pounding out the music is right over our heads."

Susan nodded. John looked at Frank. "Okay, now it's your turn."

Frank leaned closer and spoke so low that John and Susan had trouble hearing him above the din of the music. "The reason that I've decided to trust you is... my brother. He's an F.B.I. agent."

John's eyebrows furrowed in confusion. "And what does that have to do with the price of beans in California?" he asked.

"He's been working on the Coeptus Guild case," Frank replied. "I never knew it until a few hours ago. He called me to tell me that they're positive that Giovanni is being set up. They don't know how they did it, or who did it, but they're sure that's the case. He also said that I should probably get together with you, because they know you're one of the few people that they know is clean."

"And how do they know that?" John asked.

"Because they've thoroughly checked you out." Frank answered.

"They've been studying you ever since you got shot." He rolled his eyes and continued. "You're not going to like this, but they tapped your phones and generally gave you one intensive look-see.

John's face hardened once again. Frank hastily continued. "Look at it from their point of view. Apparently, they were becoming aware that something like Coeptus Guild existed even before your involvement. But they had next to nothing concrete. Your whole incident finally put a face and some definitions on something that had been something akin to a fantasy before that. Every person involved got a similar treatment. They had to know who they were dealing with. You, Giovanni, and Susan here, were all checked extensively and given a clean bill of health. Once the Judge's wife was found, they were hoping to get more answers. They didn't see this thing with the Chief coming and they want to know more about it. They sense they're close to getting some answers on this one and they don't want to let the opportunity slip."

"Makes sense," John reluctantly agreed. "But why don't they do their own investigation?"

"Tons of reasons, John. My brother freely admitted that he's not telling me a lot. But the bottom line is this, they're looking at incidents all over the country. Hell, all over the world for that matter. But man power is limited. After all, the bulk of their resources is allotted for terrorism. The reason they got me involved is twofold. One, since, for the most part, they still don't know who they can trust, I am one of the few that's considered a good guy. Second, they don't want to start asking questions themselves and alert everyone that they're being scrutinized. I can be their eyes and ears and as far as anyone else is concerned, I'm just looking into possible corruption at your department and the death of the Judge's wife."

John nodded toward his desk. "What's with the phones?"

"I got them from my brother. They're scrambled lines. Since Susan is involved, I'll get one for her too. They don't want us using our regular cell phones and land lines for obvious reasons. As I said, for the first time since they started this investigation, they feel they're close and they don't want to leave anything to chance."

John stood and looked around the room as he sorted through all the information he'd been given. Wow. He'd been wondering if the F.B.I. was doing anything about Coeptus Guild. After interviewing him a couple of times, he'd heard nothing. He knew they'd talked to Sue and her father, as well as a few other people. Even Nick had said he wasn't sure they were still actively investigating the case.

But the F.B.I. was known for not sharing well with others. They would be more than happy to sponge up whatever information they could garner from law enforcement agencies. But good luck trying to find out anything from them. The information pipeline flowed only in one direction, towards them.

He studied Frank Carlotta once again. He had good eyes, a good face. Nothing in his demeanor spoke of deceit. John's guts told him that Frank was a good, honest person. John was almost there. "What's your brother's name?" He asked Frank.

"Stuart," Frank replied.

John looked at Susan. She knew immediately what he wanted. "I'm on it," she said and moved toward her computer.

"You are one mistrusting son of a bitch." Frank smiled. "But then again, I would be too in your shoes. In a way, it makes me feel better." Knowing that nothing significant would be discussed until Susan returned, he asked, "So is there anything good in that lake back there?"

That brought about a fishing discussion that continued until Susan returned, handing John a piece of paper. John read it and asked, "Where was your brother's last posting?"

Frank first looked at John, then at Susan, in astonishment. "I see why John says that you could be useful in getting information." He looked back at John, "He was in their Denver office, in Washington before that, and in Chicago before that."

"When did he start with them?" John asked.

"1983," came the prompt reply.

John handed the paper back to Susan. "Okay, I believe you."

"Christ!" Frank said with a laugh. "I feel like I should celebrate, I'm an official member now. Is there a sanctioned hand shake or anything?"

John smiled grimly. "Yeah, well, I had to be sure. I have a few scores to settle with these people and I know how devious they are. Now, do you have any place in particular you want to start?"

The sniper watched through his scope as the cop left. He considered calling his employers to let them know about the visit. He continued to track the cop's head until he drove out of sight. In the end, the sniper decided to wait until his daily check in to tell them about the cop. He switched his sight over to the kitchen area and there he found Harvard and the woman. Her side was facing the sniper as she talked. The sniper sighted in on her temple and caressed the trigger with his finger. In his mind, he fired the weapon. He breathed a barely audible, "Pow." In his mind, he felt the recoil. He lifted the rifle slightly upward to simulate that effect. He resighted on her and saw her lifeless body tumble to the floor, her head blown to bits... in his mind.

John had a brief discussion with Susan after Frank had left. It was mostly about everyday mundane things like what was for dinner. Who was going to pick up Mary Kate, that type of thing. Then he told her, in a hushed whisper that he was going to get his equipment and do a quick scan of the house.

A proper search of a house could take hours, even days. Unlike on television, relying upon electronic equipment alone would be foolhardy. Sophisticated bugs could be turned on or off, by themselves or at preset times. Other types would silently collect data to some sort of recording device. It could then be compressed and sent out instantly in what was known a "burst" transmission. The transmitter would only be on for a few seconds at most. In that case, there would be little for the electronic equipment to detect.

The other way to detect a bug would be to place a known sound source in the center of a room. The person attempting to find the bug would then don earphones, connected to a receiver. He would walk around the room, scanning various frequencies. If the investigator heard his known sound source over the earphones, he would know that a hidden microphone was in the area.

There was other equipment, but the most reliable method was an old fashion hand search. There was no substitute for taking apart wall outlets, light fixtures, phones, sofas, chairs, and even paintings hanging on the wall. John had even discovered a microphone that had been connected to its source by ordinary looking paint that conducted electricity.

His search took him into the wee hours of the morning and when he was done, he was fairly convinced that they had no unwanted listeners to their conversations. Still, as he explained to Susan, that did not mean that they were safe. "Rifle microphones," and their ilk could still be employed.

"Rifle microphones?" she asked in dismay.

"Yeah. They're shaped kind of like a rifle with a scope.

They magnify sound from a relatively small area over large distances. It not only picks up sound directly, but can pick up the sound from the glass in a window. When you talk, minute vibrations travel to the glass and cause the glass to vibrate. Those vibrations can be picked up by a rifle mic and the listener can hear your conversation."

She shuddered. "I don't think I like hearing this. I'm beginning to wonder if I'll ever feel safe again. Makes you wonder if all those people that hear voices and say that their television is watching them are really nuts after all." She looked directly into his eyes. "They are nuts, aren't they? They can't really see you over your television, can they?"

John's face took a slightly crazed look. In a heavily accented, fake German voice he said, "Vell, ve are vatching you frueline. You have no secrets from us," and with that he gave a short, maniacal laugh.

She punched him and smiled. "I know it sounds stupid, but a lot of what you just told me sounds pretty James Bond-ish to me."

"No, your television can't see you, at least not that I know of, yet. There's always somebody out there thinking up ways to listen and see what people are doing. They've come up with some pretty clever ways. Even way back in the cold war years, they had a bug that looked like an olive. It could be placed into somebody's martini and hear everything around it."

Susan visibly shuddered. "Well, with that little tidbit of information, I'm going to bed. I'm going to get undressed in the dark, though I suppose if someone really wants to see me, that won't make any difference."

"Your one hundred percent correct on that," he replied. "But you probably don't want to hear the ways they get around that."

She shook her head and looked at him. Both of their minds were racing, and it had nothing to do with Nick Giovanni, Coeptus Guild, listening devices, or with anything outside of the two of them. John was torn. He could tell what she was silently asking him. A large part of him wanted to take her in his arms and carry her to the bedroom. But a smaller, and at this point, stronger part of him, told him, 'No.'

She could see in his eyes the battle being waged within. She decided to make the decision for him. She walked up and gave him a quick peck on the lips. She hugged him briefly and stepped away. "Goodnight," she said cheerily.

His relief was plain to see. She was both gladdened and disappointed at the same time. '*It will come*,' she thought to herself, of that she was certain. It was just that she really was a little freaked out over the thought that someone could be listening or worse still, watching them. Having his strong, capable body lying next to her would go a long way toward alleviating those fears.

"I..." he hesitantly began.

"I know," she said. "It's alright. We'll take it one step at a time. I'm a patient girl. You'll know when you're ready."

He smiled and he, in his heart, did take another step forward. This really was a very special woman. "Thank you for being so understanding." He took her in his arms and they stood there, silently, arms intertwined, for some time. They kissed. No quick peck this time. But deeply, not of passion so much as love.

When they broke, Susan felt much better, as did John. They both said goodnight and headed off to their respective bedrooms.

The sniper couldn't see that last kiss. But he did see their bedroom lights go off. He shook his head. He wondered how Harvard could have a woman like that in the house and not be sleeping with her. '*Well*,' he thought to himself, '*Harvard had better do her soon, while he still had the chance.*'

CHAPTER

8

Dawn broke, clear, bright, and cold. John was out running. He was breathing through his nostrils and his breath shot out of his nose like the steamy exhalations of some mythical dragon. The dry, dead leaves beneath his feet crackled noisily as he ran. He liked the sound. He liked the feel and smell of the cold morning air as it entered his lungs. His breath was even and controlled as the air entered and exited his nostrils and he felt as though he could run forever.

He wasn't sure how much longer he could continue to breathe through his nose however, because he had elected to push himself hard this morning. Instead of his usual path around the lake, he decided he would go up into the hills that rose above the water. He was going to traverse up and down those hills, moving forward in a serpentine fashion as he made his way around the body of water and back to his house.

It would be rough going, but it had been awhile since he had done it and he wanted to be thoroughly exhausted when his task was completed. A good hard work out was a natural drug to him that calmed him, cleaned out the cob webs, and made him think clearer. And he knew that he would need a clear mind today.

He changed direction and started up the first hill. Immediately his legs began to burn as he felt the additional pressure and soon afterward, his breathing increased to assist his heart's attempt to carry more oxygen to his muscles. He pumped his arms and pushed upward.

When he made it to the top, he turned and angled back downward. When he got to the bottom of the hill, he turned again and angled back up. In this fashion he slowly, methodically, began to make his way around the lake.

The sniper's heartbeat was also increasing, but not because of any physical exertion. '*What the fuck's he doin'*?' the sniper wondered. If Harvard continued in this fashion, it would be a matter of time before he discovered the sniper's lair. And not much time! The sniper's instructions had been clear on this point. Do not get caught! He was to use whatever means at his disposal to prevent capture. If that meant killing John Harvard, so be it.

John was on his fourth trip up the hill when he noticed that there appeared to be a beaten path through a grassy area at the top. It was obviously new and he wondered if the deer, for some reason, had decided to create a new trail.

It was obvious to the sniper now. Harvard would discover his position. He took a tighter grip on the stock of his rifle and prepared himself.

John came to a sudden stop. The leaves behind a rotted log at the top of the hill were scattered. The leaves at the center of the disturbance were matted down, as though something had been lying on them for an extended period of time. He looked around. It was a funny place for a deer to lie down. They usually liked a field of grass that could camouflage their position while they slept.

'*A wolf or fox maybe*?' he wondered. He looked closer. He could see no sign of fur. He looked around again. He could see a new path leading off into the field at the top of the hill. It was wide, much wider than one animal could have caused. He shrugged his shoulders. He decided that it was most likely caused by a pack of canines, probably wolves or coyote, all were plentiful in this area. Not fox as they were normally a solitary animal.

John never noticed that the site provided a clear view of his home. It never occurred to him to follow the path, because he assumed that whatever animal had caused the disturbance, was long gone. He resumed his run. He couldn't have been more wrong. Or more fortuitous in his decision to forget the matter at that particular time.

"Hey Nick, how's it going?" John asked grimly. He had finished his run, had showered and eaten breakfast. Now he was sitting in his office.

"About as well as can be expected," Nick answered in a glum tone. "That attorney Sue got for me called. He can't believe they're keeping me in here. Apparently the State's Attorney has convinced the judge that I'm a flight risk. My attorney got a hearing scheduled for this morning to try to get them to set some sort of bail. Not that I have the money that they're going to want anyway."

"Don't worry about it, Nick. I think we can come up with something to get you out. Now what can you tell me about all this?"

"Not much, other than what I've already told you. My mind is still reeling."

"Understandable. Let's start with the phone calls. Obviously, someone doctored the Department's phone records to show that you received a call from Sally Walton. Who could that be?"

Nick thought for a moment before answering. "Well, it would have to be someone in the computer department. They are the ones that run the phone system and keep all the recordings from the 911 line and the phone logs. It's a pretty secure area that is monitored by video and trip alarms. Access is granted via a key card. I wouldn't think anyone could get in there long enough to find and change anything. Possible, but not probable."

"Okay, so how many people work there?"

"Four, not counting the supervisor," Nick replied. "Their shifts are staggered. One comes in at 6:00 A.M. Two more come in at 8:00 A.M. The last one leaves at 12:00 A.M."

"That leaves six hours that the place is unattended Nick. That's a long time for someone to play with."

"Not really. Like I said, the place is loaded with video monitors. The feed for those monitors goes to the radio room. They see the geeks there every day so they know who belongs there and who doesn't. Even if someone managed to get in, someone would see them on the monitors and would know if they are authorized or not."

"I see your point, Nick. I can still think of ways around that, but for the time being, we'll assume that it had to be one of those five."

"Unless it was the guy that was working for Ramsey. What if he changed the records before we caught him?"

"I don't think so," answered John. "What reason would he have for changing the records way back then? I don't think this little scheme of theirs is that long in the making. No, I think this is a recent plan concocted to lay blame on you, get you out of office, and get their own stooge in. What are the names of the five that are in there now?"

Nick gave him the names. He didn't recognize any of them. "Anyone on here that you are reasonably sure you can trust?" John asked.

"Yeah, Sara Rose. She's in charge and we checked her out pretty good after the last fiasco. I've worked with her several times and I think she's pretty straight up. The guy I know least about is Dwight Chase. He's the guy that re-placed the rat we got rid of. We did a very thorough back-ground on him, but you know how that goes. We could have missed something or they could have turned him once he got in there."

"Hmm, there are a few possibilities here. I think I'm go-ing to check out Ms. Rose. We need someone in there we can coordinate with. Right now, this is the biggest chink in their armor. If we can find the mole, we can maybe work our way up from there."

"What makes you think she'll talk to you? After all, as far as she's concerned, I'm a dirty cop and everyone knows you're my best friend."

John laughed. "You know I have my way with women. I'll get her to trust me."

Nick snorted. "Christ! Now I am screwed. My fate hinges upon the man with four failed marriages being able to convince a woman to trust him. Lord help me."

They talked about personal stuff for a few more minutes. John didn't tell Nick that he was working with Frank Car-lotta. He didn't feel it was the time and he didn't feel safe discussing it over the phone. Frank was really sticking his neck out on this one and who knew who might be listening in on their conversation. Nick promised that he would call after his hearing to let him know how it went and what the bail was.

After hanging up, he reached for the secure cell phone that Frank had given him and dialed his number. They talked about his conversation with Nick and it was agreed that it would be better for Frank to approach Sara. John would attempt to talk with William Ramsey, the late Deputy Chief's son, and it was further decided that it would be best if it were an unannounced visit. They really didn't expect to get much from him but they wanted to see Ramsey's reaction to John's visit. It could go a long way in determining how much effort they should put into him.

"Oh yeah," said Frank. "One more thing, we finally got some good DNA off the other body in the woods and got a hit on CODIS. It was an ex-con by the name of Wallis Jester."

"So it wasn't Billyray Jenkins," John replied "I had a hunch it wouldn't be. Still, the timing of Jester's death still leads me to believe he was involved with all this. What was he in for?"

"He was in for burglary. He did high end jobs and was quite good. He only got caught by sheer bad luck. He had a fight with his wife and she stormed out of the house in the middle of the night. She was walking over to a girlfriend's and got gang raped in a park by a bunch of street thugs. Some guy in the neighborhood got tired of all the screaming he heard and finally, after twenty minutes, called the cops. They didn't catch anybody, but at the hospital, she got pissed. Blamed Wallis for it happening in the first place and started spilling her guts. Regretted it a few hours later and tried to take it back. But the horse was already out of the barn."

John chuckled. "Shit happens. When did he get out?"

"He got out about the same time as Jenkins," Frank replied, "and guess who his psychiatrist was at the pen?"

"Oh, let me think long and hard about that one... David Walton."

"Wow, you are a wonder! Now I see why criminals fear you."

"Yup. You got it. Just a regular fuckin' psychic. Now all we have to do is figure out how he's involved in all this."

"We'll just put it on the list. I'll assign it to one of my guys. It's pretty straight forward and would be in keeping with the investigation. Hey, my other line's ringing, catch you later."

John hung up the phone just as Sue walked in. She sat down next to him and dropped a large bundle of printouts on his desk. "By the way, I forgot to tell you that Frank was here this morning when you were running and dropped off that cell phone he wants me to use. This," she pointed to the printouts, "is everything I can manage to find on the City Council members. Two of them stick out in my mind."

John's eyebrows furrowed in interest. "Really? Who?"

Sue grabbed the top two paper clipped stacks. She handed him one of them. "Meet Lily Barrett. She owns a headhunting company that she runs from her house. She only does high end job seekers, so she makes a pretty good living. But that doesn't explain why she appears to be worth approximately fifteen million!"

John's eyes widened in amazement. "What? You're kidding me?" He shuffled through her file. "It says here her house is worth around five hundred thousand. She has a Lexus SUV. I see she has stocks and bonds worth about another five hundred thousand and a little under eighty thousand in various bank accounts. Given her occupation, I'd say she's doing rather well, but that's within reason, and I don't see the other fourteen mil that you're talking about."

Sue smiled and handed him another packet of paper clipped papers. "Kudos to me. Now meet Susan Whitaker. She owns half of an apartment building in Orlando, Florida, a house on a beach in Antigua, in the Caribbean, a rather large motor yacht, and has some sizable off shore accounts."

John looked through the papers. "Okay, what does this have to do with Lilly Barrett?"

Sue's grin got even larger. "Because, my beautiful man, Susan Whitaker died forty years ago!"

"You mean…" John began.

"Yup," Sue interrupted. "Lilly and Susan are one in the same."

"Holyyy shit."

"But that's not all," Sue continued. She handed him the next stack of papers. "Now meet Council member Bob Stark. He owns a trucking and concrete business. He too is worth a lot of money, way more than he should. But the most interesting part is that his grandfather died thirty years ago."

John looked up from Stark's file. "And?"

"And his grandfather is an amazing man. Because, from the grave, he has accumulated millions. As a matter of fact, four years ago, he became the owner of the other half of Susan Whitaker's apartment building in Orlando."

John was completely dumbfounded. This was way more

than he had ever hoped to find. He couldn't imagine how much of what Sue had found would never be allowed in court. She had to have cracked into some pretty secure and sensitive databases to get this information.

"Nice work, Sue. I can't believe you got all of this from merely sitting at your keyboard."

"Well, I did do some pretext phone calls as well, but I set up a program to look for stuff even while I wasn't at my computer. It's been going pretty much since we talked about it."

He shook his head. "Still pretty impressive. What about the Asian programmer and the lawyer? Anything on them?"

"No," Sue answered. "Both checked out okay. As a matter of fact, the programmer is living pretty much hand to mouth."

"Okay, so it's clear Stark and Barrett are connected. In my mind, the money pretty much tells me these are the two working for Coeptus Guild. But there is nothing linking them. There is no clear cut evidence of any wrong doing other than the fact they are using assumed identities to hide money. We need more. Maybe Frank's brother with the F.B.I. can help out on this one. Seems like an awful lot of money, even for a council member. What makes them worth such high payoff money? It's going to be a classic case of, 'follow the money.' With any luck, we might be able to follow this one little branch right back to the roots of Coeptus Guild."

"Oh!" exclaimed Sue. "Don't get me wrong. I don't think all of it is dirty money. Both of them made the best of what they were given and have made some very wise investments."

"Still," returned John. They had a good chunk of seed money to make those investments. What we need to do is separate the dirty money from the clean and try to link as much of it as we can back to the Coeptus Guild."

Sue looked at him thoughtfully as he spoke. When he finished, she turned her head slightly and stared into space as she continued thinking about the problem. After a while, she nodded her head as she said, "I'll see what else I can dig up, but it's going to take some time."

"Do what you can, Sue. In the meantime, I have a couple of others for you to check out." He gave her the names of the Police Department computer staff and told her of his conversation with Nick. He also told her about Wallis Jester. When he was done he asked, "Were you able to find out anything about the other ex-cons David Walton was working with?"

She shook her head. "Not much. Everything seems to be in proper order. I did notice that a couple of them had missed their check in's with their parole offices. There are warrants out for them, obviously Jester was one."

"Well," John replied, "He's present and accounted for now. Who's the other?"

"Luke Bonnais," she replied. "Before you ask, he was in for armed robbery. He was suspected in a couple of murders, but they couldn't pin anything on him. He supposedly got religion in prison and is a reformed man.

John stood up with a snort. "Not likely. I'm going over

to William Ramsey's office and try to question him. Let me know as soon as you come up with anything else." He hesitated a moment. He just had a thought and he was trying to decide if he really wanted act on it. Then he leaned down and gave her a quick kiss on the lips. She quickly kissed him back before he straightened up. "I have to go now, Sue, but I think we need to maybe have a talk tonight."

Sue stood up and put her arms around him. "Yup," she responded as she put her head against his chest. "I think it's time." She was pretty sure how the conversation would go. But the tingling in her spine and her suddenly constricted breathing betrayed her apprehension that she might be wrong. '*Oh well,*' she thought. '*I guess, as they say, "It's time to take a crap or get off the pot."*'

John pulled his SUV off his driveway and onto the road. He was heading toward the law offices of Langstrom and Associates. He had called ahead and spoke to the receptionist who confirmed that William Ramsey was in and as far as she knew, would be in all morning.

When he arrived, he parked in the underground lot and walked to the lobby of the building. A directory indicated that Langstrom and Associates took up the entire third floor. John entered the elevator and as it began its upward travel, he began to think about what pretext he would use to get into Ramsey's office. Obviously he could not announce who he really was and expect admittance. He also could not just barge in without the cops being called and John knew *that* wouldn't go well for him.

It turned out that he didn't need any kind of ruse at all. As the elevator door opened a tall young man was standing at the receptionist's desk with his back to the elevator. The man was wearing a light blue dress shirt, his trousers were held up by suspenders, and he wasn't wearing a matching suit coat. He was narrow waisted, but broad at the shoulders, and John guessed the man worked out regularly.

As he approached them, he heard the young man talking to receptionist in an intense, heated tone. "Just get in touch with him and tell him I can't make it tonight and would he like to reschedule. Period. You don't need to know anything else. If he doesn't like it, tough shit!" With that, the young man abruptly turned and headed toward the elevator, without ever seeing John. The conversation, apparently, was at an end. He and the receptionist watched as the angry young man passed the elevator and entered a men's room.

"Yes, *Mr.* Ramsey!" the receptionist hissed at the closing door.

Startled, but recovering quickly, John turned back to her. "So Bill's a little on edge today, huh?"

"Obviously you don't know him very well," she answered, while still looking at the door to the men's room. "He's *always* on edge. Especially with people he thinks are *beneath* him."

She jerked suddenly as she realized that she didn't know John and more importantly, didn't know who he was. "I... I'm sorry," she stuttered. "I... I shouldn't have said that. I'm just having a bad day. He's really a very nice guy."

The woman's face had turned red with embarrassment. She was obviously flustered and was furiously trying to backtrack. She would probably be a fount of information. He would love to talk to her more, but he didn't have the time right now. A golden opportunity had been laid at his feet and he wanted to take full advantage of it. He laughed easily as he said, "No problemo. We all have our moments, don't we?"

She flashed him a million dollar smile and said softly, "Thank you."

"That's okay. Well, I hate to go in there right now," he jerked his head toward the men's room door, "but nature calls and I don't know how much longer I can wait. Sorry if that's more information than you wanted. Wish me luck."

She laughed, her relief obvious, and said, "Good luck."

John entered the room and immediately saw that it was small. It had two urinals and two toilets. A small sink stood near the door. A scowling Ramsey was just wiping his hands on a paper towel when John entered. Ramsey looked up and it was immediately apparent that he recognized John. Ramsey's scowl transformed to a look of uncontrollable fury and pure hatred.

"What the fuck are you doing here?" Ramsey snarled. The man was visibly shaking with anger.

"I just want to talk to you for a few minutes. I won't…"

"Fuck you asshole!" Ramsey shouted as he launched himself at John.

Ramsey cocked his right fist back as he closed the two

steps that were between them. This was a confident, but very angry man. However, John's trained fighting eye immediately detected an inexperienced fighter who was telegraphing his next move way too soon. To John, it seemed as though he had all the time in the world to react.

John, who was still standing directly in front of the just closed men's room door, waited until Ramsey's punch was actually coming forward. Then, at the last possible moment, John's right foot stepped back as he pivoted to the right, presenting Ramsey with his left side. At the same time, John's right forearm came up and redirected Ramsey's blow ever so slightly to the right. Ramsey's forward motion was increased as John's left hand came up, grabbed Ramsey's extended right elbow and capitalizing on Ramsey's momentum, guided Ramsey's fist into the door.

To Ramsey's credit, he didn't scream as a sickening crunch told John that the man's hand had broken. Instead, he merely grunted and in a low tone, spat out, "Motherfucker. I'll kill you motherfucker." Ramsey then spun on his right foot and his left knee came up in an attempt to knee John in the groin.

John jumped back and with his left side facing Ramsey, dropped down, pivoting his body on his left foot. At the same time, John swung his right foot out and to the left in an arcing, sweeping motion, catching Ramsey's right ankle and knocking it out from under him. Since Ramsey's entire weight was still on that foot, Ramsey tumbled in a heap onto the hard and cold ceramic bathroom floor.

John quickly jumped up and took a defensive stance,

ready to block any further attacks. For the moment, there didn't seem to be any on the way. "As I was saying, I just want to talk." John spoke calmly but the altercation had brought forward his, until now, carefully suppressed desire to seriously hurt someone.

Ramsey slowly staggered to his feet and leaned against the wall. John could see that he was still very angry, but the anger was tempered by the pain of his recent, "*attitude adjustment.*"

"Fuck you!" Ramsey gasped. "I got nothing to say to you, motherfucker. It's too bad my father didn't take you out. He didn't deserved to have his fucking head blown off, motherfucker." Ramsey's voice cracked with emotion at the last part. "I saw the autopsy photos. It was disgusting."

"Why are you pissed off at me?" John asked in an even tone. "I didn't shoot him. As a matter of fact, he was doing everything he could to kill *me.*"

"*Because you drove him to it!*" Ramsey shouted back. "You were always on his case, always talking behind his back. You were always trying to make him look bad because you wanted his job." John couldn't believe the garbage he was hearing. Did this man actually believe that? Ramsey continued with renewed anger. "He should have killed you, you and that slut you live with. But that's all right, you'll get yours... and so will she. You're both living on borrowed time."

With that, a knowing, arrogant smile of satisfaction came to Ramsey's lips. The smile quickly faded when he saw a change come over John Livingston Harvard. His tranquil demeanor quickly left as Ramsey spoke, replaced with a darkening look that suddenly chilled William Ramsey to the very core. If someone had asked him at that moment, what color John Harvard's eyes were, he would have replied, without hesitation, "Black, black as the inside of a closed tomb."

As if by magic, John was next to him, pinning Ramsey's neck up against the wall with his left forearm. At the same time, John's right hand had reached down and had viciously grabbed hold of Ramsey's genitals and squeezed, hard. His face was right next to his. "You utter one sound," John said quietly, "and you will receive pain such that you will beg me to let you meet your father. Do you understand?" Ramsey nodded, as much as the pressure on his neck would allow him to.

William Ramsey had grown up in a cop family. Though he didn't know why at the time, his father's corruption ensured that William had never been want for anything. His father had been tough on him, but had always encouraged him to be whatever he wanted, had convinced him in fact, that he was better than everyone else. To him, people like the receptionist were there merely to serve him and didn't deserve the respect and consideration that people of a more worthy status should receive.

William had taken his assumed high bred status to heart and found that he was bright enough, good looking enough, and strong willed enough to pretty much get whatever he wanted. He didn't recall ever really being afraid of anything or anyone. He was afraid now, afraid to the very roots of his soul. He had never seen anyone look like this man who now stood clutching his balls and squeezing his throat with his forearm. As he spoke, Ramsey imagined that John's very breath was an icy cold spear that drove itself deep into Ramsey's lungs and made Ramsey shiver as though he were lying naked on some far off frozen tundra.

John Harvard had Ramsey's undivided attention as he continued to speak softly, but in a tone as hard a granite. "Now, what did you mean we are, '*living on borrowed time*?'"

"You... you... you pissed off a lot of people." Ramsey croaked out from beneath the pressure on his throat. "They want you out of the way. You're screwing up their plans."

"Whose plans?" Harvard hissed. "Whose plans?" he demanded again in a much louder and even harsher voice.

"I... I don't know. Please, please sss... stop." Ramsey gagged at a sudden increase of the pressure on his throat and scrotum.

John's mind was racing. What the hell had he uncovered? He didn't expect that he would be able to get anything useful out of Ramsey. He just wanted to see his reaction to get an idea of how much he was involved. Then again, he hadn't expected to have a physical confrontation with him. But Ramsey had started it. John could have dealt with that, could even have dealt with threats to his own life. Threatening Susan was what had made him snap. It was like de'ja vu all over again. History repeating itself. John felt the dark cloud that had descended around him but he was powerless to stop it. He could *not* let it happen again, *would not*.

John had an overpowering urge to kill this man, right

here, right now. The urge was oh so strong. But through the haze, he heard his martial art instructor's voice, "*Do not become angry. Anger does not allow you to think clearly, does not allow you to make wise decisions. Anger is the first stage of defeat. Calm yourself, calm yourself. Move with clarity and purpose.*"

John's mind closed down for an instant, as he sought to regain his tranquility. "*Show me that my life was a good trade for yours.*" His mind snapped to his dream of Emily emploring him to do the right thing. He knew it would not be possible to completely tame the anger which threatened to overwhelm him, but he knew he could get it back in its cage, at least for now.

He came back to this world a moment later and turned his attention back to Ramsey, whose face was turning a peculiar shade of purple. He saw that while his mind had been wrestling with itself, he had unknowingly placed additional pressure on Ramsey's throat and he was on the verge of passing out. He relaxed the grip of his right hand and the pressure of his left forearm, slightly. Ramsey began to breathe a little better. Though Ramsey's breath had returned, the unwavering fear however, remained. '*That's fine with me,*' John thought.

"You have to know *who*, you fucking jag off." John menacingly whispered. "How are you involved?"

"I'm really not. I…"

John's right hand gripped Ramsey's balls tighter, kneading them in his hand like a group of marbles, bringing the first tinges of tears to the lawyer's eyes. He took his left arm away from Ramsey's neck so that he could cup his hand over Ramsey's mouth, to muffle the scream he knew was coming as he increased the pressure on his balls even more. The muffled scream came and Ramsey's knees began to buckle with it. Tears were now pouring out of his eyes freely. "I'm only going to ask you nice one more time. I won't be so fucking considerate next time. I think my hand might even be cramping up as we speak. Now let's try it again, and before you answer, you should know that my unfathomable patience is almost at an end. To be perfectly frank with you, you've put me in the mood to kill some-body, come to think of it, several somebody's, and this is as good a place to start as any."

John was whispering so quietly that anyone standing next to them would have had trouble hearing him. To Ram-sey, John's voice seemed to be coming from *inside* his head. He looked into Harvard's eyes and knew, just *knew* he was only going to get one more chance to satisfy this demon masquerading as a man. The dam inside of William Ram-sey's head broke and he spent the next ten minutes blubber-ing out everything he knew about what was going on.

When he was done, Harvard let him go. Ramsey slid against the bathroom door to the floor, as though he had no bones left in his body to hold him. He was an utterly broken man.

He jerked in apprehension and tried to crawl away, liter-ally into the wall, as John knelt down next to him. "Listen to me carefully." Ramsey's eyes drifted upward to meet John's. "You listening?" John asked.

"Yy... yes." He croaked.

CHAPTER
9

John sat in his truck, head on the steering wheel, deep in thought. He had put the keys in the ignition, but hadn't twisted them forward to start it. He'd lost control back there. The urge to kill William Ramsey had been almost too strong to control. Ramsey had been unfortunate enough to be the first person from Coeptus Guild that he'd run into since the "*incident.*" The urge for some big time payback was strong, *very* strong.

He hadn't acted on those urges for a variety of reasons. Killing Ramsey would certainly have alerted them as to how close he really was. It would also have deprived him of the opportunity of getting more information from Ramsey in the future. One had to protect one's sources. Of course, leaving him alive could mean that Ramsey himself would warn them, but he didn't think that would happen. He'd seen the fearful, beaten look in William Ramsey's eyes. He'd seen it before. The look of a low life, drug addicted, petty criminal who knew the gig was up and was willing to do anything to extend their miserable lives just a little longer, at least until the next fix. He doubted that Ramsey was a drug addict and his life style didn't come close to theirs. But that defeated look was the same. No, he doubted that William Ramsey would warn anyone of his visit, or of what he had told John. *That* would definitely curtail his life expectancy and Ramsey was bright enough to know it.

His other reasons for not killing Ramsey centered around his innate respect for the law. He'd been one of the good guys his entire adult life, though his experiences with Coeptus Guild were putting a severe strain on that respect. Which brought everything back to his dream, of Emily's warning not to become one of them. That warning was never far from his consciousness.

"Show me that my life was a good trade for yours." He put his head on the steering wheel and sighed. With his arm against Ramsey's throat, blocking the life giving air from entering his lungs, John had felt so much satisfaction in the rapidly growing fear in William's eyes. So much so that it had been difficult to let up enough to let him breathe. But the image of Emily's apparition, warning him, had been enough to shake the desire for the ultimate revenge. She had become his beacon of light in all this darkness. Killing Ramsey like that would have snuffed the light out, probably forever. He shuddered to think what sort of animal he would become then. Had Gregory T. Harris been right when he had said that there was little difference between them, that they were really poured in the same mold, just different sides to the same coin? The self doubts began to rise again.

He was startled by the ring of the secure cell phone given

to him by Frank Carlotta. It seemed unnaturally loud in the stillness of his truck. With slightly shaking hands and without moving his head from the steering wheel, he answered it. "Yeah?" he said woodenly.

Frank's voice was clear and obviously excited as he spoke. "John? Listen, I got some info for you. I just got a call from the Coroner's office. Sally Walton was not put into that grave right away. In fact, they suspect that she was killed somewhere else and some time before she was buried in the field."

John's mind was quickly focused. He sat up. "What do you mean?" he asked.

Frank continued. "Turns out, when they examined the dirt around her clothing and the bones, they found it was different from the dirt at the field. They first noticed it because the dirt was much darker and had a different texture. When they looked into it further, they found that it was rich in nutrients and fertilizers. They suspect that she was originally buried in someone's garden."

"Wow," John said softly, but with little emotion. He was still feeling the effects of his energy sapping moral conundrum. "This changes things completely. How…"

"Oh," Frank interrupted. "It gets better. They also found some fly carcasses on her and her clothing. An entomologist says they are a common house fly. Conclusion to all this? She was killed in a house, laid there for some time, possibly a day or two. She was then buried in a garden for an undetermined amount of time, then transferred to where we found her."

This was an awful lot of information. A thought sprang into John's head. "Frank! You know what this means? We got proof that Nick was set up."

"How do you figure?" Frank asked in obvious confusion.

"Don't you see? The bullet they recovered from the field, the bullet from Nick's gun. If she was killed somewhere else, how did the bullet get in the field? What are they going to try and say? That he shot a corpse to death?"

"Shit! I see what you mean. That was stupid on my part. I should have made the connection sooner. I could definitely use this to get Nick released. It, at the very least, puts some serious doubts as to the validity of his charges."

"No," John replied slowly. "Let's hold off a while."

"What? Why?" Frank shot back. "He's your friend and we have information that will exonerate him."

"I know. But I want to try to get to the bottom of this. If we don't, it could just be a temporary reprieve. Who framed Nick? Who killed Sally Walton and where? We've got to find that garden."

"Yeah, okayyy! And how many gardens do you think are in this area? Thousands. Hell, tens of thousands. That could take a long time, John."

"Oh... I don't think so." John answered wryly. "I've just uncovered some information that may narrow down the number considerably."

"Care to let me in on this information?"

"Not yet Frank. You just go ahead with whatever you're working on. Let's just say that if I'm right, we'd better have this nailed down good and solid, all of our 'i's' dotted and all of our 't's' crossed." I don't want to say anything else yet, Frank, because if I'm wrong, or if I can't get something definitive, you won't want to be anywhere around me or your career will be finished. But you can help by keeping a lid on this info for as long as possible. Was there anything else of significance on the Coroner's report?"

"I haven't read the report yet, just what they told me over the phone. There was one other thing that he mentioned. They found a twig with a dried up leaf on it. They have identified it as being from a Purple Plum tree. I don't know how much use it will be. Again, though not all that common, I'm sure there are a lot of Purple Plum trees around and we don't know how much transporting was done with her before they finally dumped her in the field."

"Yeah, and again, I have some ideas on that," he said, thinking of David Walton's home. "They can get DNA off vegetation, so this may be more significant than it would appear. By the way, did you talk to that girl at the police computer department, Sara, I think her name was?"

"Oh yeah! Christ John, with the news on Sally Walton and all, I almost forgot to tell you. I was just leaving there when I got the call from the Coroner's office."

"And?" John prodded.

"Well, she seemed pretty straight up, so I took a chance and leveled with her, to a point. I told her that I suspected that someone in her department had been tampering with records, didn't say why or what records. At first she was all defensive and I thought maybe I shouldn't have been so straightforward. But then she calmed down and said that one of her people, Dwight Chase, had been acting a bit different lately. He...”

“Nick said that he’s the guy who replaced the one who was working for Ramsey.” John interrupted.

“He is. According to Sara, when he first came to work with them, he was abnormally quiet and stuck pretty much to himself. She didn’t have much of an opinion on him one way or the other. She describes him as a middle of the road IT guy at best. He’s not married and didn’t seem to have much of a social life other than work, goes home, watches TV, goes to work and does it all over again, everyday. He’s been pretty consistent until recently. Now, she says, he’s talking, inviting coworkers out for drinks, and is generally being an extrovert to the point of being obnoxious.”

“Sounds like something has definitely changed in his life,” said John. “Does she have any reason to suspect him other than that?”

“No, which is why she never even thought of him when I first asked. He’s been acting weird, but she didn’t think of him as a criminal or someone who might tamper with records.”

“Did you say anything about conspiracies or the like?”

“No, like I said, just that we think someone may have tampered with some records. I didn’t say which records or anything about Nick, but she’s a bright girl and if she didn’t figure it out at the time, I’m sure she soon will. I ended it by asking her to keep this to herself and keep her eyes open. She’s going to put a trace on his terminal. Normally, that may be risky with someone in Chase’s position but she feels that he's pretty clueless."

"Let's hope he stays that way," said John, falling back into a monotone voice that was similar to the one he used when he first answered the phone.

Frank caught the tone and quickly reviewed his entire conversation with John. He'd been a cop a long time and though it had taken him a while to catch it, something was wrong and alarm bells began to go off. There was something oddly familiar about John's tone of voice and for some reason, it was very unsettling to Frank. An odd sense of de'ja vu was settling in. Something was up with this man he was talking to.

"Hey, John, you alright?"

"I'm fine Frank," he answered flatly.

He didn't know John well, but he knew people and something wasn't right in Muddsville. He persisted. "Look, I may have just met you, but you're not acting at all like the person I talked to at your house. Now look, we have the same goals here and I've put my trust in you. You're not telling me something, something big, and I don't like it. I should be concentrating on the bad guys, but you acting like this is going to make me constantly wonder what's up with you. So I'm going to ask you one more time, *partner*, what's up?"

John didn't reply right away. Instead, he collected his thoughts as he tried to decide how much to tell Frank. If he told him everything, he'd probably commit John to a looney bin. If he told him what he had just done to Ramsey, he'd leave Frank open to all sorts of legal action.

Frank, on the other hand, knew that many times, the best

way to get someone to answer a question was to ask it and just wait, with no further comment. The other person begins to get uncomfortable with the sustained silence and feels the need to say *something*. So as John sorted things out in his head, Frank patiently waited.

As Frank also suspected, John was well aware of the technique and the silence didn't bother him at all. In fact, he was grateful for the time it gave him to collect his thoughts before answering. He decided that Frank was too sharp a guy to fall for anything too far from the truth. Besides, he was liking and respecting Frank more and more.

"Let's just say for now that this has dredged up some unpleasant memories, Frank. It's also caused some issues to come up that are forcing me to confront some demons. Don't worry, they are my issues and they won't affect you or the outcome of this investigation, at least not negatively."

Frank listened quietly, trying to put his finger on what it was about John's tone that was so disturbing. Suddenly, it dawned on him why this worried him so. Now it was John's turn to wait in silence. Frank Carlotta, in another life, or so it sometimes seemed, had been in the military. He excelled and had eagerly applied for Special Forces training, where, ultimately, he had become a sniper. He'd seen action on many fronts and had seen men react to combat. Now he knew what it was about the tone in John's voice that had seemed so familiar. He'd heard it before, and it wasn't good.

Frank wasn't exactly sure what had happened in that cabin last spring. Oh, he knew what the police reports said. He also knew that in every incident, there was so much more that went on that would never be placed in a report of any kind, at least outside a therapy room. He knew that John had killed before. He also knew from his research into John, that it had never really affected him. Something else had happened last spring that went beyond the taking of lives and Frank suspected, even went beyond his being grievously wounded.

He really needed to talk to John, to try to get him to open up and discuss it with him. But that would take time. Weeks, months, perhaps years. It was time that he knew they didn't have right now. Frank also knew that John was probably a walking, talking, land mine and he pitied any soul who had the misfortune of triggering him. Was John a danger to himself and others? That was Frank's quandary. In the end, he decided, no, he hoped, that the only people who were likely to be in danger were the bad guys. Not an entirely bad thing, unless of course you were one of the bad guys.

"Alright John, I'll go with that for now. I think I know where you're coming from, but we can talk about that later over a beer or two, or three. If you ever decide you need to talk, I'm here. Right now, we have to put all our efforts into this investigation. Go ahead and fight your demons, but don't let it get in the way of our job. Now, moving on, what are you going to do next?"

John was relieved at Frank's response and his opinion of him moved up another couple of notches. The sound in Frank's voice told John he really *did* understand and some-how, that made things just a little bit better. He cleared his throat and answered, "For starters, I'm going to check out one of the leads I just got. I'll let you know as soon as I get something concrete. You?"

"I'm going back to the office to try and dig up some financials on Dwight Chase. If Sara's opinion of him is correct, he's probably not bright enough to hide any payoff money very effectively."

"Let's hope not," John replied. "It sounds like we may be able to put the squeeze on him and find out who his handler is at least, but before you get started, call Sue. I asked her to look at the financial status of everyone in that computer department."

"Good, I'll do that."

"Oh and one more thing, Frank." John then filled him in on the City Council.

"What a can of fucking worms. The more I learn about this case, the more I wish I was sitting on a beach somewhere drinking a few cold ones and staring at the babes."

"Tell me about it. We also might know the name of another player here. Luke Bonnais. He was in for armed robbery and got paroled the same time as Jenkins. Walton was his parole officer, too."

Frank sighed and shook his head. "Do you have any *good* news to give me? Don't answer that. I'm at the office now. Keep me in your loop, will you? Later. Bye."

John returned the salutation and terminated the connection. He backed his vehicle out of the parking space and drove out of the garage.

❖ ❖ ❖

Sara Rose sat at her computer terminal, fingers flying across the keyboard in a manner that's possible only to those who have spent countless hours performing the activity. Her mind was racing just as fast. She loved computers and the rapid "rat-a-tat-tat" sound of the keys being depressed and released helped her think and was as comforting to her as any sound she knew of.

Sara Rose was both angry and embarrassed. She was very proud of the fact that she was in charge of the police department's computers. She'd reached a station in life that she had never envisioned that she could reach.

She'd been a reclusive, mousey little girl all through high school and college. She'd never related well with others, probably due to the suffocating and abusive family life that she'd endured growing up. Her father was sober only when he was working at the local hardware store, a job that he'd had since high school and a job that he hated. But he was too lazy and too unmotivated to seek employment else-where. He didn't really love Sara's mother, but she had been a nice regular squeeze for him and at the time they'd married, that had been enough.

Sara's arrival had been an unwanted surprise and in his mind, had made a horrendous life even more unbearable. So he took it out on Sara and his mother on a regular basis. He didn't hit too often, it was mostly yelling and emotional abuse. At least that's the reason Sara gave to herself as to why her mother had not left him. It was the only way she could forgive her mother for allowing it to go on, to this day actually.

An understanding aunt and uncle had given Sara a computer on her tenth birthday. Her uncle, her father's brother, owned his own company and had a very comfortable income, a fact that only served to irritate her father even more. He went totally ballistic about the computer for reasons that only he knew. She would have lost it the first day, if her uncle hadn't intervened. He had taken her father out to the garage. She could hear angry, muffled voices, but she couldn't make out what was being said. She sat in her room and calmly awaited the decision. All she knew was that when they returned, there was no more talk of taking the computer away.

She couldn't have received a better gift and she spent most of her waking hours, when she wasn't at school, shut up in her room, clattering away at her keyboard. Though the excessive time on the computer bothered her mother, her father was fine with it. Out of sight, out of mind and her mother didn't have the courage to argue with him about it. She was a very bright girl and her abilities soon grew quickly.

As the years passed, the phone in their house began to ring at all hours of the day and night as people called to ask Sara to fix their computer or network. The constantly ringing phone should have brought about a rapid retribution from her father. Strangely, it didn't. She could only guess that her uncle was somehow responsible for this phenomenon.

She had never imagined that she would ever go to college. They couldn't afford it. But one day, in her Junior year, her mother approached her and told her to start researching universities. She knew they didn't have the money, so she asked her mother where the money was coming from.

"Don't look a gift horse in the mouth," her mother had replied sternly. She knew her mother well enough to know that it would be fruitless to pursue it further. To this day, she didn't know where the money had come from. She strongly suspected that it was her aunt and uncle, but they had never given any hint as to their involvement.

When she had graduated from college, she had obtained a job as a programmer at a small company. She'd lost it when the company went under after the dot com bubble burst. Then she'd gotten the job at the police department. As she had done all her life, she stayed pretty much to herself and just did her job. She had no grand aspirations. She was just happy and content to be working at her beloved computers. And it was noticed.

The day came when it was announced that the head of the department was retiring. She was absolutely shocked, stunned, when she was called in and told that they wanted her to take over the entire computer department. She wasn't exactly elated at the proposition for she knew that it would mean interacting with people, something she had never been good at. In the end, she accepted the position and found that it fit her like an expensive glove. She grew into the job in every aspect and the decision makers who had appointed her were constantly patting themselves on the back for their wise choice.

They weren't so happy when it came to light that they'd been infiltrated by the Coeptus Guild. But her exemplary work had caused them to overlook the fact that the traitor had been one of *her* employees.

Now, it appeared, that Dwight Chase was threatening her beloved department once again. What bothered her even more, was the fact that she'd related to Dwight. His introverted nature was so like her old one that she found herself cutting him slack when she normally wouldn't have. She looked at him as a kindred spirit. She wondered if that was why she didn't question his sudden change in behavior.

Regardless, she was offended on many different levels at the prospect of another traitor in her group and she was determined to find out what the hell was going on and who, if it wasn't Dwight, was responsible. The Detective hadn't mentioned what records had been tampered with, but as Frank had guessed she would, she realized it must have something to do with Chief Giovianni's problems. Why else would a detective from another agency be involved with this?

Back when the first traitor had been discovered, she'd put *spyware* programs on all of the terminals in the entire department, except the Chief's of course. "Spyware" programs secretly recorded every keystroke, every website visited, every instant message chat, every download. Virtually nothing went on at that terminal that wasn't dutifully noted in a secret file that only she had access to. She told no one of what she had done. At first, she spent considerable time reviewing the data. However, as the months went by with nothing of

interest being documented, she began to relax, and when
Frank had sat down with her to tell her his suspicions, she'd
all but forgotten the program.

She remembered now and she was furiously accessing the
data files created by the program and began to search for
sign of accessing the phone records. She had pulled up the
records of the phone calls in question, so she knew what
time scenario she would be looking at. She had also
downloaded a copy of the nightly backup that had been
made two months prior to the suspected phone calls.

She pulled up the phone log from that backup and immediately found that the phone calls in question were not present. So now she knew beyond a doubt that the records had
been doctored.

She turned her efforts to spyware logs from Dwight's terminal. Nothing. This surprised her a little but she went on to
the next person in her department.

Direct access to the phone records were protected from
any terminal outside the computer department. A *firewall*, an
electronic barrier, helped prevent tampering by anyone other
than a determined and skilled hacker and it would take time.
Though that scenario was definitely possible, why would
one go to all that trouble if they had someone on the inside?
Given a review of Dwight's behavior in retrospect, it certainly seemed likely that it was an inside job.

As she was reviewing the spyware data for the next computer department employee on her list, she found what she
was looking for. That person sat next to Dwight. The
changes had been made two days ago, shortly after one

o'clock in the morning. That was an hour after the last shift of the day ended. She thought back to that day. The IT guy working the second shift had suddenly taken ill. He had come into work feeling fine but had been violently sick shortly after eating a snack. Dwight had been working late and had offered to take over for him.

She quickly looked up Dwight's time card data and confirmed that he hadn't signed out until almost two o'clock. *Two hours* after the last shift was over. She sat back and stared at the screen. *Idiot!* Obviously he'd been clever enough to find out the password for the person sitting next to him. Then he'd had the where with all to most likely slip something into the snack to make the man sick.

But Jesus! Have a little foresight. If he'd thought about it for half a second, he'd realize that the first thing that would be done if the records were ever challenged, would be to check the backup, as she had just done. His pathetic ruse of using his coworker's terminal was just that.

She had to get this information to Detective Carlotta. She picked up the phone and called the number listed on his business card. He answered on the second ring.

"Sergeant Carlotta? This is Sara Rose. I talked to you this morning."

"Yes Sara. What's up?"

"Well, I… after you left I looked over some records. I think I found…"

Frank bolted upright in his chair and cut her off. "Wait! Don't discuss it over the phone."

"Oh!" Sara stammered, a bit unsure of herself now. "You

don't think…"

"Look," Frank cut her off again. He didn't know if the phones were tapped or not, but the Coeptus Guild was not known for leaving any bases uncovered so he didn't want to take the chance. Poor Sara Rose had no idea who she was dealing with. "How soon can you meet me at that bar down the street from your office?"

Sara's anger and indignation at having been duped once again rapidly dissipated like fog in the hot sun. It was replaced by a growing alarm at Frank's reaction to her call. "I can be there in five minutes," she replied with a squeak. The fear in her, coupled with Frank's loud, male voice, was too reminiscent of her childhood and she was reverting back to another time, another place, another person.

"Well I can't be there for about twenty minutes," Frank said. "Let's be on the safe side and say half an hour. In the meantime, don't talk to anyone about this. Understand?"

"Yes," She answered shakily. She hung up the phone. Part of her wished that she had never looked into the records. That was the old Sara speaking. For strength, she thought of her father. Then the new Sara took over. Bastard! She swore that she would never be intimidated by anyone ever again. That included Dwight Chase and that included whoever instructed him to do their bidding. She stood up and began to gather her things.

At that moment, Dwight Chase was busy scrambling for

his cell phone. Sara Rose had been a little off on her assessment of Dwight. Conversely, Frank Carlotta had also been very right on Coeptus Guild's thoroughness. They had shown Dwight how to tap the phones at Sara's desk and a few other key phones. They didn't dare tap too many and even those taps had only recently been installed. They feared, correctly, that someone routinely *swept* the lines for taps. It was a risky business to do it even for a short time. But at this critical stage, they reasoned that it was an acceptable risk. That risk had now paid off handsomely.

It had been Dwight's idea to route the taps to his terminal, hidden in an invisible, protected file. Coeptus Guild didn't like it. The transmitters were set up on a "burst" transmission basis. At timed intervals, the gathered phone calls would be compressed into tiny data packets and sent in a one or two second "micro burst" to a receiver. But Dwight had convinced them that it might be valuable to have access to real time data as well. He further convinced them that he could do it undetected. Even the vaunted Sara Rose had missed it with her spyware program, not that Dwight was even aware of the program's existence. He had seen the county cop talking to her earlier. So he had decided to hook his earphones up to his computer and listen directly to her line as he worked. Dwight liked to listen to music on his computer so the fact that he sat with his ear phones on would not draw any undue suspicions.

His heart a skipped a beat, no two, maybe more beats when he heard Sara place the call to the cop. She knew! How? He had to let them know and he had to get out of here. He stood up so fast that his chair shot backwards on its wheels. The owner of the terminal next to him looked up in astonishment. "What the..."

Dwight looked at him, his mind racing. It had been that man's terminal that he had used. That was the man he had poisoned to make him sick. "I just remembered I was supposed to call my girlfriend this morning. She's gonna be pissed. I'm going to call her outside." He used all of his self control to look down at the man and grin sheepishly. "I don't want anyone to hear me grovel."

The man smiled. "I understand. Good luck." He shook his head as Dwight hurried away. *'Didn't even know he had a girlfriend,'* the man thought.

Before leaving, Dwight quickly bent down and started a program that would reformat his hard drive in such a manner as to make it difficult, if not impossible, to retrieve any information from it. Then, he used up the last of his emotional reserves to keep himself from running out of the building. The elevator ride up to the first floor seemed excruciatingly slow. It finally arrived and he had all he could do to keep from grabbing the door and forcing it to open faster. His reserves began to fade away to nothing as he power walked past the guard at the front desk. He had to let them know about the meeting. They had to help him get away before they came for him. He retrieved his cell phone and began to dial the number they had insisted he memorize, as he was walking out the door.

CHAPTER
10

Luke Bonnais, the recently released and presently missing parolee of the State Prison, just happened to be sitting at a fast food restaurant a few blocks from the police department when his cell phone rang. He answered it and groaned inwardly when he realized who it was. If ever the term 'snot nosed kid' could be used to describe someone, it was the caller on the other end of the line. If ever there were two polar opposites, it was Luke Bonnais and Dwight Chase.

The kid obviously had his panties in a bunch about something, though at this point Luke was at a complete loss as to what it was. The bastard was literally blubbering on in a screeching, adolescent voice that was extremely difficult to understand and extremely irritating. To Luke, it was like hearing the proverbial squeal of chalk on a blackboard and it made him cringe. God what he'd like to do to this kid. Though he usually tried to hide his abhorrence of the little fuck, this time he couldn't help it.

"Hey fuck face!" he yelled. "Slow down and try it again. I couldn't unnerstan a fuckin' word ya said." Several customers in the restaurant turned in his direction with disapproving looks. He stood up and glared at an obese man sitting close to him. The man's wife and several kids sat around him. All were looking at him with open mouths. To Luke, it looked like a nest of baby birds, open mouthed as they anxiously waited for their next meal. It only served to piss him off further. Back in the day, he would have been more than happy to walk up and punch the fucker right in the mouth, strictly as a lesson to the children of course, as to the inappropriateness of staring.

But things were different now. He needed to be low key and not attract attention. Still, he couldn't help himself as he yelled at the obese man, "What the fuck are you lookin' at, mother fucker? Don't think the little shits haven't heard that *fuckin'* word before? Fuck you, asshole." With that, he strode out of the restaurant before his temper got the best of him.

He walked to his car, which was parked about a block away as a precaution in case things got dicey. One never knew when an uninvited guest or guests might necessitate a quick departure, and having one's car parked in the parking lot right outside the door meant that leaving in it gave his pursuers the identity of his main means of escape, not a wise idea.

The whole time the discourse in the restaurant was taking place, Dwight was continuing his drivel. Slower this time, Luke realized, but his attention had been on the fat fuck, not on Dwight Chase, who didn't seem to have heard Luke's little diatribe.

"Stop!" Luke yelled. "Just stop right fuckin' now!" Serene silence greeted him over the phone. '*Now I gotta ask him a question and start him up again*,' was all he could think about. Oh well. It was what he was getting paid for. "Calm down and start again, and if you start talkin' like a runaway freight train and squealin' again, I'm gonna find ya and give ya somethin' to squeal about. Unnerstand?"

"Ye... Ye... Yes," Dwight stammered. He waited a moment then began. "It's Rose. She figured out that I fixed the records and she called the cops because they were in her office earlier today, and I just knew something wasn't right so I started listening to her phone and I heard her tell the cop, only he said to..."

"Dwight!" he shouted in exasperation as he cut the snot nosed kid off yet again. "What did I say? Slow it down! What fuckin' cop and exactly what da fuck did she say?" He was becoming a little alarmed now. Not scared, because Luke had been in some pretty hairy situations and this was nowhere near hairy. Low pucker factor as they say. Very low. But it did sound like some action was imminent and that was fine with him. He'd been looking forward to some fun.

"I don't know his name." Dwight continued in the most normal tone he'd used so far. "But I know a cop when I see one. I don't think he was from our department. Wait! Wait! ... She called him..., 'Carlotta.' Yeah, that was it, Sergeant Carlotta."

Luke knew the name. His employers had briefed him on all the players they thought he should know about. He was the one handling the dead broad and poor Wallis. Luke didn't care about many people, but Wallis was a good guy. But he'd fucked up. Blabbed to the wrong person and then tried to get himself a deal. What was it they said? '*Se la guerre.*' So goes the war. Both he and the cop were dead now. He turned his attention back to the snot nose kid, who had started talking again.

"Anyway, she called him and started to tell him what she had found. He cut her off and told her to meet him at the bar down the street in half an hour."

He was familiar with the place. "When was that?" Luke asked.

"About five minutes ago. Obviously I didn't waste any time getting out of there and calling you." Then, with a note of smugness, "I also started a program that would destroy any evidence that was on my computer."

'*At least he'd been clear thinking enough to cover his own fuckin' ass,*' Luke thought. But that didn't help his employers much. The mere fact that it had been discovered that the phone records were fake, would be enough to put a definite crimp in their little plan. It didn't sound like she had told the cop much of anything, so maybe if he could get rid of her, the plan might be back on track again.

"Hey kid, do you think she told anybody else?"

"I really doubt it."

"How hard would it be for someone else to figure it out if she wasn't around?"

"Well, it might take some time, but now that the cop knows, he'd be sure to have someone else look into it. Sara is pretty sharp and she knows the system inside and out. If she wasn't around, it would take time to get things sorted out, but they would do it eventually." Dwight was beginning to get the idea where this was going and though it frightened him, it also excited him.

For his part, Luke's brain was working one-hundred and ten percent. He wasn't an educated man, but that didn't mean he wasn't bright. He was and he'd been trying to get himself out of tight situations his whole life. He was very good at it. Which, though he didn't know it, had been a trait recognized by his employers. Which was why they had arranged to have him paroled. A plan crystalized in his brain.

"Okay kid. How'd you like for this to all go away? You can go back to work as though nuttin' happened and nobody would know nuttin'."

"How could you do that?" Dwight asked quietly.

"Here's where da rubber meets da road kid. If you want your fuckin' life back enough, you're gonna have ta help me here. You're gonna have ta step up to da plate here."

"What do I have to do?" He had a feeling he knew and he was more than a little queasy about it.

"Time's short kid. To make this go away, we have ta get rid of boda dems. I would do it myself, but I don't have da time. So here's what I want ya ta do. I want ya to get in yer car and meet me at the drug store over on Harrison. I'm gonna give ya a gun. Then I want ya ta wait for da broad at da bar. Use da gun and force her to let ya in her car. If der's a problem, just shoot her and make sure she's dead. But only if ders a problem cause I really don't wanna have a shootin' in public. I would like ta just make her disappear for awhile.

Once ya got her, call me an I'll tell ya where ta meet me. Can ya do this, kid? Can ya step up to da plate to keep what's rightfully yers?"

Dwight thought about it. He liked his job at the police department. He liked his extra income from his new employers even better. He liked the "*perks*" even better than that. On several occasions, *very* hot women had suddenly shown up on his doorstep and had spent the night, catering to his every desire. He knew that he could never get such women on his own. Yes! He could do this.

"I'll do it. I'll do whatever it takes. You can count on me Sam. What are you going to do with the cop?"

Luke snickered. The dumb kid probably thought that was his real name. "I tink da cop is gonna have a little hit and run accident. Poor guy. But we don't have time for jawin'. Get over here, NOW." With that he broke the connection and immediately dialed another number. It was answered almost immediately.

"Yes sir, Dis is Luke and we gotta sitiation here."

John was slowly driving through a residential neighborhood, attempting to find David Walton's address. Ramsey had given up Walton's name as being the one primarily responsible for getting the cons out of prison. It was another hunch confirmed. He had called the prison and was told that Walton wasn't going to be in today. As he got closer to the house, he braced himself for the meeting. He had to remain calm and avoid a repeat of the bathroom incident. Walton was the son of a judge and a government employee. Roughing him up could have some… unpleasant repercussions. What bothered John, was the fact that though he now had two confirmed Coeptus Guild members, he had really nothing concrete on who ordered Nick to be set up or who killed Sally Walton. Though Ramsey spilled forth all he knew, it really wasn't much.

As with all covert groups, information was tightly controlled and compartmentalized on a need to know basis. Each person was given just enough information to complete the task at hand. Most were aware of their group's general goals, ideals and direction, but nothing specific. Ramsey had coughed up other names as well, some of whom John recognized. Billyray Jenkins, Wallis Jester, and Luke Bonnais were all ex-cons that Sue had uncovered. Ramsey was their handler. He gave them their assignments and they reported to him.

Jester was already out of the picture, he was the dead guy in the woods. Ramsey said he didn't know anything about that situation other than he had heard that Jester had been talking to a cop and had to be taken care of. That was a surprise to Ramsey, who never would have thought Jester capable of such a thing, unless of course he'd been compromised already. Jester often spoke of the fact that prison didn't fit in with his plans and he would *never* go back there again. They all assumed at the time that meant he would *die* first.

Ramsey also admitted that the phone records had been altered to set Nick up. Bonnais was responsible for obtaining a replacement for the traitorous computer geek that had been working for Chief Ramsey. Bill Ramsey didn't know who Bonnais had gotten as a replacement, just that he had one. He'd ordered Bonnais to have the records altered a couple of days ago. *He'd* gotten those orders from Walton. He didn't know anything about how the bullet from Nick's gun had gotten in the field where Sally Walton had been discovered.

John asked him where the cons were. He told him that Bonnais was somewhere in the city. All Ramsey had was a cell phone number. Jenkins was on some sort of special assignment and that's all he knew about that. Walton had told him to have Jenkins call him directly and Ramsey was to have no more contact with him until further notice. That was fine with Ramsey. Jenkins scared the living shit out of him.

All in all, a lot of information, but not a lot of *useful* information. It was like a homeowner getting the plans for all of the plumbing, electric, and other inner workings for a house. Interesting maybe, but really of little use to the average person who just wants to live *there*.

He found the address and parked on the driveway. He sat a moment and composed himself. Regardless of what else he was, Walton was the son of a Judge. Man handling him would be different than the son of a known bad guy, attorney or not. John wasn't sure what he hoped to gain by meeting with David Walton, other than the fact that he was next on the food chain and maybe something would slip out. He also wanted to see if there were any Purple Plum trees on the property. He still wondered if David hadn't killed Sally in some sort of a lover's quarrel and there was still the matter of Tabitha Walton, David's wife. Did *she* knock off Sally in a jealous rage?

It was easy, in these cases, to think everything was a conspiracy. Did a reputed mobster wind up dead on the kitchen floor because he was a mobster? Or because he was a cheating husband who got caught by an enraged wife? A close call that showed that not everything may be as it first appeared. Was Sally just another victim of nothing more than jealousy, who happened to be in the middle of happenings of which she knew nothing about? Another twisted piece?

After collecting himself, John stepped from his SUV and surveyed the house as he walked up the stone path leading to the front door. He was surprised at the "*common*" appearance of the home. It was a small, two story tudor, its white stucco even peeling in spots. A two car garage was detached and sat at the back of the property. An older Saturn sedan sat near it. The lawn was well cared for and a well tended garden made the home seem inviting, normal. '*Not the home of a Coeptus Guild member,*' John thought. He quickly reviewed William Ramsey's comments in his mind. Ramsey had said several times that Walton was his handler and John, at the time, had believed that he was telling the truth. The house didn't fit in, but John also knew that criminals could be very discreet in their handling of money so as to *not* attract any attention.

He looked for the presence of Purple Plum trees. He wasn't sure what they looked like, but he assumed that something about them would be purple, the fruit, the bark, hell the leaves for that matter, something. He didn't see any that fit that description, but they could be in the back yard, which would make more sense actually. Wouldn't do to hide a body where the neighbors could see the actual hiding process.

He had that thought in mind as he pushed the door bell. He heard a faint West Minister chime go off somewhere in the interior of the house. The door suddenly opened a moment later and revealed the smiling face of Tabitha Walton, David's wife.

"Hello sir, and who might you be?" she asked gaily, with a light but discernible Irish accent. She stood a little over five feet tall and was more than a few pounds overweight. Her red hair was very light in color, almost blonde, and it accented the innumerable freckles that covered every bit of skin. Simply stated, she was, in John's eyes, beautiful, but with a beauty that seemed to radiate from within her.

The total effect made John want to burst out laughing and he instantly wanted to like this woman. He quickly reminded himself that she could be a killer.

"Hi! My name is John. Is Dave here?" he asked.

"No," she replied. "He's over at his Dad's. Are you a friend of his? I don't remember ever seeing you before."

John's mind was racing. He didn't want to reveal exactly who he was, but here was a perfect opportunity to get a feel for Tabitha's involvement in all of this. "No I'm not a friend. I just wanted to talk to him about Sally Walton." He kept his tone and his demeanor light as he carefully studied her for a reaction. If she was involved, even his casual tone would be threatening to her.

He noticed that the smile faded only a little. He watched her eyes. He was a firm believer in eyes, as they were rarely able to tell the same lies as the mouth. The only thing John saw in her eyes was a questioning, slightly confused look.

"Are you with the police or something?"

"Oh no," he replied with a laugh. He wanted to put her at ease and experience had taught him that more often than not, a laugh usually lightened the mood and made things seem not quite so bad. "I'm just looking into her background for my client." He was skirting the truth here, but at this point he didn't want to reveal exactly who he was. John wanted to come close enough to judge her reaction, but not alarm her to the point that she got right on the phone with her husband.

"So you're a private detective or something? Wow! That's cool! I never met a private detective before. Is it exciting?" she asked lightly as she stepped outside with him.

John could see no trace of guilt or alarm in her. Not only that, but most guilty people tried to keep some sort of barrier, mental, as well as physical, between them and anyone they perceived was threatening to them. Stepping outside of the security of their own home, was not in keeping with the actions of a guilty person. If she was involved with Sally's death, she was one mighty cool cucumber.

He laughed again as he responded to her question. "No, usually it's very boring, just interviewing people about things they almost always know nothing about."

"Well, I don't know what he can tell you about Sally's death. She just disappeared one day. Poof! Gone! He was just as much at a loss as to where she went as anyone else. When she turned up dead, he was pretty upset."

For the first time, John saw a change in her eyes, in her body language. Among other things, she looked confused, as though she wasn't sure what to say next. Her eyes strayed to some far off point. "To tell you the truth," she went on, "I... I think he took more than a passing interest in her." She looked at him again. "I don't wish ill of the dead and I certainly didn't wish any harm to her when she was alive, but I have to tell you, I was more than a little relieved when she was gone."

"I see," John said simply. She was on a roll and he didn't want to divert her. He was a little surprised at her forthrightness. After all, she really didn't know who she was spilling her guts to. Probably a result of pent up emotions. Still, this willingness to part with information was not the sign of a guilty person and he was becoming more and more convinced that she had nothing to do with this.

As if picking up on his feelings of surprise, "I don't know why I'm telling you all this." She laughed nervously. "My Lord, I only just met you. You could be a mafia hit man for all I know." She leaned against the house as though she suddenly needed support to stand up. She looked at that far off point again and said, "Her discovery the other day brought back all the things I felt at the time. I thought I was going to lose my husband." She laughed nervously again. "You are just the unfortunate soul that brought all those feeling bubbling up like a shaken bottle of champagne."

"That's alright." He said and decided not to pursue anything else with her for the time being. It was time to go find her husband. He would prefer not to talk to him at the Judge's house. Maybe he could head on over there and sit on the house until David left. He smiled at Tabitha and in his most charming voice, said, "I seem to have that affect on women."

She laughed and her eyes became lighter again. "I'll bet you do."

All John could think of was that it was going to be a shame when she found out that David Walton's cheating on her was the least of his transgressions.

Sara Rose left the Police Department building and began walking in the direction of the bar where she was to meet Sergeant Carlotta. She was deep in thought as to how she was going to present her findings. She was going to drive, but decided that she could think better if she walked, and after all, it was only four blocks. Her head was down, looking at the sidewalk and moving at a moderate rate, deep in thought. She was in her own little world, completely oblivious to happenings around her.

Luke Bonnais was sitting in his blue Ford Explorer SUV,

parked on the street about a block away from the bar where Sara was to meet Frank. He knew what Frank Carlotta looked like and he even knew the license plate number of Frank's unmarked squad car. He smiled as he thought about it. The people he worked for sure had their shit together. Most times, if he needed something, all he had to do was ask. They were a secretive bunch though, which in the criminal world was a good thing. One of their hard and fast rules was that when they met another "associate," they were not to discuss anything about their work except what was needed to complete the job at hand. With most of the ex-cons and hardcore criminals, that wasn't a problem. Luke had remembered a time when he met an unusually chatty member of their team. That member didn't last too long. Poof! He was simply gone one day. Luke had briefly considered asking around to see if anyone knew what happened to him. Only briefly though. He figured that asking about it would be a sure fire way to suddenly go "poof" himself.

He didn't really know who his employers were. Hell, the only name of consequence that he knew of was the name of his handler and he was sure that the name he called his handler wasn't the man's real name. Oh, he knew of Billyray and poor Wallis Jester and a few other peons like himself, but that was basically the extent of it.

He wasn't complaining. It was the best job he ever had. His employer really knew how to take care of an employee. He looked around the inside of his Explorer. It was a nice vehicle and he really liked it. It was a shame that after he did this job he would never see it again.

His eyes returned to the building in front of him just in time to see Frank Carlotta's squad car parking on the street in front of the bar. He glanced at the light, it had just turned green for Luke. He hadn't liked this position because of the light. But the bar was located on a corner and he needed a position from which he could observe all possible parking places for the bar, including the entrance to the parking lot. He'd seen Dwight pull into the lot a few minutes before. He couldn't see where he had parked or what he was doing, but he prayed the kid would hold it together long enough to snatch the broad.

Right now though, he put his truck in gear and began accelerating, rapidly. He figured he could get up to maybe sixty or seventy miles an hour by the time he reached Carlotta, who was parked just on the other side of the intersection. The cop had closed his door and was walking alongside the car. He was completely unaware of what was about to happen. '*Perfect*,' Luke thought. '*I'll be able to squish him between my car and his, like a fuckin' bug.*' They'd have to scrape what was left of Carlotta off the side of his squad. He smiled at the thought as he concentrated on positioning his truck for the perfect strike. "He'll never know what hit him." Luke muttered to himself.

Harold Newbaucher was a fifty year old trucker who looked more like seventy and acted more like fifteen. His appearance was due to his full adherence to the adage that one should go to the grave driving full bore, totally used up and screaming, "Damn that was one hell of a ride." He used to drive big rigs cross country and at one time had made a fine living. But his heavy drinking had caused him to lose that job and a string of others. His immature and cavalier attitude toward his profession and life in general, had caused one employer after another to get rid of him, usually on poor terms at best. Now, he was consigned to driving trailers full of gravel from one lousy job site to another, a fact that had made him, along with his numerous other bad traits, sarcastic and cynical as hell. Harold did not have many, if any, friends.

He was currently driving an old Kenworth with yet another trailer load of gravel. He'd been fighting with his ex-wife for a week. She wanted *more* money for that twit daughter of hers. Of course, she claimed the child was his and therefore he was responsible for child support. He'd been denying that the child was his for twelve years now, but refused to take a DNA test to prove it. His attorney had told him that he would have to take the test or pay. "Don't trust them fuckin' things and she'd have it faked anyhow," was all he would say to his attorney's fruitless pleas.

He'd used this latest blow out as an excuse for him to stop for a quick beer, or two, not his first for the day and now he had to fly to make up time. He should have delivered this load ten minutes ago and he was still five minutes away. Even though he was in town, he pressed down further on the accelerator. The big truck picked up speed and was now careening through the city streets at almost fifty miles an hour, a totally reckless speed given the amount of time it would take to stop or even slow the massive amount of weight. And that didn't take in to account the slowed reaction time of the alcohol impaired driver.

Harold was approaching one of his favorite bars. It was just down from the police station and at night, was usually full of cops. It made him nervous to be around so many cops, but it was a good place to go during the day. It was quiet and had a huge HDTV that was great for watching a ball game while downing a few. He looked over at the parking lot and found that there were only a couple of cars in it. Harold decided that after he dropped this load, he'd stop in for a couple more quick ones that nobody knew about.

He looked back at the rapidly approaching intersection. He noticed two things in quick secession. The first was that the light had turned red and to his horror, he realized that there was no way on God's little green earth that he could even begin to stop in time.

The second thing he noticed was a blue Ford Explorer screaming through the intersection. For a brief heartbeat, Harold thought that the Explorer was moving so fast, that it might squeak through before him. He slammed on his brakes in a futile attempt to at least slow down. But the old truck's brakes didn't come on evenly and all he succeeded in doing was to throw the Kenworth and the trailer totally out of control, skewing to one side. The face of the semi was now tracking the side of the Explorer like a heat seeking missile as it went through the intersection. In the next heartbeat, Harold Newbaucher made a couple of other horrific realizations. He was going to ram that blue Ford Explorer smack dab in the middle of the driver's door. The second part to that was there was some guy standing on the street near the corner, right where Harold's inebriated brain had calculated, correctly, they would wind up in the next couple of heartbeats.

In a twist of ironic fate, it wasn't Frank Carlotta who never knew what him that day. It was Luke Bonnais.

Dwight Chase had pulled into the bar parking lot and sat, nervously waiting for Sara's car to arrive. He steeled himself as he waited, going over and over various scenarios as to how this might go down. What if she screams? What if she just floors it and gets the hell out of Dodge? What if she fights him? Though he wasn't a great programmer, he'd been one long enough to know that all programs have flaws that *will* be found by their users. Therefore, a programmer had to have the ability to foresee potential problems and re-write the program to avoid them or at least minimize their effects. That was what he was doing when his day went to hell in a hand basket.

He spotted her about a block away, *walking*. 'Oh shit,' he thought. All of his possible scenarios involved a *car*. The possibility that she would walk to the bar never occurred to him. He gripped the gun in his hand tighter as he fretted about how to handle this. Things began to happen in quick secession.

An earsplitting, deafening explosion, pain, and suddenly the inside of the car was filled with the sharp, overwhelming odor of cordite. The god damn gun had gone off! He'd accidentally squeezed the trigger. He looked down at his feet and saw that his right foot was bleeding and realized shortly thereafter that it hurt like hell.

His eardrums hurt as well, but he realized that there were other loud noises and they were coming from the other side of the bar, near the stop light, which was blocked from his view by the bar itself. He looked over at Sara, who had come to a complete standstill and was staring down the street at a huge plume of dust rising up from the direction of the intersection.

To his credit, Dwight, despite his ringing ears, injured foot and total confusion as to what had just happened, fought down the urge to panic and had the presence of mind to realize that whatever was happening at the intersection, would be a perfect distraction for him to snatch Sara. Sam, aka Luke Bonnais would be proud of him.

He immediately started his car and drove over to the sidewalk where Sara still stood, transfixed by whatever had just happened at the intersection. She didn't see Dwight or his car until he had pulled up alongside her and jumped out. Pain shot from his foot to the top of his head, but he managed not to yell out. He held the gun under his armpit in an attempt to shield it from and casual onlookers. He felt the heat of the barrel from the recent discharge on his underarm.

"Get in the car, Sara," he ordered.

"Wha... What?" She was clearly dazed and confused.

"I said get in the car." She looked at him as though he

were speaking a foreign language. "Now!" he shouted louder than he meant to. He looked quickly around to see if he had attracted any attention. It didn't appear that he had. He stole a look at the intersection and saw what had caused the commotion. A tractor-trailer rig had slammed into at least two cars and all three, at least to some extent, were currently the bar's newest patrons. The trailer had tipped and a huge load of gravel was piled on the street and sidewalk.

He looked back at Sara and realized that she was talking to him, "What are you talking about? I'm not getting into your car."

He showed her the gun, "Yes. Yes you are, and if you don't, I'm going to shoot you right here on the street." He meant it too. He'd come this far and he knew that with his injured foot, he couldn't fight with her or even run after her for that matter. At this point, as far as he was concerned, the easiest thing to do was to simply shoot her if she resisted. He didn't know what he was going to tell Sam, but he figured he'd worry about that later.

Sara saw that he meant it and reluctantly started for the passenger side of the car. She was certain that this was some hysterical, hair brained idea that he'd concocted at the last minute and she was equally sure she could eventually talk him out of it.

"No!" he said loudly. "You drive. I'll sit in the back seat right behind you." As she moved to the driver's door, he opened the back door and hobbled over to back seat. For the first time, she saw that he was injured and his foot was bleeding.

"What happened to you?" she asked.

"Never mind," he answered harshly. "Just get in before I start shooting."

"Where to?" she queried after she seated herself and closed the door.

"Just turn around and head for the interstate."

When they were on their way, Dwight reached into his pocket and retrieved his cell phone. He called Sam's number. After several rings it beeped and asked the caller to leave a message. Luke, known to Dwight as Sam, had told Dwight, in no uncertain terms, never to leave a message. Though he wanted to, he was too frightened of Sam to disobey his standing order. Damn it! Sam had told him to call when he got Sara and he had. So why wasn't he answering?

Dwight was starting to feel a little cocky. Maybe the great *Sam*, had run into problems while he, the humble programmer, had pulled off his end of the deal without a hitch. '*Well*,' he thought as a searing stab of pain emanated from his foot, '*Almost without a hitch.*'

Sara got to the interstate and per Dwight's instructions, headed north out of the city. He didn't know what else to do or where to go. He only knew he wanted to put as much distance between them and the city as he could. A wave of apprehension swept over him. What the hell's going on? He had tried more times than he could count to contact Sam as they were driving. Sam was probably going to be pissed at the amount of calls he made to him but what the hell? He had a serious situation here and his foot was really beginning to drive him insane with pain.

He made another call to Sam and still another. It just rang and rang and rang.

CHAPTER
11

After leaving David Walton's house, John pointed his SUV in the direction of the honorable Judge Walton's domicile. He arrived to find that the home was a three story, brick and stone mansion with a huge, multi-car garage that sat slightly apart from the house itself. The garage was connected to the residence by a twenty foot long portico that was partially enclosed by brick walls that extended approximately ten feet into the air, leaving another two foot clearance between it and the roof. There was a large outbuilding that sat at the rear of the property that John could only assume was a maintenance shed, housing gardening tools, possibly a tractor, and other items associated with the upkeep of such a large estate and the several acres of meticulously maintained land that surrounded it. A small lake with a huge enclosed gazebo was nestled at one of the rear corners of the property. A black, wrought iron fence, eight feet tall and supported by columns of brick and stone that matched the theme from the house and garage, enclosed the entire property.

He was viewing most of these details from his truck,

through binoculars. He had pulled to the side of the road and was currently looking for David Walton's car. Susan had provided him with a complete listing of his vehicles and he couldn't find any of them parked on the circular driveway near the front door. It was possible that whatever car he was driving was parked in the garage, but John didn't think that was likely. So where was David?

He scanned the area again with his binoculars, including the small, gravel road that led to the gazebo and lake. The view of the part of the road near the gazebo was partially obscured by ornamental trees with purple leaves. He lowered the binoculars and began to ponder his next move when suddenly it hit him. He quickly raised the binoculars again in the direction of the gazebo.

The trees at the end of the road did a fairly effective job of hiding a small parking lot near the gazebo. And those trees had *purple* leaves! He lowered his binoculars again and thought about the trees and how they fit into the puzzle. He had expected to find those trees at David's house, not here. They could be just an anomaly as they might not be the same plum trees that Debra Walton had come into contact with. On the other hand, the fact that there were Purple Plum trees on her property could mean that the twig and leaf found on her had nothing to do with her death, which voided the use of the tress as a means to pinpoint where she had been buried.

His thoughts turned to the soil that had originally attracted the coroner's attention. It had been rich in nutrients and fertilizers. He glanced up at the trees again as he thought. That may not be of much help either, as Purple Plum trees were usually used as an ornamental tree, which meant that they were often in gardens, which in turn meant that the use of fertilizers would be prevalent.

There was only one way to find out. He had to get a soil sample. The problem was that though the trees were enticingly close, there was a huge judicial barrier in between. He had no legal right to enter onto the Judge's property and therefore any evidence that he collected would be considered "fruits of the poisonous tree," as it were. In this case, the pun was appropriate. The law stated that if evidence was collected illegally, as with John going onto private land without permission, anything found as a result of that evidence was inadmissible in court.

He pondered his problem while staring out at the Judge's property. Motion caught his eye and he focused in on an elderly man coming out of the maintenance shed with a hoe. John made a quick decision and a moment later was driving his car up the long driveway toward the house.

He stopped near the house and the gardener. The man appeared to be in his early seventies, slightly overweight, but otherwise healthy. He had on a straw hat and bib overalls and was the perfect stereotypical picture of an elderly farmer.

John didn't know if the Judge was home or not, he hoped he wasn't. He got out and looked around with a perplexed look on his face, pretending not to see the man. As expected and hoped for, the gardener noticed him and approached.

"Can I help you?" the man asked John.

"Yeah, maybe. I'm looking for Dave and I was told he was here with the Judge. Have you seen him?"

"Yes," the old man replied. "They left here in David's car about ten minutes ago."

John let a look of exasperation cross his face. "Crap! You know when they'll be back?" He was quite happy that the Judge was not there.

"No," the man replied. "But I had the idea they'd be gone awhile. The Judge took a briefcase with him. Do you want me to call them?"

"You have their number?" John asked, a little surprised that a gardener would have that information.

The old man smiled. "I've worked for the Walton's for a long time. I don't mind saying that David considers me his uncle."

"Oh, I see." John looked over at the gazebo. "Say, are those Purple Plum trees over there? They sure are great looking."

The man followed John's gaze and said, "They are nice trees. You should smell the blossoms in the spring." He sniffed in air through his nostrils as though he could smell them even now. "It's good enough to be bottled and sold. Unfortunately, they only last a few days."

"What kind of fertilizer do you use?"

"Just standard tree spikes. I use plant fertilizer on the perennials you see around the bases."

"Wow. You certainly know your job. Mind if take a closer look?"

The man grinned from ear to ear, obviously flattered at John's compliment and interest. "No," he shrugged, "let's go over there."

The gardener spouted forth a fountain of information about caring for the trees and the plants that grew beneath them. John occasionally grunted an acknowledgment as he studied the ground beneath the trees. He was looking for any disturbance to the mulched area that looked like it was different, something that may indicate that it once held a body. There was nothing. It all looked perfect.

They arrived and John feigned extreme interest in the old man's jabber as he inspected the area closer. He looked back at the gardener. "The place is so perfect, they could use it as a post card." The man's face practically split from the huge smile that crossed his face. John continued talking, "You have everything ship shape, that's for sure. Anything ever screw it up so that you *really* have to work?" he grinned.

"Yeah! Sometimes it's a bitch. Storm could come through. Sometimes vandals or thieves come in here and cause havoc."

"Vandals? Thieves? I would have thought that this place has great security."

"Most times it does," the old man answered. "Sometimes though, the system fails. It's weird. For years we never had a problem. Then last fall, the system went down and we had some problems. It was like the bad guys knew it was down."

John's interest piqued. "Really? What kind of problems?"

"Well, see that tree over there, the one closest to the gazebo?" John looked over and nodded as the man continued.

"Last fall, on my day off, somebody tore out all the plants under that tree, made one hell of a mess. The mulch was scattered all over the place, the ground was all dug up, dirt everywhere, even on the lawn. I was plenty pissed I tell you. Dave saw me over here ranting and raving, came over to ask what all the fuss was about. I just pointed, too pissed off to even talk. He said it looked to him like vandals."

"What'd you say?" John queried.

"I told him that didn't make no sense. Why just that one area? He said they probably were gonna do the whole thing but they got spooked and ran."

"So, do you think that's what happened?" John pressed.

"Made some sorta sense at the time, before last spring that is."

John was becoming more certain that this is where Sally Walton had lain all winter. Right under the noses of the police. Under normal circumstances, dogs would have been brought in and they would have found her right away. But everyone, including the Judge himself, had become convinced that she had taken off with a younger man. A classic example of an investigator's worse mistake, tunnel vision, making the pieces of fact fit the puzzle where they were expected to be, not where they actually belonged. "What happened then? Same thing?" he asked.

"Not really. That's what makes me suspicious of the first stuff. Because of what happened last fall, I kinda pay extra special attention to this spot. If I didn't, I probably wouldn't have noticed. This time, all the mulch and the plants were still in place, but they had been disturbed, you could just tell.

And the ground was different, it kinda had a big dip that it didn't have before. Don't make no sense."

"Didn't anybody see anything?"

"Nope!" the gardener replied. "I asked around, nobody seen a thing."

"What about the Judge? What did he have to say about it?"

The old man shook his head. "Nuthin'. He just laughed at me and said it was probably just the ground settling from the problem last fall."

"And you don't buy that?"

"No!" the man answered sternly. "I told you. I look at that ground nearly every day, it just happened overnight." He snapped his fingers. "Like that!" said the old man.

"What did Dave have to say about it?"

"I didn't ask him. Meant to, but he's not around as much as he used to be."

"Oh?" John said as lightly as he could. He didn't want the gardener becoming suspicious of all the questions. "Why is that? Something change?"

"Since you know David, I'm sure you know what happened to the Judge's wife. She was a lively one, that one. Had this old place jumpin' I tell you. There were big parties here, hundred, hundred-fifty people. That big gazebo over there," he nodded in that direction, "it saw some mighty good times. They'd bring in these huge speakers and music would be blastin' like you were at a rock concert. There was dancin', champagne, caviar, the works. David was over here all the time. After Sally went missin' everything changed.

No parties, nuthin'."

"Wow," John said simply. He couldn't think of anything else he could ask the gardner without it appearing that he was anything other than nosey. He walked over to the area in question and squatted down. "You sure couldn't tell anything happened here now."

He picked up a handful of dirt and mulch and put it up to his nose. He took a long, inhaled breath and said, "It sure smells good and fertile. You must have developed some awesome organisms in here to break down this stuff." John liked to garden himself, but he was in way over his head with all this organism stuff and he prayed the gardener wasn't too conversant with it either. He needed an excuse to collect some of the soil for analysis.

"Hah!" the gardener snorted. "I don't know much about that. I just put down fresh mulch on a regular basis and fertilize. It comes out pretty good."

John was relieved to hear that. Now he could lay it on as thick as he needed to. He stood up and looked at the gardener. "I have a brother-in-law who works for the university. Dirt's his thing. He looks at the chemical composition, the bugs that are in it, everything. Do you mind if I take some of this? It sure would turn his crank, if you know what I mean."

The old man shook his head with a tolerant smile, "Whatever floats his boat. Sure, I don't care, take some of it if you want."

"Thanks," John replied, looking over at the gazebo standing a few feet away. "Mind if I take a look at the gazebo? It sure looks beautiful and I've never been here before."

"Naw, go ahead." Together, they walked the short distance to the building. It was large, John judged it to be at least fifty feet from one wall to the other and it was built right at the very edge of the lake. In fact, a quarter of it extended out over the water. A door lead to a short dock. It was a gazebo in name only as it was equipped with a bar, television, sound system, bathroom, and all the amenities one would expect in such a place. Fishing poles sat in one corner near the bar. All in all, a great place to entertain friends.

He looked over at the house. A gunshot in this place could easily go unheard at the house. Especially if the windows of the house were closed and other ambient noise, such as music or a television, was present. Kill Sally in this room and hide her body under the trees until it was safe to move her. Then John remembered that the coroner had said she had been indoors for some time before she was buried. He looked over toward the bathroom.

"Was this place used very often after Mrs. Walton disappeared?" he asked the old man.

"Eh, sometimes. In the summer, it was used most weekends. Not so much the rest of the year. They have windows that can be installed when it gets cold and the place has a heating system too, so they would occasionally have parties in the winter, but not often. Judge likes to come down here to fish and be alone."

"Must be nice," John said softly, as much to himself as to

the gardener. "Mind if I take a leak? Then I gotta get out of here."

The man motioned to the bathroom in acknowledgment, but said nothing. John had the impression that he was tiring of John's incessant questions. Time to get out of here before the gardner started becoming suspicious. He had uncovered a tremendous amount of information, but he feared he may have pushed a little too hard.

The bathroom was small, Spartan, but nicely done. It consisted only of a toilet, sink, mirror over a medicine cabinet, towel rack, and trash can. There was not enough room to lay a body out on the floor, but plenty of room to stuff one temporarily. The bathroom and another small room on the opposite side of the bar were the only two rooms where a body could be stored. He had noticed that the other room had a lock on it. Unless the killer had the key handy, the bathroom was the only area available that would be out of sight. Did David Walton have a key? Good question. If he was the killer and he had the key, the room with the lock would make more sense.

But he was in the bathroom now and so that is where he began to look. Sally Walton had been shot in the head. Head wounds create a tremendous amount of blood. It was nearly impossible to completely get rid of all traces of it when there was such a copious amount. He stood a moment and imagined himself carrying or dragging a body in. The door opened to the right. He looked at the space to the right of the toilet. If Sally had been dumped there, the killer might have had problems shutting the door and in any case, it would have been a little unnatural maneuvering around the door. He looked to the left of the toilet, the only other space large enough. He could detect nothing that would indicate that was where she was dumped. He stepped over to the area and squatted down to get a closer look at the oak baseboard, a likely place to catch still running blood. Still nothing. He reached into his pocket to retrieve a small knife attached to his key ring. He then flushed the toilet to cover any noise and used the knife to pry the baseboard away from the wall slightly. He peered down into the space between the baseboard and the wall. Still nothing. He moved to the wall on the other side of the corner and repeated the procedure.

This time he was rewarded with a crusted, reddish-brown chunk of something that strongly resembled blood. He considered taking some of it and reconsidered. His search would be considered illegal and therefore inadmissible in court, since the blood was not in plain sight and he had no search warrant to look for it. The fact that he was not a police officer would help. The courts gave a great amount of latitude toward John Q. Citizen in these matters. But he had a feeling that being an ex-cop, who would have known better, negated the John Q. Citizen defense. Besides, the dirt was obtained with permission and that would be enough to get a search warrant for the general grounds and that would lead to a search of the gazebo and that should lead to the discovery of the blood that John was currently looking at.

The toilet had stopped running and John quietly shoved the baseboard back into place as much as he could without causing any noise. He also made sure not to leave any prints. He didn't want to confuse the crime scene guys anymore than he had to and he wanted to stay out of this portion of the investigation so as to not taint any evidence gathering.

He walked out of the bathroom to find the gardener leaning against the wall with his arms crossed. The man smiled but John sensed that his time here was at an end. "Thanks," he said simply and headed for the door.

John began telling the gardener of his own garden at home. He wanted to put the old man at ease again. When they reached the area of the tree under which he was now convinced Sally had been buried, he bent down and took as big a handful of dirt as he could get. He also grabbed a couple of Plum tree leaves that were laying nearby. He used his other hand to fill in the small hole he'd created and smoothed everything over. He didn't want to upset the gardener by leaving a mess he would have to clean up.

He stood up. "My brother-in-law is going to have a field day with this," He said with a smile.

To his relief, the old man chuckled and smiled back. "To each his own," he said.

John continued talking about his garden as they walked back to his truck. Once there, he continued talking as he opened the rear hatch and pulled a tarp out of one of the compartments. He spread it open and dumped the dirt, mulch and leaves on to it. He then wrapped it up so it wouldn't spill and closed the hatch.

He rubbed his hands together to remove the loose dirt that was on them and extended his right hand. "Thanks for showing me around." The gardener took his extended hand and they shook. "Like I said, I've never seen this place before, heard plenty, but never seen it. I'll catch Dave at his house later." They bid farewell to each other and John got into his truck and drove down the driveway.

When he reached the road, he picked up the secure cell phone and punched in Frank's number. He had to tell him what he had found and he wanted to get the soil and leaves analyzed right away. Once the match to the leaves and soil found on Sally Walton was confirmed, it would be an easy thing to obtain a search warrant for a more extensive search. He pondered how they could link it to David Walton as he waited for Frank to answer the phone. He didn't.

When the voicemail picked up the line, there was no greeting, only a 'beep' to indicate that the caller should leave a message. "Frank, I know where Sally was buried and I have a soil sample with some leaves that need to be analyzed to confirm the spot. I think she was probably murdered at the area as well. However, I'm not sure we want to play our cards just yet. Give me a call and let's talk about it. Later."

John was a little surprised that Frank hadn't picked up the phone, but he realized that Frank could be in an interview or on the phone with someone else. He turned his thoughts back to what he had just learned and pondered about how the Judge fit into all this. Was he, on some level, aware of his son's activities? If he was, how far would he go to protect him? Who killed Sally Walton? The Judge in a jealous rage? David? If it was David, and John was leaning in that direction, was it a lovers quarrel or did it have anything to do with Coeptus Guild? If not David, who? Still so many questions. Locating the scene of the crime helped a lot, but they were still a long way from solving any of this.

He steered his truck toward the County Sheriff's Department, hoping he would be able to get hold of Frank by the time he got there. He picked up the secure phone and called Sue. She answered on the second ring.

"Hey, it's me," said John. "How ya doing?"

"Oh hi," she answered. "I'm good, thanks. How have your interviews gone?"

He gave her a brief run down on what he had learned from the gardener and Ramsey. He didn't, however, let her know just how "*intense*" his run in with Ramsey had been. He didn't think she'd see the humor in it and truth be told, he was not proud of his loss of control.

"I think I'm going to give Ramsey a call and quiz him some more on who killed Sally Walton. If I know who killed her and why, it could lead me to who framed Nick. He says he has no idea who planted the bullet in the field."

"I'm a little confused as to why he would talk to you. Doesn't he hate you because of his father? I remember some of the news reports at the time and he certainly didn't have anything nice to say about you."

John thought a moment before answering. He really didn't want to lie to Sue. "Well... let's just say... that we came to an understanding... and leave it at that."

She thought back to the look of cold determination that she had seen on John's face months before at the cabin where he had killed all those people while trying to save her from the clutches of the Coeptus Guild. She shuddered and decided she didn't want to know how William Ramsey and John had come to their *understanding*. Moving on, she asked, "Do you think he knows who did it?"

"I'm not sure. He kind of skirted the issue when we talked, but it doesn't hurt to ask." He thought about Ramsey's terrified, rat in a hole look. "I think I can get him to open up about it. Especially now that I know a few facts that I can use to make him believe that I know more than I actually do."

It was an old ploy, the investigator would act like he already knew the basic story, sprinkling in a few known facts to shore up that misconception. The trick was to convince the subject that all that was wanted at this point were a few details to fill in the gaps. Hopefully, the subject would decide that everything was out in the open and there was nothing to gain by further denials. All that remained was some hope of leniency by cooperating.

"By the way," John continued, "have you heard from Frank? I really need to get hold of him for those tests and I want to fill him in."

"No, I haven't heard a thing. Did you leave him a message?"

"Yeah, I did. Alright, if you hear from him, have him call me ASAP. I'm gonna call Ramsey now. I'll talk to you later."

"Okay. Keep me posted and John... you be careful. Do you have your gun?" She knew that John never carried it unless he really thought he might need it. If he had a gun with him, it would both relieve her and frighten her at the same time. Relief because he had it and terror because that meant he thought he might need it.

He paused a moment before answering. "Yes Sue, I have my Walther PPK with me. Don't worry, I'll be fine."

Her heart skipped a beat at the news. "Please don't do anything rash, John. I know how badly you want these people, but I... I don't want to lose you. I don't know if I could handle that."

Quietly, John said, "I have to go now," and then to get her mind off it, "Just make sure that if you hear from Frank, have him call me. Okay?"

"Yes."

"Good, I'll talk to you in a little while." He hung up the phone and looked up Ramsey's office number. He dialed it and waited while the receptionist answered and went through her standard greeting. It sounded like the same woman he had seen earlier when he was there.

"Hi," he responded in a happy, light hearted tone. "Is Bill in?"

"Yes... would you like me to put you through to his voicemail?"

"No, I need to talk to him."

"I'm sorry, but he's asked not to be disturbed."

"Is he in a meeting or on the phone? If he's on the phone, I'll hold," John persisted.

"No, neither one. He told me to hold all calls and cancel all his meetings for today. He's been in his office all morning. He didn't even go to lunch so I think he must be work-ing on something important."

"Okay. I understand. But I *really* need to talk to him. Can you at least tell him I'm on the phone? I'm sure he will take my call."

"Well... okay. Who should I say is calling?"

John thought a moment. "Tell him it's the gentleman that he spoke to this morning, the one who said he might be calling back for more information."

The receptionist put him on hold and John listened to an entire Three Dog Night song before he heard the line being picked up.

"What do you want?" asked William Ramsey. He sounded terrified, disgusted, more than a little on the drunk side, and depressed all at the same time. If circumstances were different, John might even have felt sorry for him, but he didn't.

"Hi Bill," he said softly. "I need to clarify a few things about Sally Walton's death."

"I told you everything I know. There's nothing more I can give you." Ramsey's voice grew stronger and harder with each word he spoke.

"Listen, *Bill*, I don't think you did. Perhaps I need to see you again, just to make sure that you understand the impor-tance of staying on my good side." There was silence from the other end. That was a good sign. It meant that Ramsey's brief show of defiance was crumbling already. Time to has-ten that process along. "Yeah, I think that's it. We need to see each other again. Apparently, I didn't get my message through the first time. I was on my way somewh—"

"What do you need to know?" Ramsey interrupted. There was still a trace of defiance in his voice, but mostly, there was fear.

John hesitated before answering to give himself a chance to calm down a little. Much to his surprise, his show of force for Ramsey was not all show. He *did* want to give Ramsey a little *tune up*. His inner demon had reared and wanted blood. A moment later, when he felt he had safely put the beast back into its cage. He continued. "Now, as I was saying. I want to know more about Sally Walton's death."

"I don't know anything. Please, I'll tell you anything you want to know, but I don't know anything about her."

John had something here. He knew it. Ramsey was scared shitless and John believed Ramsey when he said he would tell him whatever he wanted to know, *except about that*. Ramsey was lying about that. To John, who had interrogated hundreds if not thousands of suspects, it was as obvious as a grease smudge on a white dress. John doubted that Ramsey would have pulled the trigger himself and he doubted he was high enough up the food chain to have ordered it. He pressed on.

"Listen you little shit head, I know all about it. I know that she was shot by the lake at the Judge's house. I know that she was hidden in the gazebo bathroom for a couple of days before being buried underneath a Purple Plum tree next to the gazebo. I know all the players." He lied about that last part. He was taking a chance. John had learned early on that it's never a good idea to outright lie to the subject of an interview. If the subject realizes that it's a lie, then everything else that the interrogator has said is put into question and everything goes downhill from there. But John needed to know and time was of the essence. He finished by saying, "All I need to know from you is, why? I've got conflicting statements as to why. Fill me in, will you. Or is it worth me seeing you again to keep it to yourself. If I have to meet with you again, I'll find out what I want to know, but you probably won't care for my methods."

John had no conflicting statements. But by saying that he did, he implied that other people had already talked and that would hopefully cause Ramsey to reason that there was no rationale for holding back any longer.

When he answered, Ramsey was obviously starting into a total breakdown. He was starting to sob when he blurted out, "It wasn't his fault. Walton ordered him to do it. And what was he to do? If he didn't do it, he would have been the one to get hit."

He, thought John, his mind racing over the possibilities. Who's *He*? Ramsey continued and even though his breath was coming in ragged sobs, his voice became angry. "You would have liked that wouldn't you? Then he never would have been able to get up to that fuckin' cabin so you could have him executed." With that, Ramsey's grief overtook him.

Well, that confirmed that it was Chief Ramsey who shot Sally. He waited a moment to give Ramsey time to calm a little, then he asked harshly, "Why was your father ordered to kill her?"

"Why do you think? Isn't it obvious? She was caught, that's why."

Caught? Caught doing what? What the hell was Ramsey talking about? He had to tread carefully here. This was uncharted territory. Was she caught stealing? Or were she and David finally discovered? There were so many possible scenarios. Was it a love triangle? In that case, either Walton could have ordered her killed. But if it was the Judge, he probably would have done it himself in a fit of jealous rage. He shook his head in confusion.

"It seems that Ms. Sally was involved in a few, unsavory things," John said. "I have conflicting reasons as to exactly why David ordered her to be taken out. What's your version?"

Ramsey laughed. A short derisive laugh with no humor in it. Then he said, "I don't know who you've been talking to, Mr. Know-it-all, but there's one answer that should be way above the rest."

"I see," said John simply.

"No, I don't think you do see. She would have ruined everything. She had guys talking to her. She was only found out by mistake, at the last minute. That's the only reason my father agreed to take her out. Do you think he wanted to do it? I don't care what you think of my father. He was a good man who got pushed by the wrong people. You! Them! Everybody! If she blew it all up, we all would have gone down, including me. And *that* was something my father wanted to avoid at all costs. I meant everything to him. That was the *only* reason he would agree to snuff out a fuckin' *cop!*"

With that, Ramsey slammed down the phone. But it didn't really matter at that point because John Livingston Harvard was speechless. He quickly pulled to the side of the road and stopped, too stunned to safely drive.

A *cop*? Sally Walton was a cop? For who? Just when he thought the pieces of the puzzle were dropping into place quite nicely, all forming a total, neat picture. It was the ultimate twisted piece. It was so twisted in fact, so unexpected, that it warped the entire puzzle.

For almost an hour, he sat on the side of that road, his mind whirring and clicking as it resorted everything he thought he knew and trying to see where the pieces now belonged. In the end, he decided it was imperative that he talked to Frank Carlotta. And even more important, that they contact Frank's brother with the F.B.I., because someone had been hiding some things. And if they were hiding little things, like the fact that Judge Walton's wife had been a cop, what else were they hiding?

CHAPTER
12

"I have to go to the bathroom," Sara Rose announced. They were still driving north and all traces of the city had passed from view long before. She looked at Dwight in the rearview mirror as she said it. He had moved over to the passenger side of the rear seat and there was no response, even though his eyes were open. The gun lay on the seat next to him. He didn't look good. He was pale and he was sweating profusely in spite of the fact that he had ordered her to turn on the air conditioning almost an hour ago. She was freezing. He obviously, was not.

"Dwight!" His eyes rolled toward her. "I have to go to the bathroom and I will not pee my pants."

Dwight didn't feel very good. He couldn't decide which was throbbing worse, his foot or his head. In fact, the pain was so overwhelming that he could hardly think. But now the bitch in the front seat was saying something, asking some sort of question. "Wha… what?"

"I… said… I… have… to… go… to… the," her voice raised several decibels and became harsher to emphasize the last word, "*bathroom!*" she barked out forcefully. Sara was becoming less frightened as she began to realize that she could take control of this situation, if she handled it right. She had been around cops long enough to know that hostage negotiators liked to keep the hostage taker busy with mundane stuff. Make them have to solve problems like eating, drinking, going to the bathroom. Make them tired and mentally exhausted. Which, she reckoned, in Dwight's case, wouldn't take much.

For his part, Dwight didn't want to think about such things. On the other hand, he had a natural aversion to someone pissing on the seat right in front of him. He forced himself to think about the problem. "Okay. Get off at the next road that looks kind of barren."

A few minutes later, one such road came into view and she turned onto it. "Now what?" she asked.

He looked around. Small natural fields and towering pines were on both sides of the road. It was dark enough that any occupied houses would have revealed themselves. There were none. He looked ahead and saw what appeared to be a long unused driveway or small road. "Turn in there," he said as he pointed to it.

"Look, I'm not going to the bathroom in the woods."

Dwight picked up the gun from the seat and pointed it at her menacingly. "*You'll do as I say!*" he shouted. She noticed that the gun shook in his hand and she decided that was not a good thing.

"Alright, alright. Just put the gun down please. You're scaring me." Thankfully, he complied.

She pulled onto the tiny road and drove a few feet down

it before stopping. The road had obviously not been used in some time and it was so narrow with overgrown vegetation that the grass and branches brushed the car as she progressed. It made a high pitched squealing sound as it scrapped along. She smiled at the sound and hoped that it was scratching the shit out of it. Dwight either didn't notice or didn't seem to care as he sat up in his seat and leaned forward. He grabbed the back of Sara's seat for support.

"Now, just step outside and do your thing, right next to the door."

"I don't want to pee right in front of you," she protested.

"Tough shit!" he spat back. "You don't have anything I haven't seen before and besides, you have other things to worry about other than being embarrassed."

She nodded and pushed the door opened. She stepped outside and began undoing the buckle that held her pants up. She looked towards Dwight and noticed that he had the gun pointing directly at her once again. "If I even think that you're going to run, I'm gonna kill you right here." She thought about telling him that he was in no condition to drive with that injured foot and obvious weakness, but decided against it.

She turned away from him, dropped her pants and squatted, using her door as support while she completed her task. When she was finished, she pulled up her pants, re-buckled them and got back into the car. "Hope you enjoyed the show," she said through tight, thin, lips.

She backed up and started to turn in the direction of the main road that they had been on. "No!" Dwight commanded. "They might be looking for my car by now. I want you to take back roads from now on. Go down this road for awhile, then head north."

Sara did as she was told and a short time later, they were on a paved, two lane road heading north. Her mind raced to come up with another problem for him to solve. She looked down at the gas gauge. *Damn*! It was still almost half full. Unfortunately, it looked as though Dwight had filled it recently. In his condition, maybe he wouldn't remember. She decided to chance it. Sara looked at him again through the rear view mirror. The gun was back on the seat and his eyes were barely open as his head lolled back and forth against the window with the movement of the car.

"Dwight, we have another problem here."

His eyes opened fully and he stiffened his neck to still his head as he looked at her. "Now what?" he drawled.

"There aren't many gas stations out here and we need gas. Do you want me to head back toward the main road?" she asked demurely.

To her dismay, he started to lean forward in an obvious attempt to look at the gas gauge. Reflexively, she stepped on the gas so the forward momentum of the car added to the resistance of his attempt. Fortunately, he didn't notice and the effort proved too much for him as he fell back against the seat. To her relief, he made no further attempts. "No. Stay on this road for awhile. We're bound to come to some small town."

"But Dwight, that could be miles and what are we going to do if we run out of gas?" Again the questions. '*Keep him active*,' she thought. '*Don't give him time to rest and collect himself.*'

"Sara!" he snapped, "Just do as I say."

Eventually, they did come into a small town. So small, in fact, that Sara was surprised that they actually had a gas station. But they did, a small two pumper with a tiny building beside it.

"Is this one okay?" she asked.

"Yeah," he responded. "Pull right up next to it and use your credit card. If you move more than one step away from the car, I'll shoot you. And don't talk to anyone."

She did as she was told and pulled up next to one of the pumps. She turned off the car immediately so that he wouldn't see how much gas they had left. Much to her delight, she noticed that the pump did not accept credit cards. '*Thank God for small towns*,' she thought. "Dwight," she said, "we have another problem. The pump doesn't accept credit cards."

His exacerbated voice reverberated throughout the small car. "Jesus fuckin' Christ! What else? How much gas do we have left?"

"We're on fumes," she lied. "And you know how long it took us to find this one. I doubt we'll make it to another one before running out."

Dwight mulled this over for awhile before saying, "Fine. Fill the car up. When you're done, I want you to pull up right next to the front door. I go to the range regularly and you'll not be more than twenty feet from me. I won't miss. Leave the doors open so I can hear what you're saying. If you try to warn anyone, I'll not only kill you, but I'll kill whoever else is inside. So you have not only your life in your hands, but theirs as well. Understand?"

"Yes," Sara replied quietly, not knowing that Dwight was totally lying about going to the range. In fact, the only other time he'd handled a gun, was when one of the ballistics experts at the lab showed him a gun that had been used in a homicide. It was heavy and it had, quite frankly, scared the shit out of him.

She filled up the tank, quickly entered the car and moved it over to the station door before Dwight could read the pump and see how little gas she had really put in it. "Remember what I said," he said quietly as she got out.

She walked in. At first, she didn't think anyone was there. It was quite small with a rack containing post cards and a shelving unit containing what she was sure would be stale candy. Little toy rubber Indian hatchets hung on yet another rack.

She was startled when an old, wizened head poked up over the back of the counter. As the head continued to rise, she saw that it was attached to an equally wizened body. "Oh, sorry," said the old man. "I'm 'fraid I took a bit of a nap. How can I help ya?"

Sara smiled. "I just got gas and I'd like to pay for it," she said as she handed him her credit card.

The man looked surprised. "Ya did? Wow. I didn't hear a thing." He looked around. "Can't find my glasses. He bent over to look at the readout for the pump. His nose was almost touching the glass before the numbers came into view.

He stood up and proudly announced, "That'll be seven dollars please."

Sara handed him her credit card. He took it and walked over to an old fashion credit card 'swipe' device and swiped it through. He also punched her card number into a more modern instrument that was hooked up to a modem. They both waited while the thing binged and bonged its way through the approval process. When it was done, he handed Sara the multilayered card form for her signature. She signed it, then flipped it over and wrote on the back, "*Help me. I am being kidnapped by Dwight Chase. I think he shot himself in the foot. We are heading north in his car.*"

She handed the form back to the old man, note side up. He promptly turned it over, tore off her copy and handed it to her. Dismayed that the old man had not so much as glanced at the note, she took the original back from the man, saying, "Oh, wait, I want to be sure I gave you the right credit card. One of them is completely paid off and I don't want to use it anymore." She took it back, looked at the front briefly before turning it over and handing it back to the old man, again, note side up. This time, she practically hit him in the nose with it. "Good, it's the right one."

She quickly returned to the car and pulled out of the lot. She didn't want the old man to react to the note in front of Dwight. She needn't have worried. Though the old man noticed that something was written on the back of the form, there was no possible way that he could read it without his glasses. He was a bit curious about what it said, so he began looking for them. By the time he found them, on the floor behind his chair, he had completely forgotten about Sara Rose's note. Five minutes after that, he was sound asleep.

William Ramsey poured himself yet another shot glass of eighteen year, single malt scotch. He savored the taste as he sat in his office chair and pondered his situation. His broken right hand hurt like hell. It was swollen, throbbing actually, but he hadn't done a thing to ease his discomfort. In spite of this, he smiled, though it was a sad, depressed smile. So that son of a bitch Harvard thought he had all the answers did he? Well, he was wrong on one very important point. Harvard had pushed his luck a little too far when prodding Ramsey for answers and Ramsey picked up on the mistake as soon as Harvard had said it. Now the question was, what could Ramsey do to screw up Harvard?

He was afraid of Harvard, he admitted it to himself. Other than his father, he had never been truly afraid of anyone. He recalled the look in Harvard's eyes as he had him pinned against the bathroom door, choking the life out of him and squeezing his balls until Ramsey was sure they would burst like a ripe watermelon under the wheels of a semi. He shuddered. The man was a killer, no doubt about it. Not only that, but to him, it looked a lot like Harvard was thoroughly enjoying himself. This was the sort of man that would tear out the beating heart of an enemy and eat it before the man's dying eyes, just to see the look of terror.

Would Harvard realize his mistake and return for clarification? Ramsey was sure he would, and he was just as sure that Harvard would carry out his threat of great bodily harm and probable death. He shuddered again. At that point, the scotch soaked brain of William Ramsey came to a conclusion, one way or the other, he was almost assuredly, a dead man.

That point being a given, he next turned his thoughts to ways he could fuck up John Harvard. On a sudden impulse, he picked up the phone and dialed. A moment later, a voice came on the line. "Yes? What do you want?"

Ramsey hesitated before answering. By telling this man all about the events of the day, he was putting the last nail in his coffin. Coeptus Guild would never let him live, knowing that he had already betrayed their trust and fearful of what else Harvard could get out of him. But what difference did it make if it was Harvard or Coeptus Guild that did him in? Dead is dead. And this way, he could at least have revenge on the man who had taken down the Ramsey clan. And so, he began to speak, holding nothing back.

When he was finished, the man at the other end of the line told him that they needed to talk about this further, right now. The man informed Ramsey to stay put and he would be right over. Ramsey, knowing it would never be the man himself who would enter his office and knowing equally as well what the *meeting* would mean for him, agreed and hung up the phone.

He poured himself a fresh jigger of scotch and sat back in his chair. After awhile, he spun the chair around so that he could look out his window at the city. It really was a beautiful view. His office overlooked the river and he watched as a brightly lit boat slowly made its way upstream. He gingerly held the scotch in his right hand as he reached into the credenza in front of him and removed a revolver.

It was one of his father's guns, a six inch Colt Python, .357 magnum. He put it in his lap and stared at it for a long time, caressing the finely machined instrument of death with the fingers of one hand while holding the tumbler of scotch in the other. He had a sudden epiphany as he stroked the weapon. His father hadn't killed Sally Walton or anyone else for William. Deep down, he always knew that. All his father ever cared about was himself. For the second time that day, he began to cry, silently this time, with a steady stream of drunken tears rolling down his cheeks and on to his three hundred dollar, custom tailored, dress shirt. His father had been an evil man. But, if nothing else, William was a master of denial and he had convinced himself that his father was a good man and that in turn, William was a good man as well. The fact of the matter was, William was evil too, just like his father. But unlike his father, he was a coward as well... and William knew it.

William Ramsey finished his scotch and put the glass down on the credenza. He picked up the gun and put it in his mouth. With one last look at the brightly lit boat, he joined his father, wherever that was.

After hanging up the phone with Ramsey, the man he

had called dialed another number and gave instructions to the recipient of the call. After finishing those instructions he hung up. '*That wraps up that little loose end,*' he thought. Then, he turned his attention to that royal pain in the ass, Harvard. He just knew that Harvard would prove, *awkward*. That's why he had taken precautions. Now, he was glad he did. It was obviously time for Harvard to have a little attitude adjustment of his own. He knew the dangers of sending someone to confront him directly. Therefore, the only other alternative was to go at the problem indirectly. The best way to deal with a well defended castle was not to batter away at the main gate, but to take out the support for the fortress and let it disintegrate from within.

He picked up the phone and dialed another number. It was answered instantly. The recipient of this call was different than the first. He was far more dangerous, extremely dangerous and like a Bengal Tiger, had to be handled firmly, but cautiously.

"Yes," the Bengal Tiger said simply.

"Be ready," the man said. "It will probably go down tonight or tomorrow morning at the latest. Make sure the job is done. Make sure your escape route is clear."

"Yes," The Bengal Tiger said again.

The man hung up. Now he needed to decide who would handle the next phase. That *was* being handled by Ramsey, but now the man would have to make the arrangements himself. He picked up the phone again.

❖ ❖ ❖

The sniper, aka, the Bengal Tiger, put the phone down and picked up his rifle. He looked through the house, searching for the woman and the kid. He hadn't seen either one for some time. Eventually, the women came into view as she moved to the kitchen sink. The sniper zeroed in on her skull and placed his finger on the trigger. There was no wind and this would be an easy shot, an easy kill. He began to slowly squeeze his trigger finger back. But he stopped, just before the point where he knew it would cause the release of the firing pin which would end the life of Sara Browning. Not yet. Not yet.

"… We interrupt your regularly scheduled programming to give you an update on the tragic and violent crash in the center of town earlier today, when a semi-truck, loaded with gravel, went through a red light, broadsiding a SUV, killing three people instantly and injuring three more. One of the injured persons, a man, has just died. Here with us now is the acting Chief of Police. Chief, can you tell us a little bit about what caused this accident and will there be any charges?"

The acting chief spoke. *"Well, all we know at this point is that a semi-truck loaded with gravel blew through the stop light here at a high rate of speed. Our traffic crash investigators report that their preliminary results show that the semi was traveling somewhere between fifty and sixty miles an hour when it hit a Ford Explorer that was also going through the intersection at a high rate of speed. Those two vehicles then collided into a parked, unmarked county squad car. They continued on and eventually crashed into the bar here, striking three patrons who were sitting next to the window. One was killed instantly and one of the other victims has just died. Both of the drivers are also dead."*

"Chief, do we know anything about the officer whose squad car was hit?"

"Yes we do. He was Sergeant Frank Carlotta of the County Sheriff's Department. Fortunately, he was able to jump to safety, suffering only minor injuries. He's still at the hospital but we expect him to be released shortly. We credit him with giving first aid to the victims and with providing us with invaluable information on the accident, as he saw the whole thing."

"Can you tell us what he saw? Our viewers would like…"

Susan Browning was listening to the television with half an ear as she was folding laundry and thinking about John. She'd heard about the accident earlier but hadn't really paid much attention to it. At the mention of Frank's name, however, that inattention changed dramatically. She hurried to the secure cell phone and called John. She was almost ready to hang up, thinking he wasn't going to answer, when she heard the call go through and his voice came on the line.

"Hello?" He sounded distracted. Confused? She couldn't quite put her finger on it.

"John? Are you alright?"

"I'm fine Sue, just a bit taken aback. I just found out that Sally Walton was apparently a cop."

"What!" She exclaimed. "Are you sure? That doesn't make any sense. Who did she work for?"

"I don't know. Ramsey just told me. He said that's why

she was killed. She had been talking to people and had found out just a little too much about Coeptus Guild. His father killed her on Walton's orders."

"Oh my God! Listen John, the reason I called was to tell you that Frank was involved in a huge accident in town. Four people were killed and he was injured. According to the news, he's still at the hospital."

"Shit!" he said as he put his truck into gear and pulled back on to the road. "I'd better head over there. Do you know how bad he is?"

"Not really," Sue said. "According to the news, he only suffered minor injuries and should be released soon."

"Let's hope that's the case. Do me a favor, will you? Dig into Sally Walton's past as much as you can. I suspect she was working for the F.B.I., in which case I'm not sure how much I'm going to find out from them. Don't take anything you find at face value. If I'm right that she was working undercover for a Federal agency, they'll have a legend for her and everything will appear to be in proper order."

"A '*Legend*?'" she asked quizzically.

"Oh, sorry. A Legend is a fabricated life made up to give an agent a cover story for an assignment. Depending on how sensitive the case is, they will make up birth certificates, driver's licenses, high school diplomas, arrest records, even prison time. I've even known them to make up fake year books to back up the story. What you need to do is try to back up everything you find with third party witnesses. For example, if you find that she graduated from say, Wexford High School, find other people who also graduated from there. Call them with a cover story and see if anyone remembers her. Do you see what I mean?"

"Yeah, I do. I'll get right on it as soon as I get Mary Kate to bed. By the way, she wants to talk to you."

"Okay. Put her on the line."

A small voice came on the line a moment later. "Daddy? What are you doing?"

"Hi Angel. I'm just going to talk to a friend of mine."

"So you won't be home to put me to bed?"

"No, I'm sorry sweetheart. But I'll check on you and give you a kiss when I get home."

She laughed at this. "Okay, but make sure that you tell me that you love me, too."

Now it was his turn to laugh. "I will Mary Kate. Don't I always tell you that I love you?"

She laughed again. "Yeah, but I like to hear it."

He chuckled as he replied, "Alright Angel, I have to go now, you have a good snooze, okay? I love you."

"Love you too, Daddy. Bye," and she hung up the phone. He smiled as he put down his phone. She was truly his light in the darkness.

He pulled into the parking lot of the hospital a short time later. He walked in and asked for Detective Carlotta, telling the nurse that he was working with him on a case and it was important that he see him. She dialed Frank's room and spoke with him. She hung up the phone and told him curtly, "He's in room 204." With that she turned and walked away. He watched her walk away and decided that she was apparently having a bad night.

He found room 204 and walked in. Frank was dressed, but lying on the bed. There were three other guys in the room. All looked up at John's entrance as Frank asked grimly, "How ya doing, John?"

"The question is, how are you doing? When are they going to let you out of here?" he asked.

"A few bumps and scrapes, but nothing to write home about. No broken bones or anything. I'm all ready to be released. I'm just waiting for the doctor to come in and sign the form. My insurance company says that if I don't get the official release before I walk out, they won't cover my expenses."

"Just trying to cover their ass I suppose. What happened, anyway? I kind of heard of a big accident on the news, but I had no idea you were involved until a little while ago when Sue called me."

"Well, I had just parked on the corner near the bar by your office." Frank answered. "I got out and was walking along the car when I heard the noise of a big semi lockin' 'em up. I looked up and this truck was barreling through the red light. The driver was obviously trying to stop but he apparently hadn't been paying much attention cause from the time he locked his brakes to the time he hit, couldn't have been more than a second or two. Anyway, all he succeeded in doing was to lose total control and ram into the side of a Ford Explorer that looked like it was heading straight for me. The semi knocked the Explorer to the side, but now the semi was turning sideways and heading right for me."

"That's not a good thing," John said with a grim smile.

"Yeah, I thought it was all over but the crying. But the good Lord was smiling at me I tell you. The trailer had turned sideways and was beginning to tip. Just before it got to me, I decided to dive straight at it, through a rapidly decreasing space *under* the tipping trailer. It was weird. I don't even remember making the decision to do that, I just did it, like someone else had control of my body for that split second. Anyway, it worked. I went under the trailer just as it would have hit me and just as it took out my poor squad. If I'd stayed where I was, I'd have been done for, either squished by the gravel, the trailer or up against the side of the building."

"Wow," John said in amazement. "That sounds like a good script for a movie."

Frank smiled. "Doesn't it though?" He looked over at his fellow detectives. "Hey guys! Give me some time with John here will you. There's a few things I need to talk to him about."

They all said their good-byes and filed out. After they were gone, Frank looked at John and said, "John, do I have a lot to tell you. This all started when I got a call from Sara Rose, the computer girl. Remember I told you she was going to look at Dwight Chase's records?" John nodded.

"Well she did and I guess she found something because she called me and started to tell me on the phone. You and I both know that Coeptus Guild taps phones at the drop of the hat and I have no doubts they could do it at a police station. So I stopped her and told her to meet me at the bar just down the street. That's why I was there when the accident happened. To meet her."

"Have you talked to her since?" John asked.

"That's the problem, John. She's disappeared. Her car is still in the lot at police department and she never went back to the office. We've called her home phone and her cell phone. Her cell phone's still on her desk."

John said, "I can't see her going anywhere for any length of time without her cell phone. To most people, it would be like leaving without your wallet or your purse."

"Exactly, but that's not all. Dwight Chase is also missing. Not only that, but before he walked out, in one hell of a hurry we're told, and he destroyed all the information on his hard drive."

John didn't like how this was shaping up. "This isn't looking good, Frank. Not good at all."

"Well, ready for the Coup de Grace?"

"What?" John queried with dread.

"Remember I told you that it looked as though that Ford Explorer was heading right for me?"

John nodded.

"Well, the driver was killed. When your boys pulled him out of the truck, they found that he had a gun on him. They decided they should figure out who this guy was, pronto, so they ran his ID right away, looking for next of kin, anything. It didn't check out. Then they ran his prints. You'll never guess who they came back to."

John thought a moment before answering. "Billyray Jenkins."

"Close, Luke Bonnais."

John whistled. "It looks to me like he was trying to take you out. That means they're getting nervous." He thought a moment. "Trouble is, he's dead. That means he couldn't have taken Sara Rose. So who did? And where's Dwight Chase?"

"Good questions all. I've…" Frank's cell phone rang. It was his department issue phone, not the secure phone. "Yeah." As he listened, he looked up a John. "Really?" he said into the phone. "Okay. Don't treat this as a suicide. I suggest that you put your best guys on it, Sheriff. You know his Dad was tied into some pretty serious shit. Maybe this is a part of that. Maybe it's not related, but I'd treat it as a homicide if I were you. If nothing else, you know the press is going to eat this up, so it's best that we do this by the book."

He listened a little longer then said, "Okay, good." He nodded his head in agreement to whatever was being said. "I agree. Thanks for keeping me informed, Sheriff. I'll be leaving here soon and heading back to my office… Okay, bye." He hung up the phone and looked at John. "Christ, this day just keeps getting shittier by the minute. That…"

John had a sinking feeling that he knew what had just happened. This was bad, very bad, on many different levels. He interrupted Frank. "Don't tell me. William Ramsey just killed himself."

Frank looked surprised. He sat up in bed. "Yeah. How in the hell did you guess that?" His surprised look suddenly changed to suspicion. "Oh please tell me you didn't have anything to do with this."

John rolled his eyes upward and Frank groaned, "Oh no."

"Look Frank, here's what happened." John went on to relate everything that had occurred, including his visit to David Walton's house and the Judge's house. When he was finished, Frank fell back onto the bed and stared up at the ceiling.

"You certainly have been a busy little bee, John. You apparently pushed Ramsey a little too far though."

"I apparently did, though I didn't think I'd pushed him *that* hard. That's not the big question." Frank's eyes rolled back toward him. "The question is, Frank, who knew that Sally Walton was a cop. Did you?" He studied Frank carefully as he waited for his answer.

"No, I certainly didn't. That throws a whole new light on things."

"Well somebody did. I think it has to be the Feds. Do you think your brother knew?"

"I don't know. I'll call him. Let me borrow your secure phone."

John's head wrinkled in confusion. "Where's yours?"

Frank smirked. It fell out of my pocket at the accident. It got a little crushed."

"I see." John tittered as he handed him his phone. "Destruction of Federal property. They'll send you up the river for sure, Frank."

"Yeah, yeah. Just give me the fuckin' phone," he said as he snatched it out of John's outstretched hand.

He punched in a number and a moment later he said, "Hi

Stu. Listen, I got a bit of a problem here. Did you know Sally Walton was a cop?"

John waited patiently as they talked for several minutes. It became apparent that Stuart Carlotta was denying any knowledge of Sally Walton's profession. It was equally obvious that, at least on the surface, Stuart agreed to look into it. Frank thanked him and snapped the phone shut. He did not give it back to John, but instead put it into his own pocket.

"He says he'll look into it," he said to John. "I think we're going to be together for a while and I'm hoping to get a call back soon. I think you need to take me back to my office and we need to have a big pow wow. No sense keeping this under wraps any longer. You beat the bushes to see what popped out and now all the animals were scrambling. We need to get Nick out of jail and we need to look everything over and come up with a plan."

As if on cue, the doctor walked in. "Hello Sgt. Carlotta. How are you feeling?" he said with a huge smile on his face.

"I'm fine doc, but I'm in a huge hurry. Something just came up and it's really important that I get back to my office right away."

The doctor's happy smile changed to a look of concern as he looked down at Frank, saying, "More important than your health, Sergeant?"

"Well, yeah. There's already been more than a few murders on this case, possibly one a little while ago and there's a great possibility that if we don't put this together there's going to be a whole lot more, real soon."

"I see," said the doctor gravely as he removed a pencil

light from his breast pocket. "Alright then, keeping your head still, follow my pencil."

Sara was tired. Not only that, but every mile of road that passed between them and the city, was another mile that the police would have to search for her. She had to get Dwight to stop. She looked in the rearview mirror at him. Man, was he pale and his shirt was soaked in sweat.

"Dwight," she said softly. "Look," she said with concern in her voice, "we need to stop. You need to get medical attention."

"Forget it," he snarled. "If I go to a hospital, they'll report it to the cops. You know as well as I do that they're required to report gunshot wounds." It was the first time that he had confirmed that he'd been shot.

She let the concern literally drip from her voice. "But Dwight, you look really bad. Maybe we could find a private doctor somewhere. We could tell them that you accidentally shot yourself while you were cleaning your gun."

He laughed sarcastically. "Yeah right, as if that wasn't the oldest story in the book. No way sister. Forget it."

She thought a moment. "Alright then, let's at least get a room somewhere so we can clean it. Maybe get some aspirin for the pain. Some hydrogen peroxide to clean it out with. I won't try to escape, I promise. I've always liked you Dwight. You're like me in many ways. I was always real quiet. And nobody ever took me seriously." She lied about that last part, but he didn't know that. She was trying to connect with him.

"Really?" he asked. "I never saw anybody not take you seriously."

"That's only recently. But not so long ago, I know everyone used to laugh at me. They put me in charge of the computer department only as an interim thing while they looked for someone else. I took over and they just kind of forgot about me. When they finally remembered, they figured they might as well just keep me in there. I did pretty good and now things are different. So I know how you feel."

It was almost all a complete pack of lies, but again, Dwight didn't need to know that. Her ploy appeared to work.

"Okay." he said. "We can get a room, but I don't want to let you out of my sight. I'm not stupid you know. Find a hotel with an office close enough to the parking lot where I can see and hear you, otherwise, forget it."

They both knew that the area was filled with that type of hotel. They were small, usually run by mom and pops, and were designed for summer vacationers wanting to get into the cooler woods for swimming, fishing, and other sundry activities that took place around the lakes and streams. She soon found one. "How's this?" she asked.

He looked around. There did not appear to be any guests at the hotel, which wasn't unusual at this time of year. It was in between seasons. Too late for vacations and too soon for hunters. "It's fine. Now just pull up as close to the door as you can get, just like at the gas station."

She did as she was told. She got out and walked into the small lobby. No one was there, but there was a small bell type ringer sitting on the counter with a sign saying, "Ring bell for service." She punched the little button on top twice and was rewarded with a cheery, "Ding ding."

A frail woman in her sixties came out of a room in the back with a happy, "Hello," and an inviting smile. She had a dishcloth in her hands and was wiping them as she approached the counter.

"Hi," said Sara. "We'd like to get a room."

"How many people?" the old woman asked.

"Two," responded Sara. She looked over at Dwight and saw him in the back seat, watching her intently.

"How many days would you like to stay?" the woman queried.

"I don't know, probably just one." Sara answered, fervently hoping that it wouldn't even be for the night. The woman asked her for her credit card as she handed Sara a form asking for her name, address, etc.

Suddenly, they both heard a man shouting. "Hey! What the hell you doing in there? What are you doing with that gun?" They both turned to see an elderly man, most likely this woman's husband, Sara decided, looking into the window of Dwight's car.

Sara's heart leapt as the rear door flew open and Dwight stepped out, the gun pointing straight at the man's chest. "Dwight, no!" Sara shouted as she ran toward them. She had abrupt feelings of guilt. If her "*Master*" plan to get away from Dwight caused these poor people to be murdered, she would never forgive herself. "Dwight, stop!" she pleaded. "Please don't harm these people. They didn't do anything. *Please*."

Dwight was shaking. The adrenaline, the pain from his foot and head, and the pure effects of the shock that he was suffering as a result of his wound were more than his body could handle. The adrenaline was already wearing off and he suddenly felt himself getting rapidly weaker. He fought unconsciousness and rubbed his face and eyes as he attempted to clear away the fog. He slowly moved his head toward Sara. "If I kill them, it's… it's your fault," he said weakly.

Sara was trying desperately to calm herself and get her brain functioning rationally. "Listen, Dwight, just stay calm. It's alright. You're in control here. You have the gun, remember? Nobody's going to try anything. Let's all stay calm and go inside where nobody can see us. Okay?" She didn't want to go where nobody could see them. But right now, she felt it was more important to calm him down. She didn't want these poor people to pay the price for her freedom.

Dwight slumped back against the door of his car. He could hardly stand. For a brief moment, Sara hoped against all hope, that he was going to pass out, solving their problems nicely. But he didn't. Instead he looked at her again and said, "Help me Sara. And if you try to pull anything, I start shooting, understand? And I start with those two." Though increasingly disoriented, he instinctively knew that Sara felt responsible for the old couple.

She nodded and walked over to him. She placed his free

hand over her shoulder and assisted him as they made their way into the hotel office. She was startled by the cold wetness of his skin. "*Clammy*," she believed was the technical word for it.

When they entered the office, Dwight motioned to the back room, which was actually the entrance to the living quarters. "In there," he said. Then he looked at the old couple who were now embracing. "You two go first. Do as I say and you two will die of old age." A thought came to him and he managed a feeble grin as he added. "Instead of lead poisoning."

They did as they were told and all four walked into the apartment the old couple lived in. Sara help him over to a couch, where Dwight stretched out. She started to stand up, but he reached out and grabbed her wrist. "No. You stay right here with me." He looked around and his eyes focused in on the floor where they had just walked. There was a trail of blood, punctuated by one bloody foot print wherever he had stepped. It was like a huge arrow, pointing right to him. He looked at the old man. "You," he said. "Pull up a chair near my feet."

The man, while still embracing his wife, picked up a small chair from a table and walked over to the foot of the sofa. He placed the chair on the floor and sat down. His wife followed.

"Now you," Dwight said motioning to the old lady. "You go clean up this blood before anybody sees it. If you try *anything*, I will kill your husband. Do you understand me?"

The old woman nodded in acknowledgment. Though scared, she was oddly calm. She was one of those elderly people who understood that she most likely had only a few more years to live. Ten, fifteen, maybe twenty, but she doubted she had that long. Though she didn't particularly want to die, she'd come to grips with that impending doom and was as ready for it as she could be. Her husband was another matter, she did not want to be responsible for *his* death. So Dwight's reasoning was sound and she rose and began preparing a bucket, soap, and a large, yellow sponge.

Dwight Chase felt like he was in a nightmare. He was having trouble accepting that this was actually happening to him. When he showered and prepared himself for work this morning, he never imagined in a million years that he would have been found out by Sara Rose, shot himself, kidnapped Sara Rose, kidnapped two old people, and was now lying in a two bit motel, possibly dying. He was in way over his head. He needed help from someone he could trust. Someone who knew how to handle these things. He fumbled for his cell phone and tried once again to reach Sam, aka Luke Bonnais. He was sure, as with all the other attempts, that he would fail.

So imagine his surprise when he heard the call go through and he was greeted with a gruff, "Hello."

Hope washed through the exhausted body of Dwight Chase. "Sam!" he yelled eagerly. "Am I glad to hear you!"

So further imagine Dwight's chagrin when a voice that he didn't recognize, a voice that definitely didn't belong to Sam, a very official sounding voice, asked, "Who is this?"

CHAPTER
13

John and Frank entered the Sheriff's department and walked directly to Frank's office. John sat down as Frank closed the door. He called the lab and told them to send a man to his office for some evidence. He made another call and made arrangements for a lab technician to come in and analyze the dirt John had collected, *immediately*. Frank made it clear that he didn't care that the guy was probably at home relaxing after a hard day at the lab. He wanted the dirt analyzed... like yesterday!

He hung up the phone and looked at John. "I think it's time we spring Nick. They know that we're on to them and I don't see any advantage in keeping him in any longer."

"I agree. We have to act fast, before all the rats can scurry back into their holes. Nick might be able to help us, though I'm not sure how fast he can get his privileges back," John returned.

Frank rolled his eyes. "Really. Especially since the city council has to approve it and we already know that two of them will vote against it, though I suspect that those two will be no shows. I'm gonna call a couple of my guys in here to get started on a search warrant for the Judge's place. Then I'm gonna call the State's Attorney and tell him what we have. I don't see any reason why he shouldn't drop all the charges against Nick. In the mean time, why don't you call Nick's attorney so that he can get started on the process for getting Nick released on his end."

"Sounds good to me," John replied. "I've got a feeling this is going to be a long night." Frank grunted an agreement and picked up the phone. Before he could even start dialing, the door to his office burst open and two detectives rushed in. John recognized one of them as being a City detective. They both looked at one another in obvious surprise that the other was present.

"Frank!" said the County detective, with a note of urgency. "We just got a hit on Sara Rose's credit card. She got gas a little over an hour ago at a gas station up in '*Hicksville*.'"

"Did you call the place?" Frank asked.

"Yeah, we did. Some old man answered the phone. He said he remembered her stopping in, but couldn't tell us much else other than the fact that she wrote something on the back of the credit card slip."

"What did she write?" John broke in.

The County detective smiled from ear to ear as he looked at his notes. "She wrote, '*Help me. I am being kidnapped by Dwight Chase. I think he shot himself in the foot. We are heading north in his car.*'"

"Holy shit!" Frank exclaimed. "Why didn't he call us immediately?"

"Because he lost his glasses and couldn't read it. By the time he found them, he had forgotten about it until we called," said the County detective.

"Did he see Chase?" John queried.

"No, all he saw was a car and he could barely see that. He's apparently blind as a bat without his glasses. All he could tell us was that it was some foreign job and it was brown, the same color as Chase's."

"Get up there right away," Frank ordered. "Before you go, call up the state and get a chopper in the air. Also get it out on the police bands." He looked at the City detective. "Can your department contact all the news channels and get it out on the air?" The man nodded. "Then get going, both of you."

When they left, Frank looked at John. "We may be over-playing our hand a bit. But I for one don't want to take any chances with Sara's life. If we lose some of these scum-bags because we're alerting the entire world that we know what's going on, so be it."

John nodded in agreement. "Like I said, it's going to be a long night. Now let's get going with those phone calls."

It was 4 A.M. and a lot had been accomplished since John and Frank had first arrived at the Sheriff's office. The dirt John had collected had come back as a match with the dirt found on Sally Walton. Chemical analysis revealed similarities too great to ignore, as well as physical characteristics. Detectives had drawn up a search warrant for Judge Walton's property, including the gazebo and they were currently rousing the duty judge out of bed to sign it. A force of street cops, detectives, and crime scene people were being assembled to serve the warrant as soon as it was ready. They wanted to act fast, before news of this got out.

Another judge had been roused as well and Nick had been released. They had briefly considered calling for a middle of the night, emergency meeting of the City Council to get Nick reinstated. But because of the probable fact that two of their members had been compromised, it was decided to hold off until after the search warrant was served.

They used the information garnered by Sue to delve deeper into the backgrounds of Lily Barrett and Bob Stark, the two council members with aliases and a lot of money. They managed to turn up enough information that the State's Attorney felt they had enough for a warrant to tap their phones. They were now under twenty-four hour surveillance as well.

Search warrants for the home of David Walton were also being drawn up. A contingent of deputies had been assigned to keep tabs on David and his house. Frank and John didn't plan on serving the warrant right away because they were also obtaining a warrant for eavesdropping devices on his home. They knew it wouldn't take David long to find out they were searching his father's estate and they wanted to see who he talked to and what he had to say about it. Then they would serve the warrant on his house.

The Sheriff's resources were stretched to the limit. There

wasn't a single detective that was home sleeping at the moment and a good portion of the patrol division were in the mix. In fact, Frank had enlisted the aid of the State police as well. They were also using a couple of detectives from the city, but there was still the trust issue, so it was decided that the city cops would play only a limited part. Even for those who had been thoroughly vetted, there was the thorny issue of appearances. No matter what part they played, some would say that they were biased and trying to cover up malfeasance in their department.

At this point the throttles had been pushed fully forward in a race to uncover as much information as they could before Coeptus Guild had time to counter. The Sheriff himself was in his office, monitoring the progress. The ramifications of this investigation were clear. The case was huge and it involved a lot of high profile people and he understood that the public, the voting public, would be watching him and his department closely. His future as Sheriff hung in the balance on this one, and he knew it.

Frank and John were sitting silently in Frank's office. There was a lull in the action and both were currently engrossed in their own thoughts. The stillness of the early morning hour was suddenly broken by the loud, penetrating ring of John's secure cell phone. Frank had held onto it after getting it from John at the hospital. The phone was laying on Frank's desk. He picked it up and flipped it open.

"Sergeant Carlotta," Frank answered.

"Yeah Frank, it's me." It was Stuart Carlotta, Frank's brother.

"What'd ya get for me, Stu?"

"I'm still not sure who was running her, but she was definitely a Fed, almost certainly CIA."

"CIA?" said Frank with surprise. "Why do you think that? Why would they want an agent married to a judge?"

"In answer your first question, I'm thinking CIA because I'm not getting anything officially here other than the fact that she started through Quantico a few years ago. She never finished. I called in a couple of markers and found that the reason she didn't finish Quantico was because she was pulled and sent to Camp Peary, That and she has a really great Legend, better than we would normally do."

Frank grunted in acknowledgment. Quantico was the FBI's training center in Virginia. That showed Sally had clear roots to a Federal level. Even more impressive was the fact that she went to Camp Peary, otherwise known as the "Farm." It was the CIA's equivalent to Quantico, but with a different curriculum. The Farm turned out covert agents, trained in everything from stealing secrets to propaganda techniques. Lock picking, photography, evasive driving, bomb making, gathering information at parties, everything a good spy would want to know.

Sally's Legend was another matter. A "*Legend*" was spook speak for an assumed identity. It meant that an entire life's history would be made up and it would have to stand the scrutiny of some very intelligent people. A good Legend could take two years or more to produce. Frank didn't know what Sally Walton, or whatever her name really was, had been involved in, but the government had spent a lot of time and a lot money on her. Now she was nothing more than a bag of bones in the morgue. To put it mildly, somebody was probably very pissed. A lot of money had been spent training those "bones."

"I don't suppose you know who she was watching, what her assignment was?" Frank asked.

"I don't know who, exactly, but I know what her assignment was."

"Well? Come on Stu, cough it up. I know you like to keep me dangling with all your important FBI stuff, but I'm tired and we need to get moving." The strain and exhaustion in Frank's voice was plain.

Stu retorted, *"Sorry Frank.* I really didn't mean to upset you. I'm tired too, you know. I've been working hard on this and I've managed to find out quite a lot of information that I'm really not suppose to know. We're supposed have this new found brotherhood since 9/11, sharing information and all. But for the most part, I don't see it. It's four in the morning, my ass is on a bit of a limb here, so cut me some slack."

"Sorry too, Stu." Frank hesitated, then questioned, "Well?"

Stu sighed. "Sally's real name was Paula Dale. Coeptus Guild grabbed her brother some years back and things didn't go so well. They blew him and his kids to smithereens with a car bomb. The kids were probably a mistake. His wife was running late, as was he and she asked him to drop them off at school. The bomb was set on a timer. Normally, her brother would have been well off to work, alone, at the time of the explosion."

Frank whistled. "I think I see where this is going."

"You think right." Stu continued. "It turns out that her brother had been confiding in her about what was going on all along. She didn't know the name, Coeptus Guild, but she knew what they were all about and more importantly, she was the one who advised him not to play along. After the explosion, she went straight to the police with what she knew. They looked into it and guess what? As usual with these guys, the cops didn't find a trace of anything. She screamed at anyone who would listen, including us, but unfortunately, we didn't do much better and we pretty much wrote her off as a nut job. Then we started to get in more cases eerily similar to her brother's. We eventually sent a couple of agents out to talk to her. They came back saying that not only was she not a nut job, but that she wanted to help in any way she could. One of the agents was nearing retirement and had seen a lot of cold war action. He knew what a properly motivated person could accomplish and he decided Paula Dale was properly motivated. We looked into her further and found that she was a pretty smart cookie to boot. You fill in the rest."

"The oldest trick in the book, a honey pot." Frank answered. A "*Honey pot*" was a female agent that was willing to go to any length, even use her feminine charms, to get her mark to do or say whatever she wanted. "But why the Judge?"

"Think about it," Stu responded. "If this is the CIA's operation, they must think there are international links. After all, what do we have in this area to warrant such attention?

Whatever is going on, it must be substantial for them to have devoted such resources. It looks as though there are four main players in the area, the two council persons, William Ramsey and David Walton. All of them are married. With that line of thinking, if they were trying to get to David Walton, they had to place her close. That meant she either had to replace his current wife or the next best thing. The Judge was single and about as close as you can get without actually living in the house. With her married to the Judge, she had access to David, which meant that since he was David's best friend, she had access to Ramsey. In addition to that, the council members were all invited to the Judge's lavish parties. I'm sure Paula saw to that. If you think about it, it was near perfect placement."

Frank was silent a moment. "All this was going on and you didn't know anything about it?" he asked in obvious disbelief.

"No Frank, I didn't," said an exasperated Stu. "They told me what I originally told you, that they wanted us to stay very low key and not have any overt involvement in your area. It was felt that the alarms for Coeptus Guild would remain silent if we worked through a few reliable locals instead. They trusted you because you are my brother and they had thoroughly checked you out. When Paula turned up dead, they agreed to let you bring John Harvard into the mix as well. You know *somebody* here *must* have known what was going on. But I swear Frank, they didn't tell me about it."

"Okay Stu, I believe you, let's move on." With that,

Frank filled his brother in on everything they were doing. He ended by asking Stuart to look into the background of the two council members. The F.B.I. is stellar in such matters.

"Sure. It looks as though you have everything else covered. We should be able to look in to it without undue notice, though at this point I think the time for being stealthy is well and truly over."

"Thanks," Frank said. "Also, can you keep on looking into Sally's assignment? As you say, I don't see any advantage in trying to keep it quiet any longer. Speed is what's important now. The rats are running for their holes right about now, or soon will be. We have to snatch them up before they're gone and it's a lot easier to hunt if you know who your quarry is."

At that moment, Frank's office phone rang. "Hold on Stu. My other line's ringing." He put the secure cell phone down on his desk and answered the ringing phone.

"Carlotta."

It was the detective who had been in his office earlier and was leading the search for Sara Rose. "Frank, one of the State choppers found Chase's car. It's parked right outside the office of a small motel up north."

The tiredness was suddenly gone as Frank spoke again. "That's great! Okay, listen, you're going to have to handle this thing. I'm too involved in other stuff right now. Call the news stations and tell them to sit on it until we get Sara back. You tell those State guys to back off. Monitor it so they'll know if Chase tries to leave. But I don't want him to know he's been found. Assemble a team and get S.W.A.T. up there as soon as possible. Notify the locals but tell them we'd like to take the lead on this. Oh, and by the way, I want Chase very much alive, if possible. There's no telling what information we can get from him on this mess."

"I got it Frank. We're on our way up there now."

"Good. Notify State first and get going with your other plans. I gotta go now. Bye." He hung up and looked at John as he picked up the cell phone again. "In case you couldn't tell, they found Sara."

"I figured." John said. "It looks as though things are finally starting to pop."

Dwight Chase's head was about to split wide open from the pressure of his brain against his cranium. At least that's what if felt like to him. There was a solid line of pain starting at the hole in his foot and leading straight upward through his entire body, through his skull and out into space, as though he had been skewered like a pig on a roast.

It was making it difficult to think clearly. Everyone else in the room realized this as well. He was still lying on the sofa. The old couple were quietly clutching each other on a nearby love seat. Sara was sitting on a chair staring at the television. Dwight had insisted that it be turned on. He wanted to see what the news stations had to say about Sara's abduction and to get a clue as to where the cops were in the process of finding them.

There was nothing. Absolutely nothing. The only news they could find had to do with the fatal accident in town. Dwight was shocked to see the mangled wreckage of Sam/ Luke Bonnais's Explorer. He didn't know for sure that it was Sam's truck, but the location and the fact that Carlotta's car had been involved, was just too great of a coincidence to ignore. Now he knew why Sam hadn't contacted him. With that knowledge came the horrifying realization that he truly was now on his own.

It appeared as though the fact that Sara was missing had been overlooked by everyone because of the gruesome accident that had caused so many deaths. But Dwight knew that wouldn't last long. He knew that Sara was single and he figured there was a good chance that her abduction wouldn't be noticed until tomorrow morning, when both he and Sara failed to show. He had until then to come up with a plan. He had to think! But he couldn't. The pain engulfed him like a smothering sack.

Unlike Dwight, Sara's brain was the antithesis of his and was thinking quite clearly. Though feigning nonchalance, she was watching him very closely, looking for a chance to overtake him. He always held his gun in his right hand and was never afraid to point it at anyone. She assumed, a little bit incorrectly, that meant he wouldn't hesitate to use it. Sara also knew that Dwight was in bad shape. She couldn't believe he had lasted this long. She had felt certain that he was about to fall asleep while watching the news. But he had become abruptly alert and agitated when they began showing close ups of the mangled vehicles from the accident at the bar. Upon seeing them, he suddenly sat up and leaned forward. His already ashen face turned even paler as he watched. Sara turned her attention back to the television and studied the footage as she carefully listened to what was being said, trying to determine what it was that upset Dwight so much.

"Dwight," she said, looking back at him, "do you know somebody in that accident?"

He returned to his previous prone position and muttered, "Just shut the fuck up!"

He laid there for some time, staring at the ceiling. Eventually, his head rolled away from the television and remained still for some time. His head didn't move for what seemed like hours. Asleep? She wasn't sure, but she thought it likely. If only she could get close enough to snatch the gun from his hand, this would be over. She slowly rose to her feet. Nothing. She slowly stepped forward, stealing a glance at the old couple. They said nothing but were watching her intently.

Another step, still nothing. Sara couldn't see them, but the old couple suddenly came to life, frantically waving their arms in a vain attempt to get her attention. The old man quietly jumped up and this Sara noticed as she was stepping forward once again.

She turned her head in the direction of the elderly innkeeper and saw that he was pointing downward in her direction, alternately showing his open hand in a "stop" motion. She finally understood that for some reason, he wanted her to halt her next step, but it was too late as she was already far too committed and could not pull back. She stepped down and was rewarded with what seemed like the loudest *"creak"* of protesting wood and nails that she'd ever heard in her life.

Dwight instantly rose up to a sitting position and she watched in horror as his gun rose up. To her, the hole in the barrel of the gun seemed big enough to stick her head in. A deafening roar and a blinding light filled the room. The sharp smell of cordite assailed her nostrils. She heard the television suddenly explode behind her and an instant later, she realized that to her relief and amazement, the bullet had missed her.

Dwight screamed. "What the fuck are you doing?" The gun waved about wildly, as if searching for a target on its own but thankfully, did not fire again. "What the fuck are you doing?" he reiterated.

Only then did he notice that the old man was also standing. Reflexively, without thinking about it, he snapped another shot off in the direction of the man and his wife. Shattering glass announced that this bullet had also missed its mark and had passed destructively, though harmlessly, through a window and into the night air.

Everyone froze while Dwight attempted to rise to a standing position. He succeeded only briefly, before falling back with a loud, "Ahhh! My god! Fuck, that hurts!" In pain, his head had briefly turned away as he struggled to get control of the pain. He looked back at Sara. "Sit the fuck down, now!" he ordered firmly. He looked at the old man. "You too." he said in a quieter, but no less menacing tone.

No one knew if Dwight had missed his targets intentionally or not. No one was anxious to find out. Truth be told, Dwight didn't know either. There had been no thought or intent, other than getting control of the situation, behind either of the shots.

Dwight couldn't help himself, his screams turned to a quieter, but incessant moaning. After some time of watching this, the old woman spoke in a soft, motherly tone. "Young man, you need to take something for that pain. I can see it's driving you crazy. Why don't you let me get you some aspirin or something?"

Dwight looked at her with suspicious eyes. He wasn't sure if she was sincere or not, but the thought of some aspirin was enticing. Why hadn't he thought of that before? "Alright," he agreed. "But be quick about it. And if I even *think* you're pulling something, you'll never see your husband alive again. Got it?"

She nodded and rose. She quietly walked out of the room to the adjoining kitchen. Her hands were shaking as she opened the cupboard containing the aspirin and other various cold remedies. She found the aspirin immediately and placed it on the counter. Then she continued to rummage through the cabinet until she found what she was looking for. Her husband's over the counter allergy medicine. Her eyes went to the warnings printed on the label. "Marked drowsiness may occur. Avoid alcoholic drinks. Alcohol may increase drowsiness. Do not use when driving a motor vehicle or operating heavy machinery."

She and her husband had often joked that a couple of

these capsules and it was good night, no matter the time of day. She poured a small glass of water. Her hands shook as she opened several capsules and dropped the powder in. She wondered if they were enough. She opened four more and dropped them in, hoping that there would be no after taste that the young man would detect.

"Hurry up in there, granny!" Dwight shouted.

"I'm coming," she shouted back as she silently removed a spoon from the drawer and stirred in the contents of the drink. She put the spoon in the sink, picked up the glass and the aspirin and returned to the room. "Here," she said as she handed him the glass and the aspirin. He didn't take them.

"Put them on the arm," he said, motioning to the arm of the sofa. "Then go back over and sit next to your husband."

She did as she was told. She breathlessly watched as Dwight put the gun down and picked up the aspirin and glass. She thought her heart would stop as he took his first drink. He didn't seem to notice anything awry. He downed the second pill, drinking the entire glass as he did so. The cool water felt good to him. He leaned over and put the empty glass on the floor. "Thanks," he said begrudgingly.

"That's okay," the old woman said pleasantly. "You know, my Papa was an army medic and he once told me that one of the best pain relievers was a good old shot of whiskey. Would you like some?"

Dwight eyed her suspiciously. "What, are you trying to get me drunk or something?"

"Oh no. I wouldn't do that. Drunk people make bad decisions and I certainly don't want you to make any bad decisions. I don't think that would be in our best interest. Do you?" she asked rhetorically. "I just don't believe you would be so excitable if you weren't in such pain."

Dwight thought about the logic of that for a moment. It made sense and he so wanted this pain to go away, or at least subside. He nodded his head. "Okay, but only a couple."

The woman rose again. "What would you like? We have some scotch, bourbon, and rum. We may even have some tequila."

Dwight wasn't a big consumer of hard liquor, though he had heard that scotch had a calming effect. "Scotch," he said simply.

The old woman walked over to the liquor cabinet and removed a bottle of twelve year old scotch. She grabbed a shot glass and walked over to Dwight. She filled the glass and handed to him. "I don't know how much experience you have with this, but it's best if you just down it, unless you're one of those people who truly love the taste."

Dwight took the glass and after a moment's hesitation, quickly lifted it to his mouth and emptied it. The golden liquid burned and he could feel it, like a fiery stream of molten lava as it worked its way to his stomach. Normally, he didn't think he would like the taste or the sensation. But under his present circumstances, it felt good. It temporarily overrode the pain from his wound and seemed to peel away the numbness he felt in his head. He handed the glass back to her. "One more," he said. "Then I'm done."

She smiled as she poured another. "Here you go young

man, drink up. I'm sure you'll feel much better shortly."

He took the glass and downed it in much the same manner as the first one. He handed the glass back to her. "Thanks again. Now go back over there by your husband."

She took the glass and went back to the love seat. She sat down and patiently waited for the booze and pills to have their effect. An hour later, Dwight had not moved for some time. She decided to test him. "Young man," she said. He did not stir. "Young man!" she shouted. There was still no response. The hotel phone rang and she stood up. She looked over at Sara and said. "I believe you can safely remove his gun now sweetie." Then she walked over and answered the phone.

"Overlook Hotel," she said calmly.

"Ma'am, this is Detective Cheruba from the Sheriff's Department. Please don't show any response to this call. We know that there is a man with a gun in there. We have your hotel surrounded, but we need to know if everyone is alright and what the situation is. If everyone is okay, nod your head and tell me that you have no vacancies. If everything is not okay, ask me what date we will be arriving."

The old woman smiled. "Well as you can plainly see Detective, we have plenty of vacancies and please, feel free to come right in." A shocked Deputy listened as she continued. "The man you're looking for is taking a nap right now and I really don't think you will have a problem with him." She looked over at Dwight and saw Sara removing the weapon from Dwight's unresisting fingers. "As a matter of fact, the woman he was with just relieved him of his pistol, so unless he can wake up and shoot you with his fingers, you have nothing to worry about."

Frank placed the phone back on the cradle and looked at John it disbelief. "I don't believe it. What a fuck up. Our guys just went in to the hotel and got Chase." He began laughing.

"Is he alive? How's Rose?" John asked, wondering what was so funny.

"Oh, he's alive." Frank replied, still laughing. "Sleeping like a baby, but alive. In fact, everybody's just fine, including Rose. The asshole shot himself in the foot just before he nabbed her. They headed up to that hotel where we found them and took the owners, an older couple, as hostages. There he is, with all these hostages and apparently not a clue as to what to do next. He's in pain. So what does the old lady do? She offers him some aspirin with a glass of water, but not before loading the water up with some allergy drugs to put the asshole to sleep. She follows that up by convincing Chase that a couple of shots of scotch would also help."

John shook his head, smiled, but didn't laugh. "It never ceases to amaze me how just plain stupid some of these guys are, just no common sense. Here's a guy who's probably brighter than you and me put together, and this is the best he can do."

"Go figure. Sucks to be him." Frank looked at his watch. "We've got all our warrants and our guys are assembled and ready to go. I think it's time we get moving." Why don't you head over to David Walton's house. I'm going to your house to get the other secured phone from Sue. Then I'll head on over to the Judge's house to monitor the crime scene guys. Why don't we meet up there? Oh, and can you drop me off at the maintenance area? I've got to pick up something to drive."

They walked out together and John drove to the county garages where Frank picked up a spare unmarked car. Frank then headed for John's house to pick up the other secure phone while John headed for David Walton's home. He arrived in the area and located the jump off point where all the squads were collecting prior to serving the warrant. Several of the Deputies were standing in a group, talking. As John pulled up, one of the older men, with whom John had worked with in the past, walked over to him.

"Hey Bill," John said as the man approached his open window.

"Hi John," Bill replied with a smile and leaned down to put his elbow on the door. "Frank said you'd be working with us on this. Good to see you."

"Good to see you, too. Are you in charge of this group?"

"Yeah, I guess. Frank's gonna head up the one at the Judge's house. As usual, he gets the good stuff and I get the little shit." Bill shook his head good-naturedly. "You two certainly dug up some crap on this one. Ya know, you guys really make an ideal couple. You're both really good at sticking your noses into places where you're not wanted. First you get all shot up. Then some asshole tries to run Frank over. You guys ever think of retiring?"

John snickered. "Naw. What would you have to do if we weren't around stirring up trouble?"

"*Humph*," came Bill's reply. "Maybe *I* could retire, if I knew I wasn't gonna have to be around to clean up after *you*."

At that moment, Bill's radio crackled and he answered it. John could hear the Deputy on the other end. "*Subject just left his house, heading eastbound. Do you want us to stop him?*"

John wondered what the hell was David Walton doing leaving the house at this hour. John interjected before Bill could reply. "No! I'll follow him. I want to see where he's going."

"You want backup?" Bill asked.

"No. I'll handle it. Your cell number still the same?" John saw his chance at another *interview* and didn't want anyone else around.

"Okay," Bill responded. "Let me know if you need any help and yeah, my number is the same. You'd better get going."

John threw his SUV in gear and squealed out of the parking lot. He soon located Walton's car and began following. It appeared that David was alone and it soon became apparent that he was heading for his father's house. John dialed Bill's number. "Bill, this is John," he said when Bill answered.

"In trouble already?" Bill asked.

"Funny. Listen, I think he's heading for his Dad's house. Can you call the crew over there and tell them to hold off on that Warrant? I need to talk to this guy first, alone and before he knows that his whole world is about to come crashing in."

"Sure, can I go ahead with this one?"

"Give me about fifteen minutes. I just don't want his wife calling him either before our little chat," John responded.

"You got it."

"Thanks," said John and hung up. A few minutes later he watched as Walton drove through the open gate at the Judge's house. John doused his lights and followed. Walton proceeded up the driveway but instead of heading for the main house, he turned and drove in the direction of the gazebo. '*How appropriate,*' John thought. His pulse quickened as he closed the distance to his quarry.

He watched as Walton stopped in front of the building and got out. John half expected him to walk over to the Plum tree, returning to the scene of the crime as it were. Instead, the man walked off to the dock and sat down, staring out over the water as though waiting for someone to arrive.

Though the ever increasing morning light was probably sufficient to cover his brake lights, John used his emergency brake so the bright braking lights would not come on. He stopped his vehicle and quietly got out. He looked for movement in and around the main house and saw none. No lights were on that John could see. That was good. It meant that he would have some *alone* time with David.

Walton seemed not to notice John's approach and jumped up with a totally startled reaction as John said quietly, "We finally have a chance to talk." Walton recovered quickly as his hand dropped to his waistband.

In a reaction honed through years of experience and practice, John's Walther PPK pistol was pointed directly toward Walton's head in the blink of an eye. "Freeze!" barked John. Walton's face was an interesting mixture of emotions. In a heartbeat, John had seen it go from the pure shock of John's unannounced presence, to one of pure disgust, with a slight hint of anger and finally, upon seeing the Walther, to one of pure horror. The ending result was a fascinating combination of all of them. In other circumstances, John would have found the face comical. Now, he did not. He quickly looked down at Walton's waistband and saw the butt of a semiautomatic pistol.

"What are you doing here?" Walton hissed. "This is private property. You have no right to be here. I'm gonna have your ass for this." Walton's face was beginning to settle on anger. Like John, his public service had caused him to be around guns and criminals most of his adult life. John's Walther had caused only a temporary scare.

"Really? I don't think you're in a position to make any demands," John stated. The cold, unreasoning anger was bubbling to the surface. The demon within was clawing to get out once more. This was one of the men responsible for *her* death. *He* was part of the group that had framed Nick. *He* was the one helping to provide the minions the Coeptus Guild used for their purposes. Sick, perverted individuals like Billyray Jenkins and Luke Bonnais, who had no moral compass and no compunction about doing whatever it took to get what they wanted or felt they needed.

"You have no right to be here, Harvard. It's trespassing and furthermore, you're pointing your gun at a prison psychiatrist. That ought to get you some serious time behind bars." He began the sentence boldly. But he noticed that as he continued to talk, a look overcame the man holding the gun pointed at his head that didn't seem to be of this world.

It was the same look his friend, William Ramsey, had seen in the bathroom. It was cold. And as he talked, David Walton became what he should have been all along—afraid, very afraid. As he finished his last sentence, the anger left him like the wind suddenly gone from a becalmed sail, listless and flopping about, with no current purpose.

"I think that you should tell me why you killed your father's wife," John said harshly. Confusion now played across Walton's face.

"Wha... What are you talking about? Sally? Why would I kill Sally?"

John studied Walton carefully. He truly seemed surprised at John's accusation. On the other hand, the man was a trained criminal psychiatrist. If anyone would know how to fool an interrogator, it would be him. "Because she was a Fed! She was on to you and your group and you had to silence her. So were you there when Ramsey shot her? Did you two rape her first so that you could finally get what you wanted from her?"

"What are you talking about? Giovanni killed her. It was all over the news. They found a bullet from his gun near her body."

The man was good, John had to give him that. "That's bullshit!" he shouted. "You know that Nick was framed. Well guess what? We know it, too. We found the phone records were doctored at our office. She and the Chief never talked. Furthermore, we also know she wasn't shot in the field. She was shot right over there," without taking his eyes from Walton, he motioned with his head toward the gazebo. "Furthermore, we know that she was buried under that

Plum tree next to the building. Handy place to store a body until springtime, huh?"

David Walton was clearly taken aback and for the first time, John began to doubt his conviction that David had anything to do with it. But it all made perfect sense. Walton used his position as psychiatrist to get the people out that he wanted. He was best friends with the Ramsey's, known Guild members. And, last, but certainly not least, Ramsey told John that it was... *Walton*?

A thought began to creep into his head as David Walton spoke. Walton's head was looking downward and he looked as though he were remembering something. "You say she was shot in the gazebo last spring?"

He looked at John as John nodded in affirmation, only now putting the final pieces of the puzzle together. He lowered his gun. Walton's face suddenly turned to alarm once again. John was confused. He no longer had his gun pointed at him, why...

John's internal warning alarm suddenly blared at full volume and he began to spin, just as something cracked his head and blinding lights tore through his retinas. He fell to the ground, barely able to hold on to his gun. A figure was standing near him. John desperately tried to focus as his gun was suddenly kicked from his grasp.

"You know, I just knew I should have had you done away with a long time ago. My mistake. As punishment, I believe it's only proper now that I personally take care of the situation. So I guess, Mr. Harvard, that I will have to kill you myself," said the voice of Judge Raymond P. Walton... the Third, no less.

CHAPTER

14

John's muddled brain tried to make sense of the current situation. He was confused. William Ramsey had told John that it was Walton. In a flash of realization, he understood as the pieces began to fall into place. Ramsey had always referred to his handler as "*Walton*." John had committed a cardinal sin for investigators. He had allowed his preconceived notions of the case to cloud his judgment and drop the name "Walton" into his mental slot reserved for *David* Walton, not *Judge* Walton. This changed everything. He now understood William Ramsey's sudden mood swing in their last conversation, from fear to almost cockiness. Ramsey had realized John's mistake and knew what the consequences would mean for John. He had taken that little victory with him to the grave.

"Dad?" John heard as he tried to focus in on the Judge's form. David too was slowly getting a picture. "Dad? It was you? You killed her? But why?"

"Oh you poor, poor, well meaning boy." The Judge's head shook from side to side in silent denial of what he perceived to be his simpleton son. "She was a cop. I don't know how much she'd discovered, but she'd managed to turn that fucking cockroach Wallis Jester. She was using what she learned from Jester to try and turn Deputy Chief Ramsey. Right there in that Gazebo. She was desperate enough to even allude to promises of a carnal nature, if you know what I mean. She wanted him to turn very badly. I think she thought that would have been the last piece she needed to come after me."

He laughed. "If she'd had a little more patience, it just may have worked. Ramsey always was more than a little smitten with her." He looked his son straight in the eyes. "As, I believe, were you. In any event, she got Ramsey to come out here and it didn't take him long to figure out what was up. He called me down here and I watched as he worked her over in an attempt to get her to spill everything. I'll give her credit, she didn't budge an inch. The old name, rank, and serial number game. In the end, I told him to go ahead and have at her. He couldn't get her clothes off fast enough and by that time she was too weak to put up much resistance. He spent some time with her, used her in every way possible, which I thought was very fitting and proper. When he was done, I put a bullet into her fucking head. Felt good. I went back up to the house and slept like a baby while Ramsey buried her. It was getting too close to daylight to transport her and Ramsey had to get up north to clean up," he gestured toward John, "that other mess. So I thought she would do just fine until we had the time to move her. You wouldn't understand. Your friend Bill did.

He was strong," he looked at his son in disgust, "not like you."

John's vision was rapidly getting better. He'd heard everything, but he continued to let his head flop around like fish out of water. He didn't want the Judge to know he was regaining his senses. As he was writhing in apparent pain and disorientation on the ground, John turned away from the Judge. Using the conversation between the two Waltons as a distraction, he removed his phone from his pocket, quickly dialed Franks department cell phone and pushed the send button and waited until he heard Frank's, "Hello." on the other end. He then stuck the phone in his shirt to conceal it. He prayed that Frank could hear them and would be able to understand what was going on. Through his partially open eyelids, John saw anguish and confusion in David's eyes.

"But, but, I *don't* understand."

"And I doubt you ever will. Now be quiet, boy, I have some matters to attend to." He looked down at John. "Can you hear me Harvard?" John slowly nodded. "Good, because you have caused me and my friends considerable trouble. Now I'm going to have to take some drastic steps that will, in the end, cause me great pain. I want you to have a little pain as well."

He looked over at his son. "Dave, please be so kind as to hand me your gun."

"What? Why do you need my gun?"

"Because, my dear boy, I'm a little nervous with all these guns laying about and Mr. Harvard here is an expert at getting his hands on them and that usually doesn't bode well for people he perceives as being, *bad.*"

"But Dad, I'm…"

"David!" the Judge said sternly in a slightly raised tone that many a father has used with their children when they aren't acting accordingly. David quietly handed him his weapon.

The Judge now retrieved his own cell phone and dialed a number. A moment later, he spoke into the phone. "Go ahead. Both of them. Let me know when it's done." He listened as the recipient of the call apparently spoke. Then the Judge said, "Well then, take her out first. Then hoof it on down there and take out the kid. She shouldn't present too much of a problem." He then terminated the connection and looked at John.

"That was a little surprise I have planned for you." He looked at John's confused face and grinned. "I've had a sniper watching your property for a few days now. I had planned on using him, if I needed to, to send a message for you to back off. But unfortunately, for all of us really, I misjudged you and things have progressed much too far. The horse, so to speak, has already left the barn. No sense closing the doors now, eh?"

John began to sit up, suddenly remembering his jog… yesterday? Was it only yesterday? He remembered the spot where he had thought some animal had been laying. That spot, he suddenly realized, would have had a perfect view of his property! He couldn't get there in time. But… "So you're going to have the sniper kill an innocent woman and a child?" he said loudly. "What, from that view on the ridge on the Northwest portion of the lake? Your sniper left a fairly clear trail leading right up to the log he's using as cover." He prayed Frank was getting all this.

The Judge's body suddenly went tense as he saw John's attempt to rise up to a sitting position and he took aim at John's head. "Stay down Mr. Harvard or I will shoot you now."

"As opposed to what? Later? At your convenience? In case you haven't figured it out. There are a boat load of cops just down the street, just waiting to bust in here. They'll hear the shot and then it's all over for you. You're definitely going down and the only thing killing me will accomplish is to get you the death penalty."

"And when they get here," said the Judge, smiling, "I'm going to tell them the tragic tale of how I was forced to kill you." Sticking David's gun in his waistband, the Judge bent over and picked up John's Walther PPK. "You see, Mr. Harvard, I happened to come down to the gazebo this morning to smoke a cigar and take in the sunrise, which happens to be true. I saw you pursue David up here and you got very angry with him. The next thing I know, you pulled a gun on him. As a matter of fact," Judge Walton exchanged the gun in his right hand for John's gun. "You shot him."

With that Judge Walton put two .380 caliber slugs into his son's chest. As David fell wordlessly to the dock, the Judge turned back to Harvard, not even seeing the body hit the ground. He continued talking in a slow, calm manner, as if nothing untoward had just happened. "Unfortunately, I got here a little too late. But then, you saw me and tried to take me out as well, I think I may have startled you. After all, everybody knows how trigger happy you are. Unfortunately, I had to defend myself. So you see, I must shoot you now, so the timing of the shots the cops hear will coincide with my story, you understand."

Judge Walton quickly moved his own gun back to his right hand and raised it to fire. But the man he'd assumed had been knocked senseless, was suddenly moving with the quickness of a Cobra. Too late, he finally understood why John Livingston Harvard was such a dangerous man. In the time it took him to switch guns, John quickly started to raise his prone body from the ground. John realized that he didn't have time to get up entirely so he used his momentum to propel him far enough forward to deliver a kick to the Judge's groin.

The kick only partially hit its mark, but it was enough to bend him over and make him stagger backward. John used this advantage to grab the Judges right hand with both of his. Quickly pressing his thumbs to the knuckles of the Judge's right hand, he then twisted the hand back and to the side, causing a great deal of pain to the Judge's wrist. As the gun fell out of his hand, John heard bones snapping and knew that the Judge's wrist was broken.

Judge Walton fell to his knees in pain, screaming in agony. John reached into the Judge's pocket and retrieved the cell phone he'd used to call the sniper. John hit the redial button and handed it to Walton. "Now call off your dog."

The Judge struggled to compose himself. A moment later, he took the phone with his left hand and listened.

"Yeah, it's me." He looked straight into John's eyes as he said, "I don't think I'll be able to call you for a while, so I just wanted to make sure that you carry out your orders... no matter what."

With that, a smile, and a quickness that belied his age, the Judge terminated the connection and threw the phone into the lake. He started to say something but never got a chance to finish, John was on him like a cat, grabbing this head with both hands. He leaned over Walton and said, with a venom laden voice, "For that, I'm going to snap your neck like a fuckin' chicken." He started to quickly move his hands and arms in a movement that would indeed, efficiently perform that very action.

Suddenly, he heard the words from his dream, "*Show me that my life was a good trade for yours.*" He hesitated. What good would it do to kill the Judge now? He was no longer a danger and killing Walton would not stop the sniper. He thought of Mary Kate and Sue. He suddenly put their faces on the many gunshot victims from his own past, dozens and dozens of them, all with the face of Sue and his daughter. The countless bodies he had seen lying on the autopsy table, eyes sightless, naked, skin pale, cold... dead. There was only one reason to kill the Judge now, *revenge*, because he *wanted* to. He *wanted* to have the pleasure of hearing this man's neck snap and the sound of his last breath going out of him. This was it. This was judgment day. In spite of his dream, John could see no way he could control the urge to make this man pay. Gregory Harris had been right after all.

❖ ❖ ❖

Frank Carlotta answered his cell phone and froze. The voices he heard were muffled and difficult to hear. He pulled to the side of the road, shut off his engine and listened intently. He heard John's voice and two others, one of which sounded like Judge Walton. A chill went through his bones as he realized the Judge had just given the order to kill Mary Kate and Susan. Then, he heard John's voice quite clearly. *"So you're going to have the sniper kill an innocent woman and a child? What, from that view on the ridge on the Northwest portion of the lake? Your sniper left a fairly clear trail leading right up to the log he's using as cover."*

He knew instantly what John was doing. He also knew that he was the only chance Sue and Mary Kate had. Shortly after that, he heard the Judge explaining how he was going to murder John and get away with it. Then, two shots and the sounds of a scuffle. The phone went dead.

Frank quickly exchanged his cell phone for his radio microphone. He radioed his dispatcher and soon learned that John was at the Judge's house and that the deputies were waiting down the street for John's signal. *"Go! Go! Go!"* he screamed into the mic. "Get in there now!" Then he quickly informed the dispatcher what was going on and ordered squads to John's house. "Run lights and sirens until you get in the area, then douse them. Call the house and warn them."

He waited for what seemed like hours, but in reality was less than a minute. His heart sank when the radio room informed him that there was no answer. "Call the city and see if they can send some units too. I'm going to be on foot, so tell them to watch for me."

Frank analyzed his position. He was within a quarter mile of John's home when he had pulled over. He was roughly familiar with the terrain. As a patrolman, he used to roust teenaged lovers from the field that led to the woods overlooking the lake. He was at John's house for the first time just yesterday. While waiting for John to arrive home, he remembered scanning the lake and the surrounding hills. His years as a special forces sniper were so ingrained, that he couldn't help but pick out sniping positions. With John's description of the sniper's lair, Frank instantly remembered the position on the northwest side of the lake that John was talking about.

He threw his car into gear, doused his lights and accelerated to a small dirt path that he knew would lead him into the field and then into the woods. He did not dare take his vehicle further than the field because he didn't want the sniper to hear the sound. He drove as fast and as close as he dared before quickly braking to a halt and silently exiting his squad. He took off running in the direction of the lake, praying he was in time.

The sniper put his cell phone down for the last time and smiled. Finally he could do his job and get the hell out of here. It had gotten cold during the night and though the sniper had taken what he thought were proper precautions, he was freezing his ass off. The ground had acted like a huge heat sink, draining the warmth from his body. Little chills periodically ran through him.

He had seen the woman scurrying about the kitchen just before Judge Walton had called. Of course, he didn't know his handler's real name but it didn't matter. Like the recently departed Luke Bonnais, he knew only that the pay was good and that was all that mattered.

He picked up his Remington Model 700BDL rifle and peered through the Leupoid sight. The woman was no longer in the kitchen. The sniper knew Susan's habits however and knew she would return shortly. The sniper put the rifle down and waited. He took the time to collect his gear in preparation for a quick departure and thought about what was to come. He had planned on leaving the area fast. The one thing that worried him was that if he had to go down to the house to kill the little girl, that would set his carefully laid plans back a little.

He shrugged his shoulders. No sense thinking about it anymore. Billyray didn't do a lot of worrying. He usually thought ahead only enough to accomplish his goals. He knew the layout of the land, he knew his basic plans for escape, and he knew what he needed to accomplish. With any luck, the little girl would hear the commotion of the woman crashing to the floor and would come to investigate. That would solve his problem nicely.

He had just finished packing when he saw her come back into the room. He quickly picked up the rifle and soon found her in his sights. She was standing next to the sink, stirring a freshly poured cup of coffee. There was absolutely no wind.

He couldn't have asked for better conditions. He took a deep breath, then slowly let out half of it before bringing his breathing to a complete halt. He sighted in on Susan's forehead, just above the bridge of her nose and began to slowly squeeze the trigger. A split second later, the Winchester .300 magnum round was on its way and there was no force on earth that could stop it.

Frank was standing still, breathing heavily. He was looking at a motorcycle, covered with brush. It was yet another coincidence that was too great to ignore. He didn't want to waste any time, but on the other hand, he wanted to take away the sniper's main means of escape. Five seconds later, he'd disabled the bike and was racing toward the sniper's position.

He slowed as he realized he was getting near the hilltop. He was standing at the edge of a grove of trees. A field, approximately seventy-five yards across, stood before him and the stand of trees that stood like sentinels watching over the lake. John had said there was a trail leading to the sniper's roost. He looked around and soon found it. His trained eye followed it through the ever increasing light. It led like an arrow, straight to the sniper. The man had obviously been using the same path to get in and out of his position. Frank drew his weapon, but hesitated as he studied the terrain. Frank had his Glock nine millimeter, which was an effective weapon, up close. For combat purposes, he didn't like the current distance.

The sniper, on the other hand, had a rifle that was made for shooting at a distance. Its main drawback was that it wasn't good for close in fighting. Frank assumed the man probably had a sidearm, but it would take time to drop the rifle and bring his pistol into action. Frank's best option was to close the distance as quietly and rapidly as possible. He started forward. He abhorred the thought of crossing an open field, especially standing up. But time was of the essence. He was half way across before he was able to tell that the man was looking through his sights. The sniper's back was to him and the man obviously hadn't detected Frank's presence. But a split second later, a thunderous boom announced to all, that he was too late.

The big Remington bucked in his hands and he momentarily lost sight of his target. As Billyray reacquired the kitchen area, he breathed a sigh of relief. Another chill from the god damn cold had uncontrollably coursed through his body, just as the gun had gone off. But the area of the kitchen sink was clear and he could see Susan's crumpled body lying on the floor. Now if the little brat could show up, he could be out of here in a minute.

As if on cue, Mary Kate came running into the kitchen in a nightgown. She saw Susan lying on the floor amid copious amounts of blood. She froze, just stood there, screaming at the top of her lungs. Billyray was too far away to hear the screams, but he could see the reaction. He smiled and quickly focused in on the little girl's head.

Suddenly, seemingly out of thin air, he heard a very official voice behind him. "Police officer! Freeze!" Billyray couldn't believe it. Where the fuck had he come from? But Billyray had the survival instincts and reflexes of a ferret. Instead of turning to face his opponent as most people would have done under the circumstances, he grabbed the log in front of him and a second later, had slithered over it. He heard a thud, instantly followed by the sound of Frank's nine millimeter. The log shuddered beneath him. Billyray had an added advantage, the log he'd been behind was located at the very top of the hill and now the terrain itself afforded him added protection. He was safe, but only for a moment. He had to locate the cop and take him out.

He drew his gun, an Israeli made "Baby," Desert Eagle .45 semiautomatic, from his waistband and peered around one end of the log. Nothing. He listened. Nothing. Billyray didn't understand. Most cops would be yelling, noisily moving about and blazing away like John Wayne. He knew how cops reacted and it had always made them easy prey. He had killed a number of them. This man, however, was different. This man, was like a ghost.

The *ghost* was, at that moment, laying in a depression. He was listening for his opponent, as well. Though he'd wanted to be a little closer before he initiated a confrontation, he really thought he was close enough to have the sniper dead to rights. But upon hearing Frank's voice, the man had moved unbelievably fast, moving over that log quick as a rabbit. Frank had fired one shot in hopes of stopping him, but it had gone into the log right between the rapidly disappearing legs. He had seen enough to know that he had to be careful with this man or he would wind up dead.

He tried not to think of where the sniper's bullet had gone, who it was that was now most likely dead. Frank wanted to call in the troops, the need for stealth being at an end. But he realized that he couldn't do it without betraying his position. He peered over his depression, looking for any signs of the sniper. Nothing.

Frank called upon all his years of military sniping experience as he thought it out and listened for sounds of the man moving away. The sniper would, most likely, either shoot it out with him or head back to his means of escape, the motorcycle. The sniper had to know that whatever he did, his window of escape was closing fast. Frank's biggest problem was the fact that the ground dropped off rapidly on the other side of the hill. That meant that the sniper could possibly move either way without Frank's knowledge. A heavy carpet of leaves helped matters some, but they were last year's leaves and not as *crunchy* as he would have liked. He decided that he needed to check it out. His sniper training dictated patience, but he instinctively knew that this man realized that he too was in a time crunch. He too would have to move faster than he wanted. Hopefully, that made them both even.

Frank elected to start moving toward the right side of the log. For the sake of speed, he rose to a crouch and began moving as rapidly as he could. He spotted a large oak tree near the ridge that would allow him to look down on the sniper's last known position.

He reached it a few seconds later and found, as he half expected, that the sniper was gone. Frank decided to take a chance and threw caution to the wind as he sprinted in to the field and toward the hidden motorcycle. He prayed he had made the right decision. If he didn't, the sniper would be long gone.

He was twenty-five yards away from the bike when he was rewarded with the sweet sound of a motorcycle engine attempting to cough to life. Frank knew that it wouldn't. The heavy brush that the bike had been enveloped in now prevented him from actually seeing the sniper.

A movement at the edge of the brush caused Frank to abruptly hurl himself to the ground. It was a fortuitous move for as he hit the ground he heard and felt a bullet whiz by his recently vacated space. It was followed by the thunderous report of the big .45 and he knew that he had no time to lose. He snapped off three quick shots in the direction of the movement and began rolling sideways to the nearest tree.

Frank reached the safety of the tree and readied himself for another onslaught. It didn't come. He thought he had heard a slight groan as he had fired, but he couldn't be sure. Once again Frank had a feeling that he needed to move forward. He rose and dove to the left of the brush that had hidden the motorcycle. His line of sight moved up and caught the movement of the sniper disappearing over a hill. Frank ran in that direction, noticing an increasing amount of blood on the ground. He *had* hit him!

Frank slowed as he reached the crest of the hill the sniper had gone over. He wasn't anxious to test his luck again. He slowed a little and approached cautiously until he could see the bottom of the hill. Nothing. At that moment, a movement out of the corner of his eye caused him to hit the dirt once again. He heard the .45 roar, but had no idea where the round went.

He looked up just as the .45 boomed again. Dirt sprayed up near his face. The debris showered his face and he suddenly found that his eyes were full of dirt. He couldn't see anything!

He tried in vain to force his eyes to open. He heard a sound off to his right. Out of sheer desperation, he fired four more rounds in that direction. This time he definitely heard the sniper groan. Frank prepared to fire what was left in his clip when the sound of the man running away told him that the fight was over for now. He rolled onto his stomach and frantically tried to clear his eyes. It was no use. He reached for his radio and called in his location and status.

Billyray Jenkins had no idea who the demon ghost was that had found him. He only knew that the man was no ordinary cop. The man seemed to know his every move even before he did. He also knew that he wanted nothing more to do with him.

He stumbled toward the road. Frank had hit him in the left shoulder back by the motorcycle. Billyray thought he had him for sure at the ridge line. But the man seemed to have a sixth sense and suddenly dove out of the line of fire. But Billyray followed it up with more shots as Frank lay on the ground, one of which had kicked the dirt in his eyes. Billyray had debated whether to finish him or just leave him. He had elected to finish the demon and had started toward him. Then, inexplicably, the demon had suddenly brought his own gun up and began firing.

How could he do that? Frank had hit him in the right leg and Billyray decided that he needed to let it be and get the hell out of there. Just as he got to the small hill at the edge of the road, he looked back to make sure he wasn't being followed. A protruding rock caused him to stumble. Normally, Billyray could easily have caught himself, but his injured leg was becoming more and more useless. He fell right at the edge of the sharp rise and tumble forward onto the road.

He heard screeching tires and looked up to see a Chevrolet Impala attempting to stop before hitting him. The driver almost succeeded. Billyray turned away and the car came to a stop, punching against his left ribs, breaking three of them.

The driver, a fresh faced young man in his mid twenties, jumped out and ran to the front of the car. He knelt down next to Billyray. "Hold on Mister," he said, not even sure that the injured man was still alive. "I'll call an ambulance." Still kneeling, the young man removed a cell phone from his belt clip and began dialing. He never saw the big .45 and probably never felt the hollow point slug that entered the front of his head and removed a significant portion of the back of his skull, taking a substantial amount of gray matter with it.

CHAPTER
15

The city hospital was a very busy place on this particular day. Frank Carlotta was having his eyes washed out by an intern. Mary Kate Harvard was being examined by a child psychiatrist. Susan Browning had a team of doctors conducting surgery on her. Billyray's fears had been justified. The wracking chill that had quivered through his body just prior to the gun going off had indeed affected his aim. Just an infinitesimal amount, but enough to cause only a *glancing* blow to Susan's head. Her prognosis was good.

Unlike Susan, David Walton's outlook was not good. He had just come out of surgery and was in intensive care. He had taken two bullets to the chest, one of which had nicked an artery. Amazingly, he was still alive, but his doctors weren't at all sure that he was going to make it.

Judge Walton was having his jaw wired shut after John's huge fist had crashed into it as he lay on the dock. His wrist had already been put in a cast and the Judge was not feeling very well in general. However, it was better than the alternative. A Sheriff's deputy sat next to him, waiting to transport the Judge to the County Jail when the doctor released him.

The body of William Ramsey was laying in a morgue drawer and had been slated as first in line for autopsy in the morning. However, the body of a young man had been discovered hidden in the grass on the side of the road near John's home. The large caliber bullet hole in his skull was sufficient to move him to the head of the line in Ramsey's place. The bodies of Luke Bonnais and Harold Newbaucher were also scheduled for autopsies. In an assignment meeting held that morning, the pathologists all agreed that it was certainly going to be quite the "slice and dice" morning, with enough autopsies for everyone.

Dwight Chase received medical care at the hotel where he had holed up with Sara Rose. The two County Sheriff's involved reached an agreement to which Dwight would be tried for the kidnapping of Sara first, then brought back to the county of the Overlook Hotel to stand trial for the unlawful restraint of the elderly hotel owners. After reaching that agreement, Dwight was transported to the city hospital, where he lay under guard, one room over from Frank Carlotta.

Council member Lily Barrett, aka Susan Whitaker, was arrested as she boarded a plane bound for the Caribbean. Her name was listed on the flight manifest as Susan Whitaker. The interesting part of that situation was that she had a seat next to Council member Bob Stark. That was convenient. They were arrested together and their desire to sit next to each other was subsequently fulfilled, in a manner of speaking. They had adjoining interrogation rooms. Another room, close by, was filled with city detectives, county detectives, and agents from the F.B.I., C.I.A., I.R.S., and Homeland Security. All were in a heated argument over the rights to interrogate them first, like sharks fighting over a solitary bit of meat in the water.

The remainder of the City Council was in an emergency meeting to reinstate Chief Giovanni. None of them would contest the issue. They were too busy trying to cover their own political asses from the coming fallout.

Nearly every Crime Scene Unit in that part of the state was working, including an F.B.I. team that was going over the Judge's entire estate and judicial offices with a fine tooth comb. Like autopsies, there were enough crime scenes for everyone.

John Harvard was talking to Nick Giovanni in the cafeteria. John was torn as to where he should be, outside of Mary Kate's room, or outside of Sue's room. He was equally worried about both. Today's events had also solidified his feelings about Sue.

Nick was speaking in a jest filled tone, "Why is it whenever you are involved with something, chaos and bodies reign?"

John grinned. "Just trying to keep your life interesting, buddy. Wouldn't want *Chief* Giovanni bored, now would we?"

Nick smiled back. "Well, it's better than the alternative. I'm here to tell you, the inside of a jail cell is *boring* and not anything I would recommend to anyone. Any word on Sue?"

"They're still working on her. Her skull is cracked and

they're worried about her brain swelling. The bullet tore a pretty good chunk of skin and hair off her head, but other than that, she should be fine."

"She was lucky," said Nick. "The shooter was using some sort of military grade sniper's weapon. Preliminary results show that it's had a fair amount of use, so chances are the guy has had some serious experience with it. He was using a .200 grain magnum round."

John shuddered. "I don't even want to think about what that it would have done to her if she'd been hit square."

"No sense dwelling upon it. Hey! Look who's here."

John turned around to see Frank entering the room with some serious sunglasses. He stood up to greet him. "Nice shades! Where can I get a pair of those?"

Frank smiled. "Very funny. The Doc says my eyes are going to be pretty sensitive to light for the next few days, but there shouldn't be any permanent damage."

"That's good," said Nick.

"Glad to see you're free and clear," Frank replied, looking at Nick. He and John sat down as Frank continued. "I just got a call from Stu." Nick looked confused. "He's my brother with the F.B.I.," Frank said, clearing up the confusion. "Anyway, the prints on that rifle came back to Billyray Jenkins."

"All present and accounted for," interjected John grimly. Nick looked confused once again, so John explained. "We were looking into a connection between missing parolees and David Walton. All were under David's care and we were convinced that he was working with the Coeptus

Guild, supplying them with soldiers. It looks as though we were wrong, but the fact that all of them had something to do with the Guild, is too much of a coincidence to ignore. We're thinking David was unknowingly guided by his father in some way. Regardless, with Billyray's prints on that gun, we now know where all of the missing guys are, or at least were."

Nick nodded in understanding. "Sounds like you guys were really busy. And here I thought you were all home downing some brewskis while I was rotting away in jail."

John and Frank snickered. Frank continued with a more serious tone. "I'm sorry to say that Jenkins has gotten away clean. We found a dead guy just down the road from your house. The Techs say that a blood trail and tire marks on the road indicate that I hit Billyray pretty good. It looks like he fell onto the road and was almost run over by the dead guy. From there, the victim got out and either tried to help him or was looking over what he thought was a dead body when Billyray shot him in the head, pointblank. He then managed to drag the guy into some high weeds on the side of the road and take off in the victim's car. The bloodhounds found the vic when they were looking for Jenkins."

"Jesus!" exclaimed Nick. "The guy's hardcore."

"As hardcore as they come, Nick." John replied. He looked at Frank. "I don't know how to thank you Frank. If it wasn't for you, I'd be planning two funerals right now. You saved them and I will be indebted to you forever."

Frank shook his head. "I probably saved your daughter, but as far as Sue goes... you need to go to church or something. That was nothing short of divine intervention. When he fired that shot, he didn't even know I was there. I had nothing to do with the outcome. It wasn't until I saw him re-aiming that I realized he was trying to take out somebody else and took action."

"Regardless, thank you for being there in time. What's going on with the Judge?"

"From what Stu tells me, they're really on him. He's the first big wig from the mysterious Coeptus Guild they've been able to get their hands on. We still don't know how far up the food chain he is, but he's not the common grunt we've been dealing with so far. With him and the two council members, it's going to be a real feeding frenzy between all the agencies."

John asked, "Have they found out why Ramesy's number was in Sally's shoe?"

Frank shook his head. "They're still scratching their heads on that one. She apparently told her handler that she was going to try to set up a meet with Ramsey and see what information she could get out of him. She was going to put herself out as wanting a little drug action. She figured that between that and stuff she'd found out from the ex-con, if she could get him to bite on something small like that, she could use that as a club to get info on the bigger stuff he was into. But as far as her handler knew, she hadn't actually put the plan into action yet."

"So then," John said, "it would appear, the Judge figured it out. William Ramsey told me she was asking too many questions and that she had, somehow lured Wallis Jester into her web and he was cooperating with her."

"Sounds like she was very close to busting this whole thing wide open," Frank commented. "The Judge appears to be quite a ruthless individual. Look what he did to his own son. Killing Sally would be nothing for him if he even suspected what she was about." He looked at John with intensity, "I'm quite surprised and happy you didn't kill him, John."

John looked away. "I almost did, Frank. I had his head in my hands and I so wanted to snap his fucking neck." He looked back at Frank and Nick. "But I guess, in the end, my good side triumphed over the bad. Me bad."

"No," Nick interjected. "You good. I always knew you were." He smiled. "Why do you think I let you hang around with me? By the way, you're slipping." John looked at him quizzically. Nick snorted. "Unless there's something I don't know about, we got through this whole mess and you never shot anybody, let alone kill them."

John laughed. "Fuck you." A man was approaching the table with Mary Kate beside him. She broke away from him and ran to her father, launching herself into his lap and throwing her arms around him. She didn't say anything for awhile and neither did John. They just held each other tightly. The others looked on in silence, sensing the special bond between them.

Finally, Mary Kate broke away and said, "Is it really true that Sue will be okay?"

"Yes," John replied, "it's true. As a matter of fact, let's go see if we can see her yet."

They all stood up and John looked at the man who had accompanied Mary Kate with an unspoken question. To his credit, the man, the hospital's child psychiatrist, instantly understood what was being asked. "She'll be fine Mr. Harvard. We'll talk later. That's one very special little girl you have there."

"Don't I know it," said John. "Thanks." He looked down at Mary Kate. "Shall we go?"

With the exception of the psychiatrist, the entire group walked in silence to Susan's room. They were told the doctor would be with them shortly. He recognized Susan's parents, Peter and Dana. They were divorced and both remarried. They were sitting on chairs in a small alcove just down from the room and got up when they saw John approaching. Peter and John shook hands as John said, "Pete, I…"

"I know," interrupted Peter Browning. "I've had experience with the Coeptus Guild, remember?" John nodded. It was how they met. Peter continued. "I know it wasn't your fault. Shit happens."

They broke their hand shake as John said, "I don't know if I'd be as understanding if I was in your shoes. After all, if she wasn't with me, she wouldn't be in there right now." He looked over at Dana Pittman. "How are you doing Dana?"

"I'm fine John, and Pete is right. Don't blame yourself for this. It goes with the territory and if I know my daughter, once she realized what you were working on, you couldn't have kept her away, no matter what you did." She looked down. "And how are you doing Mary Kate?"

"I'm okay Mrs. Pittman. I was really scared though. There was sooo much blood. But Daddy says she's going to be all better, so I'm not very scared anymore." She reached up and took John's hand as she spoke and held it firmly. She was *going* to be fine, he thought. But right now, she needed all the reassurance she could get.

They all sat around and talked for some time before a doctor approached and informed them that Susan was awake and they could see her now. They walked in and tried to look calm in the face of Sue's appearance. Her head was swathed in bandages, which they had expected. But what took them aback was the fact that the whole picture was made worse by the obvious reality that she was going to have two huge black eyes.

John knew immediately what had caused it. Trauma, from either the bullet and or her head crashing to the floor afterward, which had caused her brain to bounce around inside her skull, giving her two black eyes as though she had been struck by fists. Though the blackness hadn't settled in yet, it was clear what was coming.

Dana rushed over and gently put her arms around her daughter. Her previous composure vanished as tears rolled down her cheeks and she said softly, "Oh sweetheart, I'm so glad you're alright."

Susan weakly returned the hug. "I'm fine, Mom. I have a headache from hell, but at least I'm breathing." She looked over at John and Mary Kate. She said to both of them, "Are you just going to stand there, or are you going to give me a hug, too?"

Mary Kate ran over and with the exuberance of a seven year old and not so gently threw her arms around Sue. "I was afraid Sue," she said.

"I know," said Sue. She looked up at John, who was over her with a strange expression of his face. "What about you?" she asked. Their eyes locked. John was in turmoil. This woman had almost died because of him. That was bad. Very bad. The thought of losing her had been gut wrenching. Sitting on top of the Judge, knowing that he couldn't kill him, in spite of what the man had just ordered done, John realized that he loved Susan Browning. He realized that he'd been suppressing his feeling for her because... why? For fear of having someone else taken away from him? Because of *Her*, Emily Stone? Because of his inner hatred and lust for revenge?

The answer, he realized, lay in all three. Emily Stone was dead. The fact of the matter was that he'd only known her for a few days. He wasn't sure why he'd been so obsessed with her after so short a time. It was something Mary Kate's child psychiatrist could probably tell him. But what mattered was that he was now ready to move on. He had controlled his inner demon and had not taken revenge when the evil inside him cried out for it. And as far as his fear of having someone else taken from him, that was something he would have to learn to deal with as well. Susan was here now. She needed *him* now. She had always been there for him and it was his turn to stand guard.

He felt as though he had been through a trial by fire... and passed. As he looked down at Susan, he was both afraid and eager to embrace her. He wished there was no one else in the room.

Everyone else in the room, with the possible exception of Mary Kate, who with a child's innocence, had no idea of what was going on other than the obvious, could see the look passing between them and understood. John broke the awkward silence and bent down to give Susan a hug. She was disappointed when he whispered in her ear, "I'm glad you're okay."

Given the look in his eyes when he was looking down at her, she'd expected something else. But she put on her game face and said, "I'm fine. I'm glad you and Mary Kate are okay."

John stood up then and watched as the other adults in the room also gave her more hugs. He noticed that Mary Kate did not leave her side, even when John sat down in an empty chair in the room. She normally would have bounded into his lap and sat there in contented silence.

After a while, a nurse entered and shooed them all out. John was the last to leave. He quickly bent down to give her another hug. "Don't worry," he whispered in her ear. "The doctor says you can probably come home in a couple of days. We'll talk then." He started to rise up, but she held him tight, not letting him go.

The nurse spoke behind them. "Okay you two. Time for that later. She needs to rest and I need to take her blood pressure."

John quickly kissed her on the lips. "Later," he said as he rose up. They looked at each other until the nurse stepped between them and began preparing her blood pressure kit. He poked his head around the nurse, caught Susan's eye and waved good bye. He then turned and strode from the room.

❖   ❖   ❖

"*John.*" In his dream, he turned and saw *her*. She was smiling. "*I knew you were a good man John. Don't ever listen to them. They are evil. They will try to twist what you know into something you don't know. Something evil. They will prey upon your self-doubts. Don't let them. You know you are good. You just proved it to them and more importantly, to yourself.*"

He tried to raise his arms toward her translucent form, but strangely they wouldn't move. "Emily," he said and tried to move toward her. But his legs didn't seem to function any better than his arms. It didn't matter. He knew that he would never hold her in his arms again and somehow he knew that this was the last time she would come to him.

"*I'm leaving you now, John,*" she said as if to confirm his feelings. "*I've served my purpose and it's time for me to go. I have saved you and you should know that you have saved me. I'll not be coming back.*" She saw the pained expression on his face. "*You have Susan now. She needs you. Go to her John and never let her go. One more thing John, watch for Billyray. Even now, as he lays in pain, he is finding that he cannot forget what happened today. He doesn't understand it. He has never been one to look behind him at things that have already happened and things that he cannot change. But they will not let him forget. Be warned John. I love you.*"

She faded to nothing then. He made no attempt to stop her. Instead, he fell into a deep and relaxing sleep. He was, at last, at peace. His inner turmoil had been quieted. All the twisted pieces were straightened out and put in their proper places. The puzzle was complete. It was the best sleep that he'd had in a long, long time.

The Twisted Series

Continues in…

Twisted Benevolence

John Livingston Harvard returns and finds himself working for the government, but this time as an undercover agent for the F.B.I. He and his partner have been tasked with uncovering the latest plot by the Coeptus Guild. Children are quietly disappearing throughout the country. Not just any children, but only those of genius IQ's from troubled or poor homes. The task force set up to deal with the Guild has uncovered information gleaned from the home of a dirty judge that the Guild is responsible and Benevolence has nothing to do with it. The project is merely fuel for the Coeptus Guild's burning desire for power.

John and fellow agent Frank Carlotta travel to a small and isolated town in the mountains of Oregon. Who in this tiny hamlet can be trusted? Like all small towns, they are suspicious of strangers but are they typical small town reservations or are there deadly Guild members hidden amongst them?

It's going to take time but they need to discover what it is that the Guild is up to. Who is friend and who is foe? With typical ruthless efficiency, the Guild becomes aware of their efforts and intend to *clean* up the entire project. The missing children are found at a rural compound but who are the real victims? Is it just the children or are there those on the staff and some the community who have been duped as well? Killing them all and letting God sort them out is not an option.

For more details and information,
visit www.SilverLeafBooks.com

ABOUT THE AUTHOR

AUTHOR PHOTOGRAPH BY SCOTT FINGER

Lew Stonehouse was born and raised in central New York and spent much of his youth sailing, canoeing, and wandering the backwoods of the Adirondack Mountains in moccasins. He is currently residing in a Chicago, Illinois suburb while raising a young daughter. After serving the public as a Deputy Sheriff for many years, he went into private practice and is the current owner of a successful private investigation agency.

The experience garnered from his eclectic career in the law enforcement and private sector, from gruesome homicides to gut busting humor, has provided him with a fountain of knowledge from which he can draw upon when writing his suspenseful crime thrillers.

CPSIA information can be obtained
at www.ICGtesting.com
Printed in the USA
FFOW02n0616090216
21264FF